ANGEL TRAIN

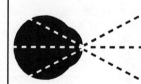

This Large Print Book carries the
Seal of Approval of N.A.V.H.

ANGEL TRAIN

GILBERT MORRIS

THORNDIKE PRESS
A part of Gale, Cengage Learning

GALE
CENGAGE Learning™

Detroit • New York • San Francisco • New Haven, Conn • Waterville, Maine • London

GALE
CENGAGE Learning

Copyright © 2009 by Gilbert Morris.
Wagon Wheel Series #4.
Scripture references are taken from the King James Version.
Thorndike Press, a part of Gale, Cengage Learning.

ALL RIGHTS RESERVED
Thorndike Press® Large Print Christian Historical Fiction.
The text of this Large Print edition is unabridged.
Other aspects of the book may vary from the original edition.
Set in 16 pt. Plantin.
Printed on permanent paper.

LIBRARY OF CONGRESS CATALOGING-IN-PUBLICATION DATA

Morris, Gilbert.
   Angel train / by Gilbert Morris.
      p. cm. — (Thorndike Press large print Christian historical
fiction)
    ISBN-13: 978-1-4104-1926-2 (hardcover : alk. paper)
    ISBN-10: 1-4104-1926-6 (hardcover : alk. paper)
    1. Overland journeys to the Pacific—Fiction. 2. Wagon
trains—Fiction. 3. Religious communities—Fiction. 4. Large
type books. I. Title.
    PS3563.O8742A875 2009
    813'.54—dc22
                                       2009020119

Published in 2009 by arrangement with Riggins International Rights
Services Inc.

Printed in the United States of America
1 2 3 4 5 6 7 13 12 11 10 09

To Bobby and Helen Funderburk —

You two have been a treasure to Johnnie and me for many years. Thanks for all the memories!

CHAPTER ONE

A slight movement to the left caught Charity Morgan's eyes. She turned quickly, then smiled at a tiny mouse that appeared from behind her walnut washstand. The small creature advanced a few steps, sat up, and primly folded its paws. Charity noted the bright black eyes, somewhat pleased with her visitor.

"So you're here again, is it?"

The music of old Wales was in her voice, though she had been born in America. Her parents had arrived in Pennsylvania from Wales along with other members of a close-knit religious group called the Pilgrim Way. It was inevitable that Charity's speech would carry the strains of Welsh.

"You've come begging. Shame on you," she whispered, but she reached over to the table beside her chair, opened a box, and took out a lump of hard cheese. Breaking off a generous portion, she tossed it toward the mouse, which stared at Charity with eyes like shiny black beads. With quick movements, the tiny beast seized the cheese, turned, and scurried back under the wash-stand.

"I don't doubt you've got some wee ones to feed," Charity murmured.

Rising from her chair, she laid the worn black Bible on the table beside her bed, then walked over to the window. The winter of 1854 had been bitter in Pennsylvania, and the ground was still frozen hard as iron. A light snow had fallen during the night, rounding the edges of the buildings and fences and giving them a peculiar grace in Charity's eyes. The huge walnut trees that surrounded the house were still bare — the leaves had all passed to the ground to make new soil — and the giants seemed to hold black branches high as if in prayer. Such a fantastic, overly imaginative notion was typical of her thoughts, and Charity sighed with longing for the spring to break up the frozen earth and bring tiny green shoots to life.

Turning to the dressing table, she picked up a mother-of-pearl comb and ran it through her brilliant red hair, which glinted with flecks of gold when the sunlight struck it in a certain way. Her eyes were a startling shade of green that flashed when she was angry or very happy. She was not beautiful; her features were too strong for that. She smiled suddenly, then shook her head.

"Nothing to buy a stamp for, are you, girl?" Summing up her opinion of her looks — which many young men did not agree with — she studied her image for a moment, almost as if she were examining the face of a stranger. Her stubborn chin reflected her character. Her lips were broad and well shaped, and her rich, smooth complexion was the envy of many women. All this did not please her, however, and she turned with a quick motion and put on her coat that hid her womanly contours. At the age of twenty-six, she was full-bodied and had quick movements.

Leaving the room, she descended the stairs to the kitchen. She paused abruptly, looking over to where her twelve-year-old sister Bronwen was curled up in a chair, reading a book. Peering at the cover, Charity said sternly, "Pa will have you for reading trash like that!"

Bronwen Morgan had the same color hair as Charity, but her eyes were a bright blue, almost electric. She looked up from the book and muttered "Well, don't tell him, Sister."

"You know he doesn't like it when you read romances like that."

Bronwen closed the book and hugged it to her chest. "I like to read romances," she said defiantly. "They're the only kind I'm ever likely to get."

"No, they're not."

"Yes, they are. I don't have any more shape than an old rake handle. I'll *never* have a bosom!"

"Indeed you will. Now don't be foolish!"

Bronwen gave her sister an envious look, then asked, "When did you get a bosom, Charity?"

Charity wanted to laugh. It was exactly the sort of question Bronwen would ask. "When the good Lord decided it was time. Now, you go start heating the water so the men can have a good bath. Get you to it now!"

Bronwen sighed, closed the book, and moved reluctantly across the room. Charity watched with dissatisfaction. Their mother had died at childbirth when Meredith had been born six years earlier. Since that time, Charity, who had been twenty when the Morgans lost her mother, Maureen, had stood in the place of a mother to her two sisters and brother. "A sorry job I've done of it," she muttered, then shook her head and threw a couple more sticks of white oak into the kitchen stove. She plucked a wool, knit cap down off a peg, pulled it over her ears, and started to leave the kitchen.

She was interrupted when Meredith came running into the kitchen, her eyes bright. She had the blue eyes of her father, and her hair was a rich auburn rather than the startling red of Bronwen's and Charity's. At the age of six, she was one of the most precocious children any of the Morgans had ever seen. She had practically taught herself to read by following along when Bronwen had read to her from storybooks. She never had a thought in her life that she didn't speak out — which produced embarrassing results at times.

Now she said, "I'm hungry, Sister."

"We'll have a good supper tonight."

"Where are you going now?"

"Going out to get a couple of chickens for the pot."

"I'll go with you."

"You don't need to." Charity hesitated and then said, "I'm going to have to kill them, you know. We can't eat them alive, can we?"

Meredith stared at her. "Don't be silly. Nobody eats chickens alive, but I want to go anyway."

11

"Well, you may go, but I don't want to hear you begging for any of them." She well knew that Meredith had named every single chicken in the yard as well as all of the livestock. She had come up with unusual names, including calling their bull Sally. The fact that Sally was a female name attached to a monstrous male did not trouble her.

"Well, come you then."

Charity walked down the back porch steps and paid little attention to Meredith's constant stream of questions and observations. She was trying to decide how many chickens she would need. It would have been an easy enough thing to decide except that her father, Gwilym, was prone to inviting expected visitors for a meal. This was well and good as a show of hospitality, but it made preparing a meal difficult for Charity. A few times she'd been forced to make portions smaller to feed the guests her father had brought.

Unfastening the gate to the chicken yard, she stepped inside, and Meredith followed. Shutting the gate, she moved over to the henhouse and took a handful of feed. The sound brought all the chickens running, clucking, and scurrying around her, and she scattered the grain with a free hand.

"That's not nice, Charity!"

"What's not nice?"

"Using feed for bait. You know you're going to kill them."

"It makes them easier to catch, besides —" Suddenly, a sharp pain caught Charity in her ankle. She uttered a cry, turned around, and saw a huge black rooster looking at her, malevolence in his beady eyes. Quick as thought, Charity reached down and caught the big rooster by the neck.

"You black devil! That'll be the last time you peck anybody!"

With a practiced motion she swung the chicken around until the head parted from the body. What was left of Judas hit the ground, then, in the way of chickens, came to his feet, and began running around, spouting blood until he finally fell over.

"Why did you kill Judas, Sister?"

Charity laughed. "Because he was a bad rooster. Now, we've got to have another one." She reached down but stopped when Meredith said, "Don't get Ellen. She's my favorite."

Straightening up, Charity smiled and grinned. "All right then. You pick another one of these old chickens."

"I don't want to. The Bible says, 'Thou shalt not kill.' "

"That doesn't mean animals."

13

"It doesn't say that."

"Don't you remember, Meredith, we read in the Bible about how the Jews in the Old Testament would sacrifice animals — lambs, bulls, and birds?"

Meredith stood in the middle of the yard, staring at the black body of Judas still twitching. "Do chickens and animals go to heaven when they die?"

"I don't think so."

"Well, I wouldn't want to go to heaven if Benny wasn't there." Benny had been her pet rabbit, and Meredith had not yet gotten over the loss of him.

Charity bent over and put her arms around the child. "Well, don't you worry about it. Whatever heaven is like, it's better than we think it is. Now, you run inside and peel some potatoes."

"All right, but don't kill Clara either."

"I won't kill Clara." Charity watched as Meredith left the chicken yard and ran lightly toward the house. When the door closed, she stood for a moment pondering. *Where does that child get her imagination? From her mother, I guess, as I did.* She looked around at the chickens and then settled on one. "All right, Martha. I guess you had a full and happy life. Come here."

The kitchen was pleasantly warm as Charity and her two sisters finished the cooking. A big red dog came through the door and nudged Charity, begging for some of the leftover dough.

"Sam, you go lie down. You're not going to get anything to eat." Sam eyed her mournfully, then dropped his head. He put his tail between his legs, slouched toward the wall, and fell down as if shot.

Bronwen laughed. "You hurt his feelings, Charity. See how sad he looks."

"Well, his feelings are too sensitive. As a matter of fact, he's not the only one."

"I hope you're not talking about me," Bronwen said sharply.

Suddenly, Meredith said, "They're coming! I hear them!"

The three pulled on their coats, stepped outside, then advanced to the front of the yard. It was a part of the day that Charity loved, for the men always came home singing. Not all of them were Welsh, but many were, and they made a fine, strong male choir. She stood there, smiling slightly, listening as they sang "A Mighty Fortress Is Our God" by Martin Luther. The sound rose, filling the world, it seemed. Some of the voices were soft and gentle, mostly sopranos of the teenage boys who had already started work in the mine. Then there were the tenors rising above the others, the baritones who added body, and finally under all, the bass singers seemed to carry all the rest of them.

The men made a blackened army, for every face and all the hands were black with the coal that they dug from the bowels of the earth. She saw her father, Gwilym, and her brother, Evan, separate themselves and wave good-bye to their comrades. They broke off the singing, and as the others trooped by toward their homes, they came forward.

Gwilym Morgan was not a tall man, but heavy with muscle from a lifetime of digging coal. There was no excess flesh on him, and his teeth seemed very white against his coal-stained face as he smiled. "Well, Charity, I hope it's a good supper you've got for us tonight."

"Yes. You go get cleaned up, Pa."

She turned to Evan and saw that beneath the black mask of the coal stains his face was dissatisfied, and he seemed depressed. "I've got some of your favorites tonight, Evan."

"That's good." The voice seemed nearly lifeless, and as Evan moved past her to enter the house, Charity watched him with fear. She knew, as did they all, how Evan hated the coal mines and wished for something better. Charity wished he could have gone to university. He could have been anything, for he was an intelligent young man, but this had not been possible.

Pushing the thought aside as best she could, Charity went into the kitchen, shooing the girls ahead of her. They set the table and made the tea. She left the kitchen and went to the room built especially for the men to bathe. There were two enormous tubs, and the two men were already submerged in soapy water. Charity placed fresh underwear and other clothing on a table.

Evan cried out, "For heaven sakes, woman, is a man to have no modesty!"

Charity's green eyes glittered, and she uttered a laugh. She had a deep voice for a woman. "Oh, you're modest is it now? Maybe you don't remember who changed your diaper for a couple of years."

"That's — that's different!"

Charity picked up a bucket and scooped up the water as Evan lowered himself farther until only his head was out. "Your hair's grimy." She poured the water over him, and Evan started sputtering and splashing soapy water out of his eyes.

"You drive a man too hard, Charity Morgan! No wonder you can't get a husband the way you treat us."

Charity merely laughed at him and glanced at her father who had his eyes closed and was soaking in the luxury of the hot water. "You hurry up, Pa. We got a good supper tonight."

"All right, Daughter. We'll be there soon."

Charity left the room, but when she was outside her brother's words seemed to echo. *No wonder you can't get a husband.*

She had paid little attention at the moment, but now she stood still and wondered if there were some truth in the statement. *Am I too hard? Will no man ever love me?* These questions had come to her many times, for many of the young girls she had grown up with had already married and some of them had started their families. Like many healthy young women, Charity Morgan longed for a home of her own, but taking care of her brother, sisters, and father occupied her whole life. True, she had become somewhat sharp in having to discipline at least three of them, sometimes even her father who was kind but occasionally thoughtless. *Have I become a witch they all*

hate? Men must see that in me, I suppose.
She knew that her good looks had drawn men, but not one of them had pressed to suit, and the thought troubled her that, perhaps, she had grown too cantankerous for a man ever to love. She shook the thought off and returned to the kitchen.

The girls had everything in hand. They performed the final touches on the meal, and fifteen minutes later, Gwilym and Evan took their seats.

"Sit you down now before it gets cold," Charity said.

"Smells good," Gwilym said. "You're as good a cook as your mother, Charity."

"No, no one will ever be that good. You know that, Pa."

The meal was indeed filling. All the vegetables were well seasoned; the potatoes had been boiled in their jackets and still had their flavor.

"Ask the blessing, Pa, so we can get started," Bronwen said.

They all bowed their heads, and Gwilym said, "Oh, our Father, we thank You for this food. We thank You for our family, for the goodness that You have showered upon us. Be with those less fortunate than we are and make us be ever more grateful for Your tender mercies. In the name of Jesus. Amen."

Everyone said, "Amen," and the food was transferred from large bowls to plates. The chicken was fried to a golden brown, and the flesh was tender. The platter was diminished alarmingly, and Charity laughed, her eyes sparkling. "Like a bunch of hungry wolves, you are! Look at you gobbling it down!"

Meredith held up a leg and said, "I bet this was Judas's leg." She turned to her father. "He pecked Charity, and she killed him. She says there's no chickens in heaven. Is that right, Pa?"

"Oh, there may be all sorts of animals in heaven. Maybe even dragons and things like that, that we never saw in this place."

"Really?"

"We don't know what it's like."

"Well, the streets are gold. It says that," Bronwen argued. "And there are mansions there. I bet it'll be better than this house."

"Be glad you've got a house. There are some out in the cold," Gwilym said sharply.

"I know that, but we'll have a mansion, won't we?"

"I suppose so, Bronwen, but it's not the gold in the streets I long for. It's to see the dear Savior Himself — and think, we'll get to see your mother again! You don't remember her, Meredith, but I bet she's thinking about you right now."

Meredith had a mouthful of fried chicken, but she stopped chewing. "Can they see everything we're doing?"

"I wouldn't be surprised."

"Well, I don't want them to see everything I'm doing," Bronwen said loudly.

"Then you shouldn't be doing them." Gwilym nodded sternly.

The argument went on for some time, but as Charity brought in the slices of apple pie, Evan said, "There's been more talk about hard times coming. The newspaper says we're going to have a panic. The mine might even close."

"That would be terrible," Charity said. "Do you remember when the mine closed three years ago? Many in this village went hungry."

"That's not going to happen again. The mine's in good shape," Gwilym said. "Mr. Campbell told me himself that the prices are good and likely to get better."

"That's not what the newspaper said," Evan responded. He was a fine-looking young man with red hair and blue eyes. He was lean and strong, but his expression was unhappy. He turned to his father and said almost in desperation, "I wish I could do anything rather than dig coal under the ground. It scares me sometimes, Pa."

The statement troubled Gwilym, for he himself never felt fear. He had dug coal out of the ground in Wales and then in Pennsylvania until it had become second nature to him. "Why should you be afraid? The good Lord takes care of us."

"He didn't take care of those six men who got killed in that cave-in last year," Evan said bitterly. Before his father could answer, he continued. "We stay down there, sweating hour after hour, bent double. The only time we're straight is when we're flat on our backs, and the dust of coal — it comes down on you with a touch you can feel. You know, it's like the coal was feeling you now gently, but one day he'd have you. That black coal is like the morning band of earth, and we're taking it out to burn it. I think the earth is angry at us."

"That's foolish talk, boy!" Gwilym said, and he was troubled. He did not like things to change, and it disturbed him that Evan could not accept his lot as a miner as had all of his people for many, many years.

Charity spoke a thought that had been with her for some time. "I know it's hard for you both, but there's something wrong with having only one source of income for a whole community."

"And what could that mean, Daughter?"

"Why, we're all dependent on the mine. If it closed, think of what would happen. It would be terrible."

"The mine's not going to close," Gwilym said stubbornly. He was a man of great kindness and high intelligence, but his vision was limited. The coal mine was all he had known in Wales and all he knew here in this new country. He could not foresee a time when the mines would close, and he shook his head with a hint of stubbornness. "We're going to be all right."

"I wish I could be a minister," Evan said. "But I'll never have the education for that. If I can't be a minister, I'd like to be a farmer."

"You'd still be grubbing in the dirt," Gwilym warmed.

"It's different walking over the top of the earth, feeling it beneath your feet, and watching things grow." There was a longing in Evan Morgan's voice, and he had spoken of this often before. He shook his head. "I guess I'll live and die down there, grubbing around like a mole."

Charity was refilling the coffee cups of the men, but she paused and laid her hand on

Evan's shoulder. She could think of nothing to say, and he covered her hand with his, whispering, "There's a good girl. Don't mind me."

"God will do something for you, Evan. I know He will!"

Sunday came, and the bright sun was thawing out the frozen earth. The Pilgrim Way had its services in a small building the members had built themselves. Gwilym was the preacher, an unpaid position in their tradition, and he loved it. He was more of a teacher than a preacher, but his sermons were always interesting.

The congregation filed out, and Gwilym was surprised to see two men waiting for him. "Why, good day to you, Mr. Campbell."

Angus Campbell, the owner of the mine and other properties besides, was a rather short man but so full of dynamic energy that one tended to forget his size. He had iron-gray hair, penetrating blue eyes, and a domineering attitude in the way he held himself and in the way he spoke. "A word with you in private, Gwilym Morgan."

"Why, certainly, Mr. Campbell. Come inside."

"You wait here, Charles."

"Yes, sir."

Charity watched as the two men went inside and wondered, along with the others, why the owner of the mine would single out their father. She turned to Charles. "I'm surprised to see you here, Mr. Campbell." The two had met before on several occasions but had not often spoken.

"Yes, we've just been to church ourselves."

Meredith had been watching this, and she piped up. "Are you rich, Mr. Campbell?"

A flush diffused itself along Campbell's pale features. "Why — I don't know how to answer that."

"I mean do you have a lot of money?"

Charles smiled slightly. "I know what you mean, lass, but I still don't know how to answer it."

"Don't be embarrassed. It's not a sin to be rich," Charity said. Her eyes were sparkling. She was curious about the young man. He was in his midthirties and unmarried although it was not from lack of opportunity. He was not a handsome man, and his diffidence was so different from his father's demeanor that Charity wondered how they could be of one blood.

"You mustn't mind Meredith, Mr. Campbell. She says what she thinks, and, of course, I suppose no rich man likes to admit

25

it. Don't mind her. She's curious as a pet coon."

Meredith moved so she was facing the man and looked up into his face. "If you're rich," she said in an insistent voice, "you ought to help Mrs. Patterson."

"Mrs. Patterson?"

"Oh, that's a widow who lost her husband in the cave-in last year, Mr. Campbell," Charity said. "She has four children, and things are . . . well, not too good with her."

Charles Campbell cleared his throat and said at once, "I would be most happy to help the lady." He fumbled into the inner pocket of his coat, came out with a billfold, and took out some bills. Extending them toward Charity, he said, "Perhaps you'd be kind enough, Miss Charity, to give this to the lady."

"Oh, I think you should give it to her in person, Mr. Campbell. It would mean so much that way."

Campbell seemed uneasy. "Well, I hardly think that's necessary."

"Oh, I believe it is. I'll be glad to take you to her house if it's all right with your father." She added this and saw that indeed there was a problem with the man. *I'll wager he doesn't sneeze without his father's permission!*

"Well, that would be most kind of you."

"Wait until your father has his meeting with mine, and then we'll go."

"That would be very fine."

Charity did not know exactly what to make of Charles Campbell. *With such a father as he has,* she thought, *he ought to be more dominant, but he seems as uncertain as a young, callow youth.*

Finally, when Campbell and her father came out, Mr. Campbell said, "Come along, Charles."

"Father, Miss Charity has told me of a lady who is in difficulty. I promised to help. She's going to take me to her house."

For a moment Charity thought Mr. Campbell meant to forbid the young man, but then something passed across his features, and he smiled; at least the corners of his lips turned up, although the smile never seemed, really, to reach his eyes. "Very well, but you need to be back at the house by three o'clock."

"Of course, Father."

"Well then, that's settled," Charity said. "You run along home, Evan. Watch the girls. Mind."

"I certainly will, but who's going to watch me?"

"I'll watch him, Sister," Meredith said

27

quickly. "If he does anything wrong, I'll tell you."

Charity laughed and took the arm of Charles who seemed surprised she had done so. "Now, let's go do your good deed for the day."

There was no cooking on the Sabbath day, and that night the family sat down to warmed soup. Gwilym was unusually quiet. He often started a conversation about an element in Scripture, but tonight he said absolutely nothing until the meal was nearly finished. Finally, he looked up and cleared his throat. "You've probably been wondering why Mr. Campbell wanted to speak with me."

"Yes, what did he want, Pa?" Evan said. "I don't know as he's ever gone to visit any of his workmen."

Gwilym Morgan seemed troubled. "Well, it came as a surprise for me." He turned to face Charity and said, "He asked my permission for Charles to come calling on you, Charity."

Charity's eyes opened wide with surprise. "Calling on me?"

"Yes, I thought it was a polite thing to do since it's the custom around here to get the permission from the father."

"Why didn't Charles ask you himself?"

"I don't think Charles ever does anything himself," Evan grinned. "He's still under his father's thumb just like all the rest of us."

"I think he's shy," Bronwen said. "He could hardly talk to you, Charity."

"Well, what am I to make of that? What did you tell him, Pa?"

"I gave him my permission."

Bronwen cried out, "Won't that be wonderful! If you marry him, we'll be rich! We can live in a big house and have servants."

"No." Evan was not quite so enthusiastic. "I imagine a wife of Charles Campbell will have a lot to put up with."

"You don't like him?" Bronwen asked in disbelief.

"I don't have any feelings about him, but I know one thing. A daughter-in-law would have to toe the line with Mr. Angus Campbell."

"I think you're right," Charity said. "It would be like living with a tyrant."

"That young man? Never," Gwilym said.

"No, his father. You think Charles Campbell would ever stand up to Angus Campbell? Never in a hundred years!"

Gwilym was toying with his fork. He didn't answer for a time, and then he said,

29

"Maybe a strong woman could give him some courage."

"I'll have no husband who's afraid of his own father," Charity said. Then she laughed. "I'll go walking with him though. There are some other poor women who need help. I'll see to it that he does what's right."

"You won't marry him?" Bronwen cried out in disappointment.

"No, but I won't tell him that right off. Just think of all the envious looks I'll get from the women who would like to have him. Well, they can have him when I'm finished with him."

Gwilym put his fork down, and there was an expression on his face his children had never seen before. "Well, I will go to my death!" he said loudly. "You're turning down a man who has everything?"

Charity Morgan looked at her father and said with great emphasis and determination, "He has everything except courage, and without that what good is a man?"

CHAPTER TWO

By mid-March, the iron-cold weather had passed and brought one of the mildest springs in anyone's memory. The trees had already begun to put on their tiny golden tongues, the forerunner of the leaves that would soon turn dark green and fill in the forest with an emerald spring dress. It was the time of year Charity Morgan loved best, and she had left the house seeking some of the early plants that were her delight.

The first she found was a patch of pokeweed, and the berries were already beginning. Some people, Charity knew, believed that it was a remedy for rheumatism, but it was dangerous. Some Pennsylvanians pressed the berries and used the juice for a strong whiskey they called "port wine." The large roots were poisonous, but the acrid young shoots are rendered harmless by boiling, and they could be eaten like asparagus. It was too early for that, and there was not enough so she moved on, delighted by the freshness of the spring air and the loamy smell of the rich ground breaking out of the claws of winter. She passed a patch of what she called "rattle-snake plantain," small six-inch growths with tiny greenish white flowers. She had heard that it was a sure cure for hydrophobia and snakebite but put no stock in it.

Moving on, her eyes caught a small bunch of daisy fleabane — not a particularly beautiful plant. It was called a fleabane from the belief that when the plants were burned, they were objectionable to insects, and they were often hung in cottages for the purpose of excluding unpleasant marauders. Charity passed small samples of Queen Anne's lace and a larger mass of purple-stemmed angelica. She picked none of these, but she found a group of small wood violets. She loved the delicate purple color and the fragrance and managed to find enough for a small sampling.

Finally, she made her way back to the house, and as she did, she thought of Charles's courtship. For a month he had appeared at the Morgan home dutifully, it seemed to Charity, to take her to visit his church and once to his home where she had been impressed by the ornate settings and the expensive furniture but less so by the behavior of Angus Campbell. He seemed to have been a man in power and authority for so long that he could not behave in any other way except to speak down to people. At first Charity was angry at this, but later it amused her, and she thought once of calling him "Your Majesty" or "King Campbell," but she managed to hold back this particular humor that lay beneath the surface of her personality.

One effect of Charles's courtship was that quite a few young women of marriageable age were jealous and could not seem to cover it up. This amused Charity, for she had no plans for living at the castle of King Campbell! The mothers of these girls were practically green with envy, but whenever one of them tried to find out more about the seriousness of Charles's intention, Charity merely laughed and put them off.

By the time Charity got back to the house, she found Evan in the garden. He had been breaking the soil with a sturdy horse the Morgans kept mostly for this purpose — a big gray with the name of Phineas. She stood for a while and watched the rich earth turned over by the plow, and finally she went into the house and poured two mugs of hot coffee from the pot on the stove. She brought it out and called, "Evan, come and warm yourself with this coffee."

Evan had been concentrating on the plowing, but he said, "Whoa there, Phineas," and came to stand beside her. He took the cup, sipped it, and blinked. "This is too hot to drink."

"Don't be so picky," Charity said. She reached up and pulled at his forelock. "You're going to be an impossible husband."

"I'd be the best husband in the world!"

"No, you won't. You're spoiled rotten, but I suppose since I did most of the spoiling, I'll just have to take the blame for it."

The two stood there talking. They had always been close since they were more the same age than the other children, and Charity loved her brother deeply. She found only one fault with him, and that was he lacked a sense of humor — not so much as lacked, as he seemed to keep a tight rein on it. He was a handsome young man with clean-cut features, a determined jaw, and the same red hair Charity had inherited from their mother. It was Evan who finally brought up the subject everyone did sooner or later.

"Have you decided what to do with Charles?" he asked. He held the coffee in both hands, the steam rising. There was a curious light in his eyes.

"Why, it's no decision I have to make. He comes calling, is it? What am I to do about him?"

"He must be serious. He never chased any other young woman around."

"Chased! Well, devil fly off! If you call that chasing, I'd like to know why!" she exclaimed. "He comes and sits in a chair and stares at me, and Pa has to make conversation. I wish he *would* chase a little bit. I might even let him catch me. Hasn't even tried to kiss me. Now, why is that? Maybe I'm getting old and ugly."

Evan grinned; his sister was anything but ugly. He studied her a moment, admiring the clearness of her skin, the determined line of her jaw, the beautifully shaped eyes, and the red hair much like his own. "You need to marry him."

"Marry him? What am I to do, Evan, grab him by the lapels and demand that he propose?"

"Maybe you should. He's a little bit shy."

"Boring! That's what he is."

"What do you want, an entertainer or a husband? Go to the music hall and get you a juggler or a jig dancer."

"It would be better than Charles's courtship."

Evan chewed his lower lip thoughtfully, a

35

habit he had. He grew serious and said, "Charity, if you have any feeling for the man at all, you ought to get him to propose, then you ought to marry him."

"Why are you so interested in my finding a husband, Evan?"

"Because things are looking bad. Sooner or later the economy will fail just like it did seven years ago. I was only eleven, but I remember the hard times, and you remember them even more vividly, I think."

Indeed, Charity did remember when the banks had failed. It had been a long struggle back, and although things had improved, rumors of economic failure still seized the country.

Evan continued, "You ought to do it for the sake of the family. If you were married to the son of the richest man in town, we wouldn't have to worry about Bronwen or Meredith. It's them I worry about. You owe it to them."

Charity Morgan was a good-tempered girl, but suddenly her anger flared. "Evan Morgan, I gave my life to raising the three of you. I haven't married so I could see you through your childhood. Perhaps you've forgotten about that! I don't need any sermons from you, Evan. Besides, he hasn't asked me, and I don't think he will."

Evan ran his hand through his hair and said finally, "Well, women can make men do things."

"Oh, so now it's women who are dominating, is it? That's the dumbest thing I ever heard of! You're just like an old mule, you are, Evan!"

She continued to rail at him, for his statement seemed to imply that women were manipulative and domineering. "No woman's ever made you do anything that I can remember. Agnes Fletcher tried hard to make you court her. She didn't do it, did she?"

"No, but —"

"No buts! If Charles Campbell comes and grabs me in his arms and kisses me and pays no attention to my protests, then maybe I'll think about it. But he's no more likely to do that than he is to jump over the house. Git you back to your plowing now. You're better at it than managing my affairs."

Angus Campbell ate his soup noisily and appeared to be deep in thought. Charles, who sat across the table from him, was accustomed to this. His father had two moods. Either he was talking loudly and proclaiming the truth as he saw it, or he was silent, thinking thoughts that no one dared break into. Charles ate his soup, and when the maid brought the lamb on a fine china plate and set it before him, he began to cut it. He jumped slightly when his father said, "Well, we've got to talk about this girl you're courting."

"Charity?"

"Of course! Charity Morgan. How many girls are you courting?" Angus demanded. He had beetling eyebrows that overshadowed his penetrating eyes, and he studied his son carefully. He had planned to have a houseful of sons, but his marriage had produced only one child, and then his wife died. He had finally accepted the fact that he couldn't find a woman he loved enough to live within the bonds of matrimony so he put his hopes into the one son. Now he said, "It's time for you to marry, Charles. I need grandchildren."

Charles nearly said, *You talk about me like I'm a stud good only for reproducing the Campbell name,* but lack of practice at challenging his father forbid that. He shrugged slightly and said, "She's a fine girl. I like her very much indeed."

Angus snorted. "Like her very much indeed! I hope you're a little bit warmer than that when you talk to the girl."

Charles put his fork down and stared at

his father. "Why are you so interested in her? You always wanted me to marry a woman from a good family."

"She *is* from a good family! Not a breath of scandal against any Morgans, and besides that, look at the woman. She's got good strong hips and a good bosom. Why she's made for bearing children! Fine-looking woman and has some life about her. The Morgans have that reputation. We need some life in the line, boy. Life, I tell you! She's good stock. The whole family is smart, and they're healthy."

Charles could not refrain from saying, "You make it sound like a breeding proposition as we do with horses or cattle."

"The principle is the same. If you want good livestock, breed properly. If you want a good family, you look at the woman and decide what she'll bring to the line. The principle is the same," he repeated. "Now, you ask that girl to marry you tonight, you hear me?"

"Yes, Father, I hear you. It'll be as you say."

Charles arrived in his carriage behind a matched team of bays that were the envy of horsemen in the county. The carriage was a masterpiece of art too — new and built from the finest materials. Charity was waiting for him.

"Do we have to make another visit?"

"Yes, we have to go see the Widow Chambliss. She has four small children and no help."

"Very well," Charles said with resignation. He helped her into the carriage, got in, and then, following her directions, drove to a small house on the outskirts of the village. The visit, he knew, would be like all the rest. There would be dirty, raggedly dressed children and a poor widow, and he would give money. He did not resent this, for he, indeed, found some pleasure in it, but after they left the house, charity talked about what a fine thing it was to be able to help people. Charles could not help remembering his father's commandment, and instead of going right home, he turned the horses down a side road.

"Where are you going, Charles? This isn't the way home."

"I thought I'd go by the river road. It's pretty this time of year."

It was the first time he had ever seemed to notice the world about him. One of the things Charity did not like about Charles was his lack of appreciation for the beautiful world of Pennsylvania. She said, "You like this season?"

"Oh yes, but then I guess I like all seasons."

It was a milksop sort of reply, and Charity tried to keep the conversation going. Actually, they had little in common. His world was like a foreign country to Charity. She was used to the demanding work of taking care of a family. The church was a very living thing to her, but Charles's religion seemed to be simply a matter of form, something he did, as he wore a certain suit or ate at a certain time.

Finally, Charles pulled over beside the river, which was now free of ice and made pleasant, sibilant gurgling sounds. "I love the river," Charity said. "If I were a man, I'd be a captain of a riverboat or maybe an oceangoing vessel. Wouldn't you like that, Charles?"

"I think it would be very uncomfortable."

Involuntarily, Charity shook her head. Was there *nothing* the man would grow enthusiastic over? She sat in silence, determined to let him choose the line of conversation and was shocked when he turned to her and said, "I would like it very much if you would marry me, Charity."

Charles made no attempt to kiss her or even to take her hand. It was the kind of of-

41

fer a man might make if he were seeking a business partner. He had no passion and no excitement. Charity had suspected that, sooner or later, this moment would come, and she had prepared herself for it. She had to refuse him, but she had to do it kindly.

"It's honored I am that you would ask me to be your wife, but I'm not ready to marry, Charles."

Charles Campbell suffered a shock. He had loitered in his courtship because he had doubts about whether Charity would be a proper wife for him — which meant in his mind one that would satisfy his father. It never once occurred to him that she might refuse him. He was aware that many women had in subtle ways — and some not so subtle — offered themselves to him. For Charity to refuse him was almost beyond his comprehension, and he wondered if he had heard her correctly.

"What do you mean you're not ready to marry? What are you waiting for?"

Charity hesitated. Perhaps a little of the truth would not hurt this young man who had so much — and yet so little. "Charles," she said, "a woman should love the man she marries with all of her heart. Next to God he should be the biggest thing in her life, and the man should feel the same way about the woman. Man and wife, they become one flesh. I saw a good marriage between my father and my mother. They loved each other dearly, and I vowed I would never marry until I found a man I could feel as strongly about as my mother did about the man she married." She continued to talk about what it was like to be in love.

Finally, Charles, somewhat nettled by her refusal, said, "You're romantic! You're waiting for a man on a white horse to come into your life."

"Not so. I'm the most practical member of my family. I always have been, but there is a love that surpasses friendship. A wife should be the best friend her husband has and also his lover."

Charles blurted out, "Think what you're doing, Charity. Hard times are coming. I've heard Father talking to other men of power and influence. They all know that there's going to be a break in the economy. You have your family to think about."

"Charles, the Lord is my Provider. There's a word in the Bible called *Jehovah-jireh.* It means 'The Lord is my Provider.' "

"Oh, that's well enough that —"

Charity looked him in the face and said plainly and with great force, "I would not

43

marry a man I'm not willing to share a bed with for the next fifty years."

Charles swallowed hard and could not meet her eyes. She was outspoken, but this, at least, convinced him that she would be the most uncomfortable woman to be married to he could possibly meet.

"Well, Father will be disappointed."

Charity smiled. She wanted to say something cutting, but she felt a great sorrow for this young man. She realized that Charles's wife would have to fit into Angus Campbell's scheme of marriage. He was a patriarch in the worst sense of the word.

Finally, she said gently, "Well, don't worry, Charles. I'm sure your father will survive the shock."

Those around the super table were noisy, as usual, with Bronwen the loudest. She was telling about an adventure she had on the way home from the school. Evan was quieter than usual, and Charity knew she would have to hunt him up later and find out what was troubling him. Meredith was eating noisily and without a sign of the table manners Charity had tried to teach her. Her father, however, troubled Charity the most.

"What's troubling you, Pa?"

"I've been troubled you didn't marry

44

young Charles."

"I've explained that to you."

"I still don't understand it. He's not a bad-looking fellow. He has no bad habits. He has the money to care for a wife. Tell me again why you rejected him. I think you've gone loony, Daughter."

"Everyone thinks that," Bronwen spoke up. "Everyone says you lost your mind, Charity. I think so too."

"You watch your mouth, girl!" Gwilym said sharply. He had refrained from criticizing Charity's choice, but he would not permit any of the family to criticize her because of it. "It's her life, and she's the one who will have to live with the man she chooses."

"I didn't like him anyway," Meredith said. "I think it would be unseemly for her to marry him."

"Unseemly?" Gwilym couldn't help but smile. "Where did you find that word?"

"It's in the dictionary, Pa. It means 'not suitable'."

"I think this is a sprite or an elf we're raising. She's reading the dictionary. What a strange child you are, Meredith Morgan!"

Evan had said practically nothing, but now he spoke up. "I have something to say, and it's going to be difficult." Instantly every eye

45

was on Evan. Even Meredith had noticed that he'd been quieter than usual, but it was Charity who had the only clue. He talked more to her than he did to the others of the family, and she had a fear of what he was going to say next.

Evan put both hands flat on the table and bowed his head for a moment. He was a thoughtful young man, kind, more withdrawn than Charity would have liked. "I've decided I'm going to leave here and go look for work someplace else."

"I wish you wouldn't do that, Evan," Charity said at once. "We need to stick together as a family."

"What would you do, boy, go to another mine?" Gwilym asked.

"No!" The answer was sharp and staccato. "Never again will I go down beneath the earth to work! I'll do anything but that."

It was an old argument, and Gwilym Morgan knew there was no use pursuing it further. "We need each other, Evan. You're the oldest son. You'll be the head of this family one day. You can't abandon your family. It would be like losing an arm to you."

"I know it would, Pa, but we're going to have to do something."

A gloom seemed to fall on the entire

group; even Meredith, after looking at the faces, said nothing. One by one they left the table then, but somehow a page in the book had turned, and each knew a new chapter was beginning.

Three days after Evan's announcement, Gwilym shared news too. He had taken his bath and said nothing, but finally, when all were gathered around the table and he had given thanks for the food, he said quietly, "It's bad news I have, family. The mine is going to close."

"I knew it!" Evan exclaimed. His words came in a rush. "Everybody's been saying it. What are we going to do now, Pa?"

"We're going to pray and ask God to give us guidance."

"Some aren't waiting," Charity said quietly. "The Grissoms, the Taylors, and the McDonalds — they've already left town."

"Our number grows smaller," Gwilym said, "but the Lord will hold us together. We'll call a meeting and come to a decision." He looked down at his hands ground with the blackness of the coal that would not wash out. "We need each other. That's what the church is."

Evan looked up quickly at Charity and shook his head. She knew what he was thinking, and she feared he was right.

"Yes, we'll have to seek God and find a way to keep the Pilgrim Way together," she said.

CHAPTER THREE

Stopping for a moment and bending over, Bronwen peered carefully at the small break in the earth. For a moment she stood perfectly still, her mind darting back and forth, wondering whether an animal had made it. She was keenly aware of the world she lived in — trees, grasses, reptiles, birds, and everything that occupied this particular part of Pennsylvania. She had filled the house with trophies she found, including a hornet's nest that hung close to her bed. She was an inquisitive twelve-year-old with more than her share of imagination, and this quality troubled her father who valued practicality more than romantic notions.

Straightening up, Bronwen continued her walk along the river. March was still cool, but the sun overhead was warm, and she stopped more than once simply to look up with her eyes closed and soak in the warm rays. Eventually, she saw a figure and ran forward to stop beside Evan sitting on the remains of a fallen tree and staring out over the river.

"What are you doing, Evan?"

"Nothing."

"Why don't you come home with me? Charity has made some gingerbread."

Evan turned his eyes on her and shook his head. His mouth was turned downward in a frown. "No. I'm thinking. Now get away from here, or I'll sling you in the river."

Well acquainted with her older brother and knowing he wouldn't do such an act, Bronwen took a seat beside him and for a while chattered on without receiving an answer.

Finally, he said impatiently, "Will you hush, girl? You'd talk the horns off a billy goat."

"Evan, do you think we're going to starve?"

"We might."

This was not the answer Bronwen wanted, and she argued, "No, we won't! God won't let us starve. Haven't you ever read the Bible?"

"Yes, I've read the Bible." Evan rose and gave her a disgusted look. "Good-bye now."

"Where are you going?"

"To the saloon — to get drunk."

50

Bronwen called out after him. "You'll go to perdition if you do!"

Evan glanced over his shoulder. "Perdition might be better than this place."

Bronwen shouted, "I'm going to tell Pa." She waited for a reply but got none. Bronwen pursued her walk for a time and took a shortcut home. She was headed through a section where several of the poorer houses lay on the outskirts of town, and suddenly she saw two boys older than herself watching her. One of them was smoking a cigar.

He called out to her, "Hey, Bronwen, come here."

"I won't." She knew both of the boys. The larger one was Druce Prosser, and the smaller one was Kian Madoc. Druce's father was a notorious drunk and brawler, and now Druce stood in front of the girl, blocking her way.

"Well, look at this, will you, Kian. We got a big mouthed girl here."

"You leave me alone, Druce Prosser!"

"Why would I do that?" Prosser grinned. His teeth were bad, and there was a sly look in his eyes. He winked at his friend. "Kian, what do you say we show Bronwen something?"

"I don't want to see anything from you."

"Why, we'll show you something you've

51

never seen before." Prosser grabbed her and grinned at her struggle. "You're a young woman now. You better start learning how to treat your gentlemen friends."

"Let me go!"

Both boys laughed, and Kian grabbed her other arm. "Come on in the shack. Ain't nobody home. We could have a party," Prosser said. He leaned over and whispered something in her ear, and Bronwen fought to get away, but they were too strong for her.

"Let me go!" she screamed.

"After we'll show you something. Come on, girl —"

Suddenly, a big man turned the corner. He reached out and cuffed Prosser on the ear, and the boy yelled and grabbed his ear. "You let me alone, Dai Bondo!"

"Will you have another?" The speaker, Dai Bondo, was not a tall man, but the muscles of his chest and arms filled out his thin shirt. As most men in the neighborhood, he had the grime of coal dust ground into him, and his eyes had scar tissue around them. He was a bare-knuckle fighter, a fearful one, and now he slapped Kian Madoc in the chest, driving him backward. "You rats get out of here. Crawl into your holes," he said.

"My pa will kill you!" Prosser shouted,

but he backed away.

Dai laughed at the two and said, "Away from here, or I'll break your noses." He turned to Bronwen. "Come here now, girl."

Bronwen stuck her tongue out at the two boys and skipped along beside Bondo. "I'll take you to your house," he said. "You might run into some more vermin like that."

"I wish you had knocked them both silly, Dai Bondo. They whispered dirty things in my ear."

"Did they now? I may have a talk with their fathers. Bad manners, they're having."

As the two walked along, Bronwen talked as fast as possible, and finally they reached the house. She said, "Come inside. It's some gingerbread, you'll be having."

Dai grinned. "All right, girl. I think that sounds good."

As they stepped inside, Bronwen said, "You smell that? Charity makes the best gingerbread in town."

Gwilym Morgan appeared, and his eyes opened with surprise when he saw Dai Bondo.

"Well, Dai," he said, "what is it now?"

"Pa," Bronwen said, not giving the man a chance to speak, "Druce Prosser and Kian Madoc tried to take me into their old house, and Dai Bondo gave them a thumping!"

53

Charity had come in from the kitchen, an apron around her waist. Her eyes glinted dangerously, as they did when she grew angry. "Did you give them a kick, Dai?"

"No."

"I should have been there!"

Dai Bondo grinned. "Well, you've given Charles Campbell a good kick, so I suppose you'd know how."

"Come on in. Have some gingerbread."

They all sat down except Charity who cut slices of gingerbread. As Bronwen related her adventure to Gwilym, she gave each a slice. "An extra large one for you, Dai."

Dai took a bite. "Wonderful! You ought to take some to Charles Campbell and soften the man up, don't you see?" He took another bite of gingerbread and turned his head sideways, laughter in his eyes. "People are wondering why you won't have him."

Charity was pouring tea for everyone. "I'd as soon be married to an old eel! They have more backbone than Charles Campbell."

Dai drained half his tea, boiling hot as it was, and winked at Gwilym. "She'll marry a man with backbone, Gwilym, and he'll take a broomstick to her."

Charity laughed. She liked Dai Bondo very much and was grateful to him for his help. "If you want more gingerbread and more tea, you'll say no more about Mr. Charles Campbell."

Dai nodded and continued to eat his cake. Finally, he said, "Gwilym, people are saying the Pilgrim Way will scatter like a bunch of scared crows."

"No, that won't happen!" Gwilym said firmly. "God put us together, and He'll make a way for us to live."

"If you're having my opinion" — Dai shrugged his massive shoulders — "the whole town is going to dry up and blow away."

Talk continued about the hard times and the possibility of the town ceasing to exist. "There's no way for us to make a living here, Gwilym," Dai said, and he shifted in his chair and put his big hands before him. They were scarred, and the knuckles were large and had been the quietus of many an opponent in the bare-knuckle fights. "This is going to be a ghost town in a few weeks. Seven families moved just this week."

"What do you suggest, Dai," Gwilym said, "that we quit and go away in all directions?"

"Let me show you something," Charity said. Moving quickly to the table beside the window, she picked up a newspaper. It was folded, and she placed it before her father.

"Look, Pa, I've been reading about Oregon."

"Aye, I've heard about that," Dai Bondo said. "What does it say?"

"What difference what it says! We can't go to Oregon."

"Why not, Pa?" Charity said. "There's free land there; that paper says so!"

"Does it say it's more than two thousand miles from here, and it's a blinking wilderness?"

"That's what I understand," Dai said, giving Charity a sharp look. "The redskins are thick out there."

"But there's free land there. We could take up homesteads close to one another." Charity spoke rapidly. She was excited at the news of the new country opening up on the West Coast. According to all reports, the land was fruitful and it was free. She turned her attention. "Dai, you've always talked about the mill your father owned for grinding corn. You could build one there and be a miller. No more grubbing in the mines."

Dai blinked with surprise. He was not a man who thought a great deal and had little philosophy, but the miner's life was a hard one, and the best memories of his life were those days when he was a small boy. He had worked with his father in the grinding mill.

"It sounds like a bit of heaven, but how do we get there? There are no railroads to Oregon."

"There are no roads either," Gwilym said defiantly. "There's no way."

"But wagon trains go all the time. Read what the story says."

"It's foolish, Charity. Now say no more about it. It's only a dream."

"Well, Pa, it may be only a dream, but it's more than we've got now!"

Charity was walking along her favorite pathway. It was a half mile from the village and relatively unspoiled. She had seen deer in this place, a sight that had thrilled her, and now she kept her eyes open for such a sight.

The sun overhead was warm, and she stopped for a time and breathed in the freshness of the air. Winter was gone, and the warmth of summer lay ahead, a time she dearly loved.

Suddenly, a figure appeared at the end of a lane. The man looked familiar, wearing a black suit and a hat such as no one wore in her village. As she came closer, she was delighted to realize it was her Uncle Paul Bryce. She cried out, "Uncle Paul!" and started to run toward him, but as she got closer, something happened to the man. She saw his face, a face she loved, for Paul Bryce, a brother to her dead mother, was partial to her. He was the warden at a state penitentiary not twenty miles away from the village, and he often came, sometimes with his family, to visit the Morgans.

"Uncle Paul!" Charity cried out and then suddenly stopped for there was a serious look on her uncle's face, and even as she watched, somehow he seemed to fade. Charity stood dead still and cried again, "Uncle Paul — Uncle Paul!" The figure before her motioned her, urging her to come to him but then seemed to turn into a mist and was gone.

"Uncle Paul, what's wrong?"

Abruptly, the figure before her vanished, and Charity emerged from the vivid dream with a tiny cry. She sat up in the bed and stared into the gloom. The moon outside was throwing silver beams through the window, and she found herself trembling. The dream had been so real, and she went over it in her mind. She remembered how he had motioned toward her as if telling her to come with him.

Charity had no watch nor clock, but she could tell it was close to dawn. Knowing that sleep would not be possible, she got out of bed, dressed quickly, and left her room. She went into the kitchen, started the fire, and soon made herself a cup of tea. Others would be getting up soon, but she could not think of breakfast.

She had the Welsh feelings about dreams and visions. Her mother had been an imaginative woman believing greatly in dreams and their interpretations, but Charity had never experienced a thing like this. She thought about her Uncle Paul and how deeply he had loved her mother. The two had been very close. Since her death, Uncle Paul had visited often, bringing them gifts at Christmastime, and though Charity tried to shove the dream from her mind into the dark area of forgetfulness, she knew she would not be able for it was imprinted there as clearly as if it were painted on a canvas. She knew she would not speak of it to anyone, but she longed for her mother in a painful and poignant way.

Charity walked with Meredith and Bronwen toward the house that sat off the road. It was the house of Mr. Jonas Edwards, the schoolmaster in the village. Edwards had taught Charity and Evan, and now he was in charge of the education of her two sisters. "You two behave yourselves."

"I always behave myself," Meredith said.

"No, you don't," Bronwen argued, giving her an impatient look. "In our last lesson you paid no attention. You were looking at some bugs crawling on the window."

The door opened, and Jonas Edwards, a tall man with kindly features and a shock of salt-and-pepper hair, smiled. "Well, good morning. My scholars are here. How are you, Miss Charity?"

"I'm fine."

"Come in. I'll give you a report on these two, and a cup of tea, we'll be having."

Twenty minutes later Edwards sat with Charity in the kitchen, pouring her tea. He had set the two young scholars to work, and now he said genially, "I've got a good report on your sisters. They're both bright girls. Meredith especially. I think she's going to be a scholar of some kind." He smiled. "And Bronwen . . . maybe a writer of romance."

"A scholar would be better," Charity smiled. She had always liked Mr. Edwards, and now she listened as he spoke of how well they were doing. Finally, the talk turned to the economic plight of the town. In answer to Charity's questions about what was going to happen, Edwards frowned and put his cup down. He folded his hands and shook his head sadly.

"I'm afraid there's little hope, Charity. I'm going to have to move my family soon."

"You'd leave the village? Why, you've been here my whole life."

"I know, but the way things are happening, people are leaving, and there won't be enough scholars for school and no one to pay my fees."

This was the greatest shock Charity had heard. She had been troubled, along with many others, about the fate of the village and the inhabitants, and now for Mr. Edwards to leave was worse than she had expected. Then she remembered her conversation about Oregon. "Tell me about Oregon, Mr. Edwards."

"Oregon, is it? Is your father thinking of going to Oregon?"

"No sir, he's not, but I am. We've got to go somewhere, and I barely know where it is."

"Let me show you." Edwards rose and pulled a large book from the shelf. He opened it up and turned it so she could look at it. "Here we are in Pennsylvania, and here is Oregon."

"That's a fearful long way, sir."

"More than two thousand miles."

"Pa says there's no good way to get there."

"Well, of course, you can take a sea voyage and go by Cape Horn, around South America, but that's terribly expensive. It costs more than three hundred dollars for a single passenger."

"We could never afford that."

"No, most people go in wagon trains. The trains are made up in Independence, Missouri." He put his finger on the map. "Then they follow what's called the Oregon Trail all the way along here until they get to Vancouver and then Oregon City. I've read a good deal about it."

"It's a long, long journey," she whispered. "Pa's against it."

"Well, it's not a thing to be undertaken lightly," Edwards said, shaking his head sadly, "but, in a way, the whole movement over the Oregon Trail has been good for Pennsylvania."

"And how is that, sir?"

"Well, they have to have good wagons, and the best ones, Conestoga wagons, are made right here in Pennsylvania. The wagon makers and wheelwrights are working around the clock."

"What about the land there? It's free, I've heard. I've been wondering if it might not be a place for our people to go. Free land is not to be sneezed at."

Edwards studied the young woman. He

had a real affection for her and her brother Evan and now was troubled at what she was proposing. "Well, it's called free land, Charity, but it's not really."

"How is that, sir?"

"Well, people die trying to get there — cholera, storms, Indian attacks — and when you get there, there's a forest. You'd have to fell huge trees. It's not Plains country, you understand. You'll have to hew a farm out of the wilderness." He suddenly had a thought and rose again. Going to his bookshelf, he picked two books and said, "Here, you might like to read these. This one is just a cheap dime novel."

Charity took the book. It was printed on cheap paper, and there was a crude illustration on the front of a young woman talking to an Indian woman. The title was *Esther: A Story of the Oregon Trail.*

"The story's just a romance. It's not much, but you get more of a feeling from this book." She took the other book he handed her. "James Fenimore Cooper has written a whole series of books about the frontier. I think he sort of romanticized the Indians, the natives there, but you should read it if you're interested."

"Thank you, Mr. Edwards." She took the books, turned the pages over, and knew she would read them at once. She waited until the lessons were over and then led the two girls home. They were chattering like squirrels, as young girls did, but Charity heard none of it. *So it would be a hard journey, but there would be a place for us, and we could stay together.* The thought warmed her, and she knew she would have to tell her father about it, but she rather dreaded it.

That night at supper, she waited until after the meal and then told the family what Mr. Edwards had said about the Oregon Territory.

Her father listened carefully; then his mouth drew into a tight line. "It's impossible, girl. More than two thousand miles in a wagon and with wild Indians and sickness. Don't even think of it!"

Evan, however, said, "I'd like to read one of those books while you're reading the other one. I'd like to go to a place like that."

Charity felt encouraged for she had at least one supporter, but she knew her father would have to be convinced.

Later, as Evan was helping her wash the dishes, he said, "Charity, I must leave this place."

"Where would you go, Evan?"

"I don't know," he said, and there was a grim quality to his voice. She recognized it for she had heard it a few times when he made up his mind and couldn't be dissuaded. "I don't know where I'll go, but it won't be to a mine."

"You always wanted to be a farmer."

"I could be one in Oregon."

Charity sighed and put the last dish up. "But Father's hard against it."

"Well, Oregon or someplace else. I'm not going to spend my life grubbing underground like a blind mole!"

CHAPTER FOUR

The meeting house that the men of the Pilgrim Way had built was plain — a simple frame structure with a hard pine floor and a twelve-foot-high ceiling. The furniture was as basic as the building itself. The hard pews, built of rough lumber, had straight backs so it was impossible to get comfortable in them. A waist-high table, two and a half feet square, served as a pulpit for the preacher, and the four windows on each side admitted the bright morning sunlight as Gwilym Morgan stood behind the pulpit.

Most of the people he looked out on he had known all of his life, and now he saw in their faces a nervousness and a lack of assurance that troubled him. He had prayed much over how to speak so that they would face their problems with faith in God, but he saw on every face apprehension and even fear.

The one exception was Karl Studdart, a

tall, broad man of German heritage, with blond hair and blue eyes. There was no fear in Studdart, and Gwilym was well aware that Karl thought he was a more suitable leader of the group than himself. His wife, Freida, sat beside him, and beside her Helga, their sixteen-year-old daughter. Gwilym thought quickly, *Karl wants to be the leader of the group, and in some ways he would be better, but one thing is sure, he's not afraid of this journey that we're contemplating. We can count on him.*

Malcolm Douglas and his wife, Ann, sat with their children, Will, Elizabeth, and Henry, all under the age of ten. Malcolm, at the age of thirty-two, was no more than average size. He had rusty hair and blue eyes and had originally come from Scotland. He had lost most of his accent but not all. *A good steady man but not convinced that this is the way to go. Oregon seems like a million miles away to him, but I think we can win him.*

Next to the Douglases was the Brand family — fifty-year-old Nelson; his wife, Kate; their son, Tom, a tall, good-looking boy with brown hair and brown eyes; and seventeen-year-old Alice. Brand had little boldness about him although he was one of the elders of the church and could be counted on in most things. He was timid, however, about this trip and had already spoken of his fears to Gwilym. *I'll have to win him over, but he's a good man.*

Halfway back, Frank Novak, age thirty-one, stared at Gwilym. Novak had black hair and dark blue eyes that revealed his Slavic ancestry. His wife Marva, three years younger, was a strongly built woman with dark brown hair and eyes. *It's hard to know about Frank. He doesn't talk much, but I've heard that he's opposed to this trip. He'd be a good man to have on the train. I'll have to be sure to try and convince him after the meeting.*

On the other side from the Novaks was the Dekker family. Jacob Dekker was in his midforties, a sturdy man of Dutch ancestry with blond hair and clear blue eyes. His wife, Sofie, was a heavy-set woman with the same blonde hair and blue eyes. Kirsten was their daughter, and their three sons, Hans, Fritz, and Paul, ranged from eighteen- to twenty-four-years-old. Gwilym had tried to sound out the Dekkers, but Jacob was a slow-moving man and could not seem to make up his mind.

On the same bench were Jacob's parents, Konrad and Minna. They were both short people and both had silver hair. *They're old to be making the trip,* Gwilym thought. *They're in their seventies. They'll go to be with their family.*

As his eyes scanned the congregation, Gwilym considered Nolan Cole. Cole was only twenty-eight, six feet tall, one hundred eighty pounds, and well built. He had black hair and hazel eyes. He was a strong-willed man, given to having his own way. He wasn't a good husband, which most recognized, and wasn't popular with his neighbors. His wife, Marzina, sat beside him, and Gwilym noted that they did not sit close together. He knew she was unhappy, but there was nothing a man could do to fix a mismatched couple.

In front of the Coles were York Wingate and his wife, Helen. York was not a tall man, no more than five-nine, very wiry with crisp brown hair and brown eyes. He was a doctor, and his wife had been Helen Dekker, daughter of Jacob and Sofie. Gwilym had particularly wanted this couple to go, for a doctor on a journey this long would be needed, without a doubt.

Gwilym glanced over the rest of the group and, noticing restlessness, said, "Friends, we will now stand and give thanks to our Father for His goodness." The congregation stood, and he prayed a brief prayer, ending with, "Lord, You led Abraham out into a land he had never seen. You kept him safe from enemies and wild animals, and we are asking You, O righteous Father, to guide Your people in that way. In the name of Jesus, we will ask this. Amen."

A few amens floated across the room, echoing Gwilym's benediction, and he continued, "I am well aware, brethren, that some of you are apprehensive about this proposed trip to Oregon, and you do well to be thoughtful for it is a long journey, and there are dangers." Gwilym spoke earnestly and finally he said, "As is our custom, we are one body, and there is no ruler or master here. Each man is the priest in his household, so I will now leave the floor open for discussion of the way we should take."

At once Karl Studdart stood. He had a thick neck, strong hands, and a determined look on his face. "Brother Gwilym," he said, "I have prayed much, and I and my family are agreed that we must go from this place. There's nothing for us here. The question is, should it be Oregon, and I say to you now that if that is the will of the body here, then my family and I will certainly join in the pilgrimage."

He spoke for some time with a rough sort of eloquence, and there was a forcefulness in the man that people naturally looked to. He ended by saying rather enigmatically, "We are of necessity forced to trust in our leadership, and let us pray that God will give us leadership in a way that will not guide the Pilgrim Way astray."

Gwilym nearly smiled. *This is Karl's way of saying, I am the natural born leader of this group. It's time for Gwilym Morgan to step down.* He said merely, "Thank you, Brother Karl. Now could I hear from the others? Is there anyone else?"

Sturdy and with piercing blue eyes Jacob Dekker stood up. "I have troubled about this journey, Brother Gwilym. None of us have been this way before."

"We could all drive wagons," Studdart spoke up. "That's the way we will get there."

"Yes, we can drive wagons, but we know nothing about fighting Indians or even the way. There will be decisions to make. I am not sure we are ready for this, not until we look at all other possibilities."

One by one the members rose, and each man said something. Most of them were filled with doubt, and York Wingate spoke for all when he said, "It troubles me, Brother Morgan, that none of us have been over this trail. We are not frontiersmen. I think that the proper thing would be to find men who could go with us and teach us the way to make this journey."

A murmur of ascent went over the congregation, and at once Gwilym said, "That is a wise suggestion, Brother Wingate, and we will do exactly that." He knew that the group was still divided and that some action was needed to draw them together. They were a small enough group as it was, and all of them had heard that the larger the wagon train the safer it was from Indian attack.

"We will take this day for fasting and prayer and seek God's leadership," Gwilym said. He went to the bench in the front and knelt and soon was joined by others, and the building was filled with the murmurs of intercession as members of the Pilgrim Way sought God.

None of the women had spoken in the meeting. This was customary with the Way. Any leadership the women had was the ability to influence their husbands who would then make the public announcements. Charity had listened carefully, and during the service one thing had become clear. She had not been able to escape the dream of her Uncle Paul motioning to her. She believed strongly that some dreams had meaning, and she had decided she would visit the prison.

Her father was agreeable for the Morgans had all visited the prison to bear witness of the gospel to the inmates as well as to take books, tracts, and gifts of food. "I think it would be a good thing if you would go see your uncle, but you must not be gone too long."

"Two days at the most. You know how much I enjoy Uncle Paul. I'll cook all day tomorrow to take things to the prisoners, and I'll take the buggy if it's all right."

"It's somehow unseemly for a young woman to be going about the country alone. Maybe Evan should go with you."

"I'll ask him, Pa."

Evan declined Charity's invitation, and the next day she spent cooking with Bronwen's help. By bedtime they had cooked a mountain of cookies, several cakes, and pies. She knew the inmates got hungry for sweets, and she was exhausted by the time she'd finished.

The next morning she rose early, and Evan helped her load the wagon. "I'll go with you if you think I should, Sister," he said, his eyes troubled.

"I'll be glad to have you, but you don't

have to, Evan, if you've got things to do here."

"I'm not very good at talking to prisoners," Evan admitted. "I never know what to say to them. You talk like a magpie." He grinned. "Whatever do you find to talk about?"

"Oh, it doesn't matter. They're hungry for any kind of conversation."

"Especially from a pretty woman, I would guess. You have a way with them."

Finally the buggy was loaded, and she spoke to the horses and turned to wave, "Good-bye, Bronwen. Good-bye, Meredith. Good-bye, Evan — Pa. I'll be careful."

She looked forward to the trip for it would give her time to think. She had thought of little but her dream and knew from the meeting at the church that something must happen soon. She prayed all the way to the prison, fifteen miles away, and reached it well before dark. Her uncle's house was close to the prison, which was surrounded by thick, high walls. The sight of them always gave her a chill, and her visits always brought a sense of pain that men should be locked up like animals, but she knew it had to be.

"Whoa, Queenie," she said as she pulled up in front of the house. She started to get down and saw her Uncle Paul Bryce walking rapidly out of the house.

"Charity!" he cried. "How good to see you!" He reached up and lifted her down easily. He was a tall man, lean and strong, with the reddish hair and the gray eyes that his sister, Charity's mother, had.

"It's good to see you, Uncle Paul. Look, I've got all kinds of goodies here for the prisoners. What shall we do with them?"

Eileen Bryce came hurrying out. She was forty-six, a handsome blonde with light green eyes. "Charity, I'm so glad you've come." The two women embraced, and she added, "It looks like you brought enough to feed the world."

"It won't be nearly enough, but I like to bring something. I brought a lot of tracts, too, Uncle Paul."

"Well, the prisoners will take the tracts if you put them alongside a slice of pie." He smiled. "You're getting prettier every time I see you."

"You're just trying to get some of my pies, Uncle Paul." Charity smiled and patted his arm. "Let's get these inside, or should we take them directly to the prison?"

"I think I'll take them to the prison. You stay here and visit with Eileen. You can distribute them and visit in the morning.

How long can you stay?"

"Oh, until you get tired of me."

"Well, that will never happen," Eileen smiled. She was very fond of Charity and all the other children. Both she and her husband spoiled them dreadfully every chance they got. "Come on in now. You must be tired. The food's still hot. Still on the stove." She led Charity inside, and Charity sank into a chair, accepting the food and hot coffee gratefully. As she ate, she gave Eileen the news of the family, and then when her Uncle Paul came back, she had to tell it again.

"What's happening?" he said, taking a cup of coffee from Eileen. "Is the family well?"

"Very well, Uncle Paul, but there's a great deal of difficulty facing us."

"Difficulty? What sort of difficulty?" Warden Bryce listened as his niece outlined the problem. He was a highly intelligent man and kept up with national affairs. It turned out he knew a great deal about the exodus to Oregon, and the three of them talked for a long time about the possibility. Finally, Paul said, "Well, Charity, it's a difficult trip. Dangerous, even deadly, and I'd be sorry to see you and your family settle so far away."

"We'd miss you, too," Charity said, "but

we've got to do something."

Paul Bryce had never been an intimate member of the Pilgrim Way. He thought the Pilgrims were too narrow, and he was a member of the Methodist Church as was his wife. He still had great faith in the small group, especially in Gwilym and his family. "Well," he said finally, "while you're here, maybe God will open a door."

"I was reading that in the Bible last night," Eileen said suddenly. "It's in the book of Revelation. God said to one of the churches, I forget which, I set before you an open door."

"That's what we need, Aunt Eileen," Charity responded, "a door." She hesitated. "I had a dream about you, Uncle Paul."

"Well, there are young women dreaming about me all over this country." Paul winked at her and ignored Eileen's sniff. "What was the dream?" He listened as Charity related the dream, and then he said, "So, that's why you've come."

"Well, I'm always glad to see you and to have a chance to bear witness to the prisoners and to do what I can for them. But, yes, I believe some dreams mean something."

"Well, they did to Joseph and to Jacob and to Paul. He dreamed he saw a man from Macedonia, saying, 'Come over and help us.' So if there's some reason for you to be here, we'll have to find it. Now, let's you and I go in and sit before the fire and —"

"No, I'm going to help Aunt Eileen with the dishes, then we'll all three sit before the fire."

"Good for you!" Eileen exclaimed. "He's the laziest man I've ever seen," but she smiled as she spoke, and the three immediately started clearing the dishes.

The prison had always frightened Charity, and she was not easily frightened. There was a fetid smell about the place that she thought was the smell of fear. Of course, there were other bad odors, too, that seemed to have sunk into the concrete walls of the prison, but the physical aspects were only part of the difficulty. Everything was gray and hard and cold. The strange lean faces that looked out at her from between the bars gave the appearance of vicious animals. She always managed to cover her fears and managed a smile each time she talked to one of the inmates. They came in all shapes and sizes. Some men with white hair and gaunt faces had all goodness and benevolence leeched out of them by their lives and by the prison itself. Some were very young, and she encountered one of the youngest during her morning visitation.

Her Uncle Paul had furnished a large room and had agreed to let the men come in five at a time so that she could see as many as possible. He had tables set up, and the sweets she had brought filled the tops of them. The warden had provided plates and fresh coffee for all who wished it, and, of course, they all did.

The first group of men scrambled in, wearing coarse, gray prison dress. All of them had shaved heads, which made their appearance more wolfish than was actually true.

Charity introduced herself. "Good morning. I'm glad to see you. My name is Charity Morgan. I've met some of you before, perhaps, but I want you all to taste some of my cooking. I am considered a very good cook."

The men moved forward eagerly, and Charity spoke to each one. She did not give a tract to every inmate, only those who showed an interest, and it was not until the second group of prisoners entered that she met a young man who appeared to be no more than sixteen or seventeen years old.

"What's your name?" she asked.

"Billy Watson, ma'am."

"Well, Billy, would you rather have pie or

cake or cookies?"

"Any will do me, ma'am."

"How about some nice blackberry cobbler?"

"Oh, ma'am, that would be very nice."

The other prisoners were eating wolfishly, and one of them, a big bruising man who had introduced himself as Jack Canreen, said, "Hey, Billy, you get us something to take back to the cell, and I'll let you keep half of it."

Charity turned and stared at him. "If I give it to him, he'll keep all of it."

Canreen grinned roughly. He was rough in every aspect. His face showed the marks of battle, and his hands were like hams. "Billy takes care of me. He's like my daddy, ain't you, Billy?"

Charity tried to stare him down, but his eyes were bold and innocent. "How about another piece of that cake, Charity?"

Charity did not like his attitude. She cut him another piece of cake, however, and said, "Are you a Christian man, Mr. Canreen?" The other inmates laughed, and one of them, a tall man who had said absolutely not a word but had taken coffee and a piece of pie, smiled briefly.

"No, Jack's no Christian. He belongs to the devil."

Canreen shot a glance at the tall man who must have been at least six feet three inches. He had a dark complexion and was sun-burned so that his light blue eyes seemed to gleam almost electrically. "You stay out of this, Tremayne."

The tall man took a sip of coffee, shrugged, and said no more.

Before this group left, she pulled Billy to one side. She felt sorry for the young man. "How old are you, Billy?"

"Seventeen."

"And what are you in for?"

"I was convicted of burglary. I got in with the wrong bunch, Miss Charity."

"That big man, the one called Canreen, does he bully you?"

Fear touched the young man's eyes. "Yes, ma'am, he bullies everybody — except Casey Tremayne."

"If I give you some cookies, can you hide them from him?"

"No, ma'am, he'll shake me down as soon as I get out of here."

"Before I leave, I'll have my uncle bring you back, and I'll give you something extra good. Are you a Christian man, Billy?"

"My ma was. I guess I'm nothing."

"Here, take this." She handed him a small New Testament, and he took it awkwardly.

"Thank you, ma'am, I'll sure read it."

She watched the young man go and then greeted the next group. At noon she had lunch with her uncle who did not eat the prison food but what Eileen brought in covered dishes. They had a meal of pork chops, mashed potatoes, and green salad that she was surprised to see.

"Eileen knows how to grow things," Uncle Paul said.

"She's a good cook," Charity said. Her mind returned to the prisoners. "I feel so sorry for these men."

"So do I," Paul said, shrugging his shoulders. "Most of them are here because they couldn't control themselves. Others, more or less, got caught up in the machinery."

"I think that young fellow Billy Watson must be one of those."

"Yes, he is. Doesn't have any business being here. The other prisoners brutalize him. There's nothing I can do about it, I'm afraid."

"The big man, Canreen. He bullies him."

"Canreen's a hard case. He bullies everybody."

"But not the one called Tremayne."

Paul's wife shot his niece a glance. "You met Tremayne? You get a smile out of him?"

"No, I didn't."

"You never will. He's a hard one. Canreen wouldn't bully him. He tried it once and lost a couple of teeth in the process."

"He seems angry about something, Tremayne I mean."

"Yes, his name is Casey Tremayne. He's got an interesting story. He's not from the North, you know. He grew up in the West. As a matter of fact, his folks were killed in an Indian raid, and he was raised by the Sioux until he was twelve. Then he got away from them."

"What's he in for?"

"He half killed a man. They got him for attempted murder. Trouble is, the man he shot was the nephew of the attorney general of the state of Pennsylvania. He was pretty well railroaded, and he's bitter about it."

"He looks different from the others."

"Well, that's his Western side, I guess. He's been all over the West. He was a trapper for a while, trapping beavers and prospecting for gold. He knows that country."

"How long is he in for?"

"He comes up for parole pretty soon, but he'll never make it."

"Why not?"

"He can't behave himself. He's angry at the world, and anytime anybody crosses him he lashes out and that includes guards. No way to get out of this place."

"I'd like to have that young man Billy back and give him some extra food. He took a Bible, too, but he said Canreen would take the food away if I gave it to him."

"You can have him back in. Would two o'clock be about right?"

"That'll be fine, Uncle Paul."

Late that night Charity was tired, for she had spent all day at the prison. Many of the prisoners were eager to talk, and some would listen to her urging to look to Jesus for salvation. Some rebuffed her, and some simply remained silent. She had finished dinner, and she was sitting in front of the fire with her Uncle Paul. Eileen was in the kitchen.

The two talked for a long time. Finally, Charity asked, "Do you think the dream I had about you means anything?"

"It might. Your mother would have known. She was very close to God. He spoke to her often in dreams." Charity stirred. Bryce gave her a careful look and said, "All this you've told me about Oregon, you think I can help you with that?"

"I don't know how you could, Uncle Paul."

Paul Bryce was a deeply religious man.

He believed in the supernatural, that God entered into the lives of people. His sister had been a fine Christian, and their mother had been devout. He sat silently for a time and said, "Well, if God is in it, we'll find out. Let me pray on this, Charity."

"All right, Uncle Paul. I hope God speaks to you."

CHAPTER FIVE

Charity had extended her visit to three days, and she had given away all her tracts and, of course, all the food she had brought. A feeling kept pulling at her, and each time she had thought she was ready to leave, something had prevented her. She spent a great deal of time alone, praying and seeking the face of God, as she always did, but for some reason she knew with certainty there was a purpose in her being here. She would not have put it in those terms, but it kept her at her uncle's house longer than she had first intended.

Finally, on the fourth day of her visit, she had risen early and was fixing breakfast when her uncle came in. He was dressed and ready for work in the same dark suit he always wore, and he greeted her pleasantly. But with one glance at him, Charity knew something was on his mind. He was a smiling man, as a rule, but now there was a seriousness about him. He accepted the cup of coffee she offered and said, "Sit down, Charity. There's something I may need to tell you."

"All right, Uncle Paul. What is it?"

The simple question seemed to trouble Paul Bryce. He turned the cup around and around in his hand, studied it as if there was an answer to be found in the black coffee, and finally he looked at her. "There's something that has come to me, and I wonder whether I should mention it or not. It's about Oregon."

Instantly Charity grew alert. "About Oregon? What about Oregon, Uncle Paul?"

"The difficulty seems to be getting there. From what I understand the land there is wonderful. They get plenty of rain, and crops would grow well. If a man wanted to go into logging, there's the logging industry. There's the biggest stand of timber on the continent, I believe, but getting there has been a problem for many."

Charity sat very still. Hope was rising within her, and she said, "I've been praying every day for an answer. What is it you've been thinking?"

"This may not be of God," Paul said slowly, "but it's come to me so strongly that at least I can mention it. It has to do with your making the trip safely from Pennsylvania to Oregon, and I warn you that it may be simply wishing on my part — something I would like to see happen because I want your family and the people of the Way to prosper."

"Tell me what it is, Uncle, please."

"Well, I've told you that Casey Tremayne was a Western man. He knows that country. I've spoken with him without telling him anything about you or your problem there at the Pilgrim Way. He has been over the Oregon Trail several times and knows it well. He's a Westerner. Knows animals, and I think it's possible that he might lead you there safely."

"But he's a prisoner."

"He's eligible for parole, and he'll be coming up any day now, but he won't get it — that is, unless there are special circumstances."

"What do you mean, Uncle Paul. I don't understand you."

"I've thought this out. I believe that I could get the parole board to issue a tentative or conditional parole to Tremayne and any of his fellow prisoners who have his same limitations. We have some hard men in here, men who likely will come up for parole many times and be turned down because of their behavior, but I'm in good standing with the members of the board. They usually take my advice, and I think although this is unusual, they might listen."

"Tell me what you plan. It sounds wonderful."

"Well, it's not," Paul said flatly. "It's a *possibility.* But I have thought about this. If I could get the parole board to issue a *conditional* parole, conditional for the men who are chosen, their parole will be approved after they have escorted your people all the way to the Oregon Territory." He leaned back and shook his head. "It sounds absolutely impossible, doesn't it, Niece?"

"It sounds like the only hope we have, but would Tremayne agree to do it?"

"I think he might. He's a bitter man. He's had a terrible thing happen in his life, but this may be his only chance to get out for years. If you like, we'll put it to him and let him make the decision. Maybe it's a fleece, Charity. If he says no, then it's not something that the Pilgrim Way needs to follow. If he says yes —"

"If he says yes, then the next miracle will come in convincing the members of the Way to accept him. But I believe it's the Lord. The dream about you was so real, and now this has come. Can we talk to him at once?"

"If you're sure this is what you want to do, you come along with me, and we'll put the matter to him."

James Elsworth Charterhouse looked up from the book he was reading, peering over his glasses at Tremayne. He was a slight man, no more than five feet nine inches, and thin as a rail. The planes of his face were sharp and aristocratic — high cheekbones, a thin nose, and a broad forehead. His hair was blond and his eyes a mild blue. He spoke with a pronounced English accent.

"I say, Casey, I wish you'd stop pacing the floor like a caged tiger." He waited for a response, and getting none, he added, "Have one of those lovely cookies I begged from Miss Morgan."

"I don't need any cookies. I need out of this hole! I'm going to die here."

Charterhouse shrugged his thin shoulders with an eloquent gesture. "A very wise man once said, *'Quem di diligunt adulescens moritur, dum valet sentit sapit.'*"

Tremayne gave Charterhouse a disgusted look. "And what does that mean?" He pretended to be disgusted at his cellmate's use of Latin but was actually impressed. Elsworth, as he was called, was a graduate of Oxford and picked up foreign languages with effortless ease. He spoke and read German, French, Spanish, Greek, and Latin and apparently never forgot anything.

"Would you believe me if I told you it meant, 'The snake fell out of the tree and ate the baby'?"

"That makes about as much sense as most of the things you spout off."

"Dear boy, don't be offensive! Actually, it's a line from Plautus, and it means, 'He whom the gods love dies young, while he has strength and senses and wits.' "

"Well, that's a cheerful thought!"

"Well, it's not too pleasant to grow old and sick." Charterhouse put down his book, took his glasses off, and polished them. "You're not going to die in here. Stop fighting the system and lick a few boots. You'll get a parole that way."

Casey turned to face Charterhouse squarely. "I won't ever do that, Elsworth."

"No, you're too proud. And you don't understand the dangers of pride. It's all in the Bible, old fellow — in the book of James, the fourth chapter. 'God resisteth the proud, but giveth grace unto the humble. . . . Cleanse your hands, ye sinners; and purify your hearts, ye double minded. . . . Humble yourselves in the sight of the Lord, and he shall lift you up.' That's what you need, old chap — a dose of humility."

"It hasn't worked for you, has it?"

"Not yet, but I'm a proud fellow — just like you."

Casey Tremayne grinned. "You don't belong in this place, Elsworth." He had developed a real affection for the Englishman, in part because Charterhouse had been responsible for making life in a cell tolerable. Before he had been assigned as Casey's cell mate, Tremayne had sunk into a morass of bitterness, had fought other inmates, and had given the guards a bad time. He had despised Charterhouse at first, but the Englishman introduced him to the world of books, and to Tremayne's surprise, he had developed a sharp interest in the world of literature and history. Elsworth was filled with talk, and Casey found a friend in him.

"Don't despair, Casey. This place is pretty bad, but we'll get out of here one day."

"I don't think so. It would take a miracle, and I don't believe in miracles."

"My Uncle Seedy always said, 'There's no miracle for a man who doesn't believe in them.' "

Casey laughed. "That uncle of yours is

full of wise sayings. I think you made him up so you can spout your philosophy without taking the blame for the nonsense."

"No indeed!" Elsworth protested. "Uncle Seedy is as real as you are. Practically raised me, as a matter of fact. And if you —"

Charterhouse was interrupted when a voice cut in. "Tremayne, the warden wants to see you. Get a move on." The guard was a burly giant of a man named Willy Hankins. He was a rough sort and did the prisoners no favors. Charterhouse had said of him once, "If your beard was on fire, Hankins would light his cigarette on it."

Tremayne said nothing but followed the guard down the corridor, wondering what he'd done wrong this time.

Charity sat bolt upright in a chair in her uncle's office. Bryce had ordered the guard to bring Tremayne in, and the two sat silently, both entertaining doubts and hopes. Finally, the door opened, and a guard said, "We have Tremayne here, Warden."

"Let him come in, Hankins."

As Tremayne came through the door, Charity suddenly had second thoughts about what was proposed. The man looked dangerous. He was far taller than average, and she had noticed that when he was there with the other inmates, he stood at least half a head taller than most of them. She had seen a lion once in a traveling circus, and there was something of a leonine quality in Casey Tremayne. He was not thick muscled but lithe, and his smooth movements weren't often seen in big men. His face was a mask, but his eyes were alert. They were the lightest blue possible, and though they were half hooded now as he studied the pair, she saw a hardness in him, and for a moment her heart failed her. But she was trusting God to give leadership in this matter.

"Tremayne, I have a rather unusual proposition for you," the warden said, then hesitated. "You may as well sit down. This may take awhile."

"Yes, Warden." Tremayne turned, and once again Charity noticed how smoothly and easily he moved. Most men lacked his quickness. He pulled the chair across the desk from the warden, sat down, and fixed his gaze on Paul Bryce's face. Most men would have been asking questions instantly, but Tremayne said nothing.

"You've met my niece, Miss Charity Morgan. She's the daughter of my sister who passed away. Her family belongs to a religious group called the Pilgrim Way."

Charity couldn't read Tremayne's face. She only half listened as her uncle traced the circumstances of the Way and ended by saying, "So you see, Tremayne, they're going to have to leave here, and they don't have a great deal of money. I've mentioned a possibility to her, and I'd like to lay it before you. You're up for parole, but we both know your behavior will prohibit your getting it. You understand that?"

"Yes, sir." The reply was brief and noncommittal, and Tremayne's eyes moved from the warden's face to meet Charity's. She seemed held by his intense gaze, and then her uncle continued.

"I believe I see a possibility here of getting you out of this place. It may be a pipe dream, but I want to explain it to you." Bryce leaned forward and said, "I believe I can convince the parole board to grant you a conditional parole."

"Never heard of a thing like that."

"It's never been done, but I believe I can get the board to take a chance on you and on any of your fellow inmates who would be helpful. It would amount to your taking over as scout for the wagon train and getting them safely to Oregon. If you can do that, the parole will be affirmed for you and for any of the men who make the trip and who qualify in your judgment. What is your thinking about this?"

Casey Tremayne spoke instantly. His voice was soft, and he had a slight accent that Charity couldn't identify. "I'll do anything to get out of this place, Warden. I expect you know that."

"I can't blame you for that. You have any questions about the proposition?"

"A lot of questions," Tremayne said instantly. "In the first place, what authority would I have with the wagon train?"

"Why do you ask that?"

"Because there are going to be difficulties along the way. This religious group is probably used to obeying a bishop or some such figure, a preacher perhaps. That would not work on the Oregon Trail. If an Indian attack comes, there wouldn't be time to stop and have a prayer meeting." He turned, and his lips turned up in a grin. "There are times, Miss Morgan, when action is needed instead of prayer."

Charity spoke up quickly, "I don't think there would be any problem. If I can convince my father and the elders to accept you, that would be one of the conditions they would have to agree to."

Tremayne studied her and then shook his head. "I doubt if you can convince them."

"I can if this thing is of God," Charity said in a sprightly voice. "I know you don't believe that, but I do."

Tremayne studied her carefully; his eyes seemed to bore into her very mind and heart. She met his gaze, and finally he shrugged and said, "I think I'd like to do it, Warden."

"All right. We'll get everything set up here. Here's a list of men due for parole but will never make it. They're all troublemakers. I think you know them. You can choose four or five to go with you, and you'll be their boss."

Tremayne took the list of paper, and a quick smile swept across his face. "These are the worst hoodlums in this prison." He glanced at Charity. "There are some murderers on this list. Some bank robbers. None of them are likely to join in your prayer meetings."

"That won't be your problem, Mr. Tremayne. Your problem will be to get us through safely to Oregon."

"Could I have a pencil, Warden?" He took the pencil from Bryce, made some checks, and said, "I'll take these four, and Billy Watson."

Bryce stared at him. "Watson's not exactly a tough sort of fellow."

"No, but he needs to be out of here. Never should have been sent here in the first place."

"There'll be no trouble about him. You agree then?"

"Sure I agree, but I think Miss Morgan's going to need a little miracle to get her people to agree with this." His head turned toward Charity again. "You realize you're asking a group of Bible-believing righteous folk to put their lives in the hands of a group of jailbirds."

For an instant Charity's heart nearly failed her, but she said, "I believe the Lord is in this. I've been praying and fasting, and it's all come together. I'm going back home now. You talk to the men you want to take with you, and I'll talk to my people."

"I don't think you'll have any luck," Tremayne said and shrugged his shoulders.

Charity hated to see his air of futility. He looked capable, but he was not the kind of a man she could really admire. No doubt he could shoot and fight and do the things Western men were reputed to be good at, but he did not have God, and to Charity Morgan that was a fatal flaw. She rose and said, "I'm going home, Uncle Paul. As soon as I convince our people, I'll be back."

As soon as she left the room, Tremayne

said, "Warden, is she always like that?"

"She has been ever since I've known her, and I've known her since the day she was born. She's a stubborn young woman, and I might warn you of this: If you have any idea of getting out and abandoning them, forget it. I'll put your name and the names of any who abandon the trip in every town in the West. You'll be brought back here and given a life sentence for escaping."

Tremayne seemed unimpressed. "It won't be any trouble for me. I may have to knock a few heads to enlighten some of the men I'll be taking. The only thing most of them understand is a bullet or a whipping."

"I want to tell you this, Tremayne. This girl is very dear to me. My sister and I were very close. I loved her dearly, and I still do though she's gone to be with the Lord. But my heart is with these people. They're going to be hard for you to get along with. I couldn't get along with them."

"You couldn't get along with them?" Tremayne was surprised for the first time. "I don't understand that."

"They're very . . . straight laced. There's even sort of a pride in their humility. They think that society is far too worldly, even religious groups. So they can grate on your nerves. You'll judge them to be self-

99

righteous, and I guess there's some truth to that in some cases. But my brother-in-law, Gwilym Morgan — there's not a finer man on the earth. You'll see that in him, I'm sure. He may not be much of a fighting man, but he's a good man, and his children are fine too. I'll take this as a personal favor if you can help us."

The appeal seemed to touch Tremayne. He ducked his head for a moment and was silent. Then he said, "I'll get the train through, Warden, or die trying."

"Good man. Now, would you like to meet your new employees?" He smiled as he held the list and said, "I can send for them, and you can meet them in a room here."

"Trot 'em out, Warden. They need to understand a few things."

Tremayne studied the six men who stood before him, and a sense of despair brushed against his mind. *These are the men I'm supposed to use? Well, it may work. Maybe the girl is right, and God is in all this.*

The room was stark with no furniture except one table and two chairs. The five men Warden Bryce had summoned looked uncomfortable and somewhat apprehensive. They had entered the room to find Casey Tremayne standing there, and he had ignored all their questions. Finally, the door closed, and Jack Canreen said, "What's this all about, Tremayne?" He was a huge man, six feet two, and weighed two hundred twenty-two pounds. The huge biceps strained the fabric of his prison uniform, and his strength was bull-like. His face was scarred with marks of battles past, and he looked dangerous.

Tremayne studied Canreen, who had only lost one fight, and that had been to Tremayne himself.

"I've got a proposition. The warden has made an offer to me, and I wanted to let you men in on it because you may be concerned."

"What kind of offer would he make to us?" Canreen sneered, doubt and anger in his voice. "What does he want? He ain't giving something for nothing."

"I think maybe he is this time, Jack. Let me tell you what's happened."

Quickly he outlined the details of his visit with the warden and Charity Morgan. He scrutinized the faces of the men. The three men who stood closest to Canreen were all known for their viciousness. Frenchy Doucett was a small man no more than five feet ten and weighed less than a hundred forty pounds. He was lightning quick with a knife. He wore scars on his neck as the remnant of an old knife fight, and his black hair and brown eyes gave evidence of his Cajun blood. *He's knifed two men in prison, and he claims to be a good shot,* Tremayne thought.

His eyes moved to Ringo Jukes. Jukes was an unusual-looking prisoner. He was six feet tall, well proportioned with a head of auburn hair. He had dark blue eyes and was a handsome man. His good looks concealed a vicious streak. He could be cruel and had been on more than one occasion. Like the others, he had tested Tremayne and found himself battered so badly that he couldn't work for a week.

Standing next to Jukes was Al Delaney. He was thirty-eight years old, of average size, and one eye was covered with a black patch. Of the four, Delaney was probably the most decent. He was rough and could take care of himself, but the quality that Tremayne treasured most was the fact that he had handled mules. That had been his profession, and he would be invaluable on a drive to Oregon.

Tremayne studied these four, and then his eyes touched on Billy Watson, who did not seem to belong with the others. Billy was only seventeen, a slight young man with light brown hair and mild brown eyes. He had been abused by Canreen and others, and it was for this reason rather than for his fighting ability that Tremayne had chosen him. Tremayne realized his softhearted quality, which occasionally showed itself, compelled him to give the young man a second chance. Despite his cynicism, Casey Tremayne knew that Billy was basically good.

He smiled at Elsworth Charterhouse, who smiled back.

He outlined the situation and stated his side of it. "I think most of you fellows are like me. You'd do anything to get out of here."

"There must be a catch in it, Casey," Al Delaney said. "I never heard of a prison letting guys go."

"It's all conditional, Al," Tremayne said. "If we get the train through, our pardons will be confirmed. Anybody who runs will be hunted down like a dog by the law and by me. Get that straight right now."

"Who is this bunch we are supposed to watch out for?" Canreen demanded. "A bunch of preachers you say?"

"They're Christian people, and I'm warning you right now, Jack. You'll treat them well, or else I'll leave my mark on you as I did once before."

The remark seemed to drop like salt on a wound. Casey Tremayne was the only man who ever bested Canreen in a fistfight. Both men had been bloodied and bruised, but Casey Tremayne had walked away while Canreen didn't regain consciousness for hours. He still had the scars, and now there was a challenge in his eyes.

"You think you can whip me, Canreen?"

Canreen shifted. "I'm not interested in that. I'm interested in getting out of here."

"That's smart, Jack. So I'll put this to you. Any man who disobeys me, I'll whip until he can't walk, and then he'll work the next day. I won't bust any bones."

"What if you can't whip him?" Canreen demanded sullenly.

"Then I'll shoot him in the head," Tremayne said flatly. "Let me add this. There'll be one rule about these people. You'll treat them with respect. There will be young women too. You haven't seen a young woman in a long time. If any of you get out of line with any woman, I'll cut him off at the neck. There'll be no trial. I'll be the judge, jury, and executioner. Can you swallow that, Jack?"

Jack Canreen glared at Tremayne, but he shrugged. "I'll do anything to get out of here. Even be nice to your preacher friend."

He turned and said, "What about him? He's not going to help on a drive like this." He indicated Billy Watson with a nod and waited for Tremayne's answer.

"I'm taking Billy because he's going to be a good man. He's already a better man than you, Canreen."

"Why, I could whip him with one hand."

"You probably could, but still you'd wind up on a gallows or shot by a posse. The jury's still out on Billy. He can be anything he wants to. He shouldn't have been in this prison in the first place, and I'm giving him his chance. If I catch any of you ragging him too much, I'll settle it. If any of you set out to discipline him, you get ready to pick your teeth up. Any questions?"

"Why you takin' the Limey? He'll be worthless," Canreen demanded.

"He's the only one of us who can speak Latin. We might run into some educated redskins."

"When's all this going to happen, Casey?" Frenchy Doucett asked.

"May not happen at all. The girl has to go back and convince her friends. I know all you fellows are men of prayer, so you'd better start praying she does, or otherwise we'll all probably rot in here." His voice was cynical, and he shook his head. "Don't count

105

on it. I stopped believing in Santa Claus some time ago, and that's about what this amounts to. That woman has to convince the psalm singers to trust their lives to a bunch of jailbirds."

He hesitated. "I don't believe in miracles, fellas, but maybe this is my only chance out of here so I'm going to have to believe something and this is it."

Chapter Six

On her journey home Charity felt oppressed by the enormous decision she had to place before the members of the Pilgrim Way. However unlikely, the circumstances seemed to have been arranged by the Lord, yet the closer she drew to home, the more she was aware that no one but she had ever thought of such a thing. Many people had doubts about making a trip to Oregon under any conditions, and now to put themselves in the hands of a group of criminals seemed like a nightmare.

All the way home, she prayed that God would give her a word. She had determined to fast and pray until God gave her a sense of rightness. She had always been able to find the mind of God concerning decisions. The decision not to marry Charles Campbell had been so clearly outlined from God and placed in her mind that there was never any doubt, but this was entirely different.

She reached home and was greeted with enthusiasm by the entire family who wanted a report on their uncle and aunt.

"They're both fine, and they send you their love," she said to them. She hugged her father and said, "He especially wanted me to give you a hug for him."

"He's a good man, Paul Bryce. He's like your mother. They were very close, those two."

She went to bed that night and slept little. She had not eaten anything, for she believed fasting was one of God's commandments, especially when there was a decision to be made. All night long she struggled. She thought of Jacob wrestling with the angel and remembered that during that encounter he sustained an injury and limped for the rest of his life.

O God, she prayed, *show me the way. I know there will be opposition, but I pray even now that You would touch hearts and minds and grant favor and lead us as You led Abraham to a promised land. Prove Yourself, O God, to Your servant and to Your people.*

For the next day she managed to avoid eating, and all day long she sought privacy by walking along the river. That evening, when she was on her way home, she felt weary and drained.

I prayed every prayer I know how to pray, Lord, and now I leave it in Your hands. You've told us to wait on You and to be patient, and that's all I can do. She felt physically exhausted, and the lack of food, no doubt, had something to do with that, but she had discovered long ago that intense spiritual warfare was a debilitating affair and weakened the body.

She had nearly reached home when suddenly she stopped. The spring had come and March was nearly over, but she was unaware of the greenery and the golden leaves coming out in tiny buds. It was as if someone called her name from a far distance, and there on the road she simply bowed her head. Time passed, but Charity didn't notice. Finally, a verse of Scripture came into her mind. This was not unusual. She knew the Bible so well that Scripture would often come. This time, however, there was a startling clarity. It was a verse that spoke to one of the pilgrims of the Bible. *Ye have dwelt long enough in this mount.* That was the essence. She recognized the verse but could not place it in context. Hurrying home, she went up to her room, pulled out her Bible, and began to search.

She had a faint memory, and turning to the book of Deuteronomy, she read the first six verses of the first chapter. And then she ran across the Scripture that seemed to leap off the page: "Ye have dwelt long enough in this mount."

Tears came into Charity's eyes, and she began to sob. "Thank You, God," she whispered. "Thank You for your guidance, for I take this as Your word."

She got to her feet and washed her face. It was not unusual, she knew, for people of the Way to take a Scripture as guidance. It was an enlightenment they believed in. They used the Bible for their spiritual lives as men would use a map to find their way through dangerous territory. The Bible had the truth for them. It was the Word of God, and a peace descended on Charity at that moment. She knew that although there would be difficulties and trials, there would be victory at the end. She went downstairs and found her father sitting in his favorite chair, reading the Bible.

"Pa, I need to talk to you."

"Sit down, Daughter." Gwilym looked up and saw the seriousness of her face. "You have a problem?"

"No, Pa. I think God has given me an answer to a problem."

Gwilym closed his Bible and turned to face her squarely. "What is it, Daughter?"

"Pa, will you do one thing for me?"

"Why, surely, lass."

"Will you listen to everything I have to say without interrupting, and then after I've finished, you can say anything you like and ask me anything you like. Will you do that for me?"

"Why, of course I will."

The house was empty, another sign this was a propitious moment. Charity began by telling her father about the dream, careful to mention that it had been repeated twice. She told how she had followed what she felt was the right thing in going to see her Uncle Paul, how she had explained the people's problem, and how that he had listened and agreed to pray that they would find an answer.

Gwilym sat silently, his eyes seeking his daughter's face. He knew this girl was close to God, as her mother had been and her grandmother before her. He had great confidence in Charity's ability to search the Scripture and knew that she was at least as devoted to the Word of God as he himself. He did not speak, but when she told him about Bryce's offer, his eyes widened, and involuntarily he shook his head a fraction of an inch.

Charity saw this but calmly related how

they had talked to Tremayne, and her uncle seemed assured these men would help them make the trip to Oregon. She ended by saying, "I have talked to Tremayne, and he is a rough-hewn man. He's a Western man and knows the country. He knows the Indians. He lived with them for a while when he was kidnapped from his family after his parents were killed. But Uncle Paul says that the parole board will follow his recommendations. I've been fasting and praying, Father, and I believe that this is God's answer. Now, you may ask me anything."

Gwilym was stunned. He stared at his daughter. The thing he dreaded most was telling her that she had missed God. And still he feared for the future.

"I don't see, Daughter, how it could possibly be. Even if I would agree to it, the elders and the people themselves would have to agree. You realize what you're asking us to believe? That a group of criminals and murderers could be the means of our salvation? It seems if God wanted to bring someone to help us, He could do better than that."

"God moves mysteriously, doesn't He, Pa?" Charity said calmly. "If you will agree, that's one miracle." She smiled and took his hand. "You've always been a good father and a good leader to the people. This is the hour of crisis. I believe the Lord has spoken through that Scripture: 'Ye have dwelt long enough in this mount.' We know we have to leave, and this is the only way I see us keeping our people together. Will you join me, and we will convince the others?"

Gwilym sat silently for a time, and finally he took a deep breath. "It's strange, but I've been worried sick about what's going to happen. But as you spoke and gave this Scripture, it seemed to me that God spoke to my own heart. It's like that storm on the Sea of Galilee when Jesus was asleep. Do you remember? And they came to Him and said, 'Master, master, we perish.' You remember what Jesus did?"

"Of course. He got up and rebuked the storm, and it went away, and suddenly everything was peaceful." Her eyes glowed with delight. "That's the way with you, is it, Pa?"

"Yes, it is. We both may be deceiving ourselves, but I think I see the hand of God in all of this."

"Then we'll go to the people and put it to them."

"We need to pray more. I know you've been praying, but I need to prepare myself. I–I haven't been a strong leader, Daughter."

"Pa, you've always done a magnificent job of bringing the Word of Life to us."

"That's one thing, but this is something else. I feel so unfit."

"You mustn't say that. God has put you in your place, and now it's time to leave this place as Abraham left and as the children of Israel left the wilderness and went to the Promised Land. God is in it. We'll convince them, you and I."

Every member of the Pilgrim Way was gathered at the meeting house — more than thirty families. Children were there — some merely crawlers, some at their mother's bosom. Gwilym had insisted that every member be present for the meeting, but he had said no more.

"What's this all about, Gwilym?" Karl Studdart spoke in a loud voice, and he glared at Gwilym. "Why weren't the elders told about this before it was brought to the whole group?"

"I did not call the elders because this is a matter that must be decided by the head of every family. It's a serious thing, and you will have a chance to question any of it, Brother Studdart. Now I'm going to ask you to listen to my daughter Charity. You all know her for a young woman who has been close to God. She has come to me with something she says God has put on her heart. I will ask her to tell you what has happened, and I will add this," he said, "I believe that what she has to say is from God, but each man must decide for himself. Charity, come and tell this group what God has been doing."

Women did not speak often in open meetings, and Charity had expected to be very nervous. But a calm descended on her, and she stood beside her father. "I realize that it's not customary for women to speak at open meetings, and I would not, except that God has spoken something to me that affects you all, and you all must hear it. I will be very brief and as clear as I can."

Charity began to outline the process that had taken place in her life beginning with her concern about the future of the Pilgrim Way and her fears that the fellowship would be scattered. She related her dream, stressing how the dream had been repeated, and then she told how she had acted on the dream. She spoke about how her uncle had listened and had been concerned also about the Pilgrim Way. As she said all this, she was aware that there was curiosity but little else in the faces of the people. But as soon as she related her uncle's offer to put a group of men at their disposal and that these men were convicts, expressions changed almost instantly. Some faces were filled with anger, others with confusion and doubt.

"I know this comes as a shock to you," Charity said slowly, her eyes going from face to face. "But when I got back, I fasted and prayed, and God gave me a Scripture. Just one verse, or even part of a verse. It is, 'Ye have dwelt long enough in this mount.' I shared this with my father, and we prayed together. We feel it is God's will for us to go to Oregon, and we feel that God has provided these men to help us make the journey safely."

"This is foolishness!" Studdart said loudly. He got to his feet and his voice rose. "We are to put our lives in the hands of criminals. I do not —"

"Brother Studdart, you will be seated." Gwilym's voice was cold, and he stared at Karl Studdart. It was the first time he had ever challenged anything the big man said, but there was a strength in Gwilym Morgan at that moment, and Studdart was taken aback. He started to stutter, but Gwilym overrode him, saying, "You have heard my daughter's testimony. I believe what she has heard is the word of God. This is new to you. We will dismiss without further comment, and I ask each of you to do one thing. Find a place, pray, and seek the will of God. This makes no sense, of course, in the natural, but we are not people of the natural. We are people of God, and if God wants to use these men, it is His right for He is the Lord God.

"You will remember this, however, that God chose a man called Cyrus, who was, no doubt, an idolater and a wicked man, to be a blessing to the people of Israel. Think about that," he said, "and now I will dismiss you. We will meet tomorrow night at six o'clock. During that time you will be given an opportunity to share your views, and we will make a decision.

"Now," he lifted his hands and prayed, "God, our Father, we are Your people, and we are helpless like sheep without a shepherd unless You are with us. This is a startling thing, and a thing that arouses unbelief in the heart, but if this is Your will, O God, I pray that You would speak to the hearts of men and women and young people, and that we might be obedient to whatever Your will is. We're trusting in the name of Jesus. Amen."

Charity stood still beside her father, and the two watched as the building emptied. Some people were talking loudly and others whispering. Gwilym said sadly, "I fear the outcome of this, Charity."

"If God is in it, He can speak, and He can change hearts. We're going to believe God. That's all there is to it."

The Morgans talked a great deal the following day. The younger girls were excited about making a trip; that was all it was to them. It might have been no more than a trip to Pittsburgh, which was the farthest they'd ever been away from home.

Evan, on the other hand, had serious doubts. He loved and admired Charity, but he commented, "I think it's testing God. It doesn't make any sense at all, Charity, to trust these men. Once they're out from the walls that hold them in, they can do as they please."

"They can only do what Casey Tremayne will let them do," Charity said.

"He's only one man."

Charity nodded. "Yes, that's true, but when you meet him, you'll see he has a strength that most men lack."

"You're trusting a man who tried to commit murder?"

"I'm trusting a man God has put in our way. So show a little faith, Evan, will you?"

The meeting was called to order by Gwilym, and he looked out over the congregation. "This is a time for every man who has a feeling about what we're proposing to say so. Whatever we say, let it be done in Christian charity. If you do not believe this is of God, then you have a right to say so, but I beg you not to do so in anger. We all want God's will, and though we may disagree, we are still brethren."

Charity sat perfectly still; her hands were clenched so tightly together they ached. She did not know what to expect, and when she saw Karl Studdart rise, her spirit seemed to go cold. *No, he's going to fight.*

Studdart turned to face Gwilym squarely for a moment, then he turned to face the congregation. "When I left here yesterday, I was convinced this was a mistake, a terrible mistake. I was convinced that Miss Charity Morgan had missed God and that to follow up on what she had discovered was to ignore the will of God."

Charity closed her eyes and waited for the deluge, but she was surprised to hear Studdart continue. "I must tell you that when I began to pray, I was trying to tell God what

119

to do, but He shut me up at once." Suddenly Studdart smiled and even laughed. "He told me that I was a proud man, and that I was to obey His voice and to be a part of the Pilgrim Way as we go to Oregon. I encourage the rest of you to join those of us who will be going."

"Glory, hallelujah!" The words burst from Charity's lips before she could keep them in, and Studdart gave her a quick glance and smiled as he sat down.

"I want to hear from every man, the head of every family," Gwilym said. "Those who go must know that we are headed into danger, but our God will go before us. Now, who will speak first?"

The meeting was not long. In the end eighteen families agreed to sell out and go to Oregon. Eleven decided not to go.

Gwilym said, after the last man had spoken, "Let us ask the Lord to bless those who have chosen not to go. That God will put them in the place He has for them, and let us pray for those who will go that God will give us courage and strength, and that we will be obedient to His will. Let us pray."

Tremayne was in his cell when a guard appeared. "You're wanted in the warden's office, Casey."

"I'm getting to be a regular visitor there."

Tremayne rolled off his bunk and followed the guard down the corridor. When they reached the office, the guard knocked, and Casey heard the warden say, "Come in."

When he entered the office, he saw Warden Bryce standing beside his desk — and with him was Miss Charity Morgan. He saw the excitement on her face and said, "I take it you got your miracle, Miss Morgan."

"I think it's our miracle, Mr. Tremayne. The group has agreed."

"Well, I think it's a miracle, and it'll be another miracle if you get there with this group you've chosen," Paul Bryce said. "But I believe that God has been in it. I'll leave you two alone to talk this thing over." He left the office.

Before she could speak Casey said, "I'm happy for you. I'm glad it's worked out this way, and I — well, I'm grateful for the chance at a different kind of life."

"I'm hoping that God will touch your life, Mr. Tremayne."

"I think Casey will be fine, but I want to warn you that these are rough men. I'll keep them in line. They've been warned already, and they know they'll mind me, but this is going to be a hard, difficult journey. It is for everyone under any circumstances."

Charity smiled brilliantly, and he was aware what an attractive woman she was. She was tall and shapely, and her eyes mirrored a wisdom he did not completely understand. She was watching him, and he wasn't sure what the expression in her eyes meant. It pulled at him like a mystery. He suddenly felt a slow run of excitement as though he were on the edge of a discovery.

There was a fire in this girl that made her lovely and brought out the rich, headlong qualities of a spirit otherwise hidden behind the cool reserve of the lips. She was, Tremayne saw, a woman with a great degree of vitality and imagination. He saw the hint of her will or of her pride in the corners of her eyes and of her lips. He had not been around a woman for a long time, and he was intently aware of her body, against the folds of her dress. Suddenly he realized she affected him powerfully. It fanned the hungers he had suppressed for years, and he thought there might be more problems than he had imagined.

"I know it will be a difficult journey," she said quietly. "Do you believe in God, Casey?"

He smiled and nodded. "I've given up thinking on Him, Miss Morgan, but maybe after all this, I'll have to change my mind."

CHAPTER SEVEN

Dr. York Wingate looked up from the plate of ham and eggs and watched his wife who sat across from him. At the age of thirty-five, he looked hale and healthy. He had light brown hair, dark brown eyes, and craggy features. He had been told that he was not a handsome man often enough that he believed it, but the warmth and quick intelligence in his eyes made him seem attractive. He studied his wife, Helen, who was a small, delicate woman — almost too delicate for the child she was bearing. He had seen enough women with her physical characteristics to be certain she would have a hard time when the child came, but she seemed never to fear that part of bringing a new Wingate into the world. He picked up a biscuit and nibbled at it for a moment.

"I've been thinking, Helen, about this trip to Oregon."

"What about it, dear?" Helen looked up

and gave him a quick smile. "It's going to be wonderful! We're going to love it there. There can't be many doctors, so you'll have a large practice."

York shook his head. He had tried to explain to her that Oregon was not like Boston, Pittsburgh, or other large cities. He tried again but without much hope. "It's a rural place, Helen. The biggest town in the area is Oregon City, and it's fewer than a thousand people. There aren't many women there. Mostly it's built by men who've gone to find their fortunes in a new country, but the more I think about it, the less I want to make the trip."

"I don't want to be separated from my family and from our people." She had always had a close tie with her family. The world of the Pilgrim Way was all she had ever known, and although she would never admit it to her husband, she felt an insecurity at the very thought of being parted from people she knew. Now she reached across the table and seized his hand. "I know what it is. You're worried about taking me on a trip when I'm expecting a child."

"Well, it's a rough way, and you're not a big, strong woman, Helen."

"I'm strong enough to have this baby. God gave it to us, York. He's going to be a child of promise exactly like Isaac was to Abraham and Sarah."

"I believe it's of God that we're starting our family, but you have to remember that riding into the wilderness over bumpy roads or no roads at all is not what I'd advise for a woman having her first child."

Helen shook her head, and her hand tightened on him. "We've got to go with our people. I won't be left here all alone."

Wingate knew argument wouldn't change Helen. She was amenable to most of his suggestions, but ever since the Oregon trip had come up, she had refused to listen to anything except making the trip. He made one more try, however.

"Dr. Goldsmith in Pittsburgh has offered me a partnership. There's even a house I've found that would be just right for us." He spoke urgently, but even as he did, he was aware that his words were wasted. He saw his wife, who was always ready to obey him, was not going to accept anything but going to Oregon. He tried again. "Each family can only take one wagon. Maybe two for the larger families, but no one will be able to take all their furniture."

"We could get furniture after we get there. We'll sell what we have. Furniture is not a home, York. Home is a man and a woman and babies, and that's what we're going to have." Jumping up from the table, she threw herself into his lap. He held her, almost desolate to feel the fineness of her bones and know the torment that would be coming. She held on to him fiercely, and he was nearly ready to weep. York Wingate gave up — again.

"We'll talk about it later," he said.

"No," she said, "we'll talk not about whether we're going or not, but how wonderful it's going to be when we get there. Now," she straightened up, kissed him, and said, "you have calls to make?"

"A few. I've got to go by the Morgans. Bronwen's got a cut on her hand that was pretty bad. I'll need to change the bandage."

"Tell Charity to come by and see me."

"All right, I'll tell her." York got to his feet. Words formed as he tried to think of a way to convince her that she should not make such a trip, but those words would not come out, and he said, "I'll be back early."

"I'll cook mutton tonight. You always like that, and we'll make a list of what we can take with us."

"It'll be a short list." York shrugged. He turned and left the house, and since the Morgans lived only three streets away, he didn't bother to hitch up the buggy.

The April sunlight was bright in the sky, and large banks of fleecy clouds drifted slowly across the clear, azure dome. A group of blackbirds rose from a field, their guttural cries contrasting with the twittering of the song sparrows that always seemed to be in the Novaks' yard. He waved at Irene and Daniel, the two youngsters, and they waved back.

When he reached the Morgan house, he turned in the gate and was met, before he could get to the door, by Meredith. The very sight of her brought a smile to Wingate's face for he had a special fondness for the child. He had brought her into the world, and she seemed to feel that gave her a special claim over him.

"Hello, Dr. Wingate," she cried. "Are you going to fix Bronwen's hand?"

"I expect I'll change the bandage."

"You've got to look at Sam. He's got a sore foot."

"I'll be glad to take a look." As usual, Meredith chattered as they went into the house. He wondered what it would take to get her to be silent, but then she never had been, so he pushed the thought away. Inside, he was met by Charity.

"Good morning, Dr. Wingate."

"How are you this morning, Charity?"

"I'm fine. I'm worried about Bronwen's hand."

"Well, let's take a look at it." Charity stepped aside, and Wingate set his black bag on the table. "Let's see that hand, Bronwen."

"I don't want to."

"Come now. I've got to change the bandage and see how it's doing." He waited until Charity said sternly, "Let him see your hand, Bronwen. Don't make a fool of yourself."

"I won't hurt you. I'll be very careful." He took the hand she reluctantly extended and began to remove the bandage. When it was off, he looked carefully at the cut and nodded. "It's doing fine. We'll have to put a clean bandage on it, and you'll have to be careful not to bang it around."

Meredith had crowded in as close as she could and was staring down at the wound on her sister's hand. "I don't see the bones."

"Well, thank God for that. The cut wasn't down to the bone."

Meredith watched closely, and Bronwen turned her head away, not wanting to see the cut. She had been splintering firewood with a sharp ax, and it slipped and cut her hand. As soon as he put pressure on the wound and wrapped it again with a fresh bandage, Wingate said, "There, Bronwen, you'll be good as new in a few days."

"Sit down and have some coffee, Dr. Wingate."

"That would go down all right." He put the supplies back in his bag, fastened it, and sat at the oak table that had been made, like nearly everything in the house, either by Gwilym or his father, who had been a fine carpenter.

Charity poured his coffee and said, "I've been trying to make a list of things to leave behind, and every time I put something on it, somebody insists we have to take it."

"I'm not leaving my bed," Bronwen said. "My grandpa made it, and he gave it to me. It's mine."

"I know it's yours, but wait you until we get to Oregon. Pa will make you another bed."

"I want my old bed."

Charity shook her head with a look of disgust. "It's a battle for everything. We'll have to start all over again, girl. Can't you understand that?"

"It's going to be hard in a lot of ways, this trip to Oregon," Wingate said. He sipped the coffee and blinked. "This is hot."

"Coffee's made to be hot. Who wants to drink a cup of old, cold coffee?"

Wingate smiled for there was a sharpness about Charity that everyone noticed sooner or later. "I've been trying to talk Helen out of going."

"Because of the baby?"

"Yes. It's not a trip for a woman expecting her first child to make. Unless we made very good time, which I doubt, she'd have the child somewhere on the journey. It's not something I would recommend."

"How do babies get born, Dr. Wingate?" Meredith piped up, looking up in his face.

Wingate couldn't resist a grin. The child would ask anything that came into her mind without any thought of decorum.

Bronwen spoke up at once. "You're not supposed to ask questions like that."

"Why not? How am I going to learn anything if I don't ask questions?"

Charity started to speak, but Wingate looked at her and winked. "I'll tell you what. You ask your sister Charity about things like that. There are some things that are private and intimate that should be talked over by women. Men are too rough and don't have good enough manners."

"I don't see what good manners have to do with it. Your manners are good enough for me — most of the time."

Wingate laughed. "Don't tell me about

those other times, but you just ask Charity."

"She doesn't have any babies."

"I know," Wingate said, "but she'll tell you all you need to know right now, and then later on —" He broke off as Gwilym entered the room. "Hello, Gwilym."

"Hello, Doctor. How is that girl?"

"Very good. No problem."

"Glad she didn't chop her hand off."

"Sit down, Pa. Let me fix you some coffee. Is it too early for a little cake, Doctor?"

"Never too early for your cooking, Charity."

Charity brought the cake, and as he bit into it and complimented her, Wingate saw that Gwilym was unhappy. "What's the trouble, Gwilym? You worried about this trip?"

"No, not about that but about getting rid of things here. We all need to sell our property, but who'd pay anything for a town that's going down as fast as ours is, and I doubt if we can even sell our furniture and the things we won't be able to take."

Charity had taken a seat and looked over her cup of coffee. "I've had a thought about that. What we need to do is to get everybody together, and just before we leave we'll have a sale in Pittsburgh. We'll advertise it in the paper, and everyone will come to get bargains in furniture and tools and all the things we can't take."

Gwilym had never had such a thought. His mind had been full of the trip itself, but now he said, "Well, that might not be a bad idea. I'll talk to the men about it. It would be quite a sale."

"How many families are committed to the trip, Gwilym?"

"Eighteen. The Johnsons weren't going, but they changed their mind at the last moment. That's a good thing. He's a handyman and a staunch elder too."

Wingate finished his cake. "By the way, when will the prisoners be coming in?"

"I got a letter from Uncle Paul yesterday. He says that the parole board approved the plan, and the men will be released this week."

Wingate shook his head slightly. "I feel a little bit dubious about these men."

"I think Uncle Paul made it pretty clear to them that they'll behave and get us through, or else they'll go back to prison. He said if any of them tried to run, he'd have the law run them down and put in jail for life for trying to escape."

"Well," Wingate said as he rose to his feet, "I hope they're good men."

"They're not good, or they wouldn't have

been in jail," Meredith said severely.

Wingate winked at Charity. "Well, you'll have to straighten them out and make good men out of them, Meredith. Just preach at them a little bit."

"All right."

Charity walked to the door with Wingate and stepped outside. "I wish we were leaving right away." She studied Wingate's face and said, "I know you're worried about Helen, but we'll all help."

"That's good of you, Charity. She's a fragile person, not only in body but in spirit. She has no idea about the hardships this trip involves."

"I'm not sure any of us do, but I'll stay right with her all the time."

Warden Bryce stood in front of the group of men who had gathered, and not for the first time wished that he had never mentioned this possibility to Charity. It was too late now, however, for the board had already approved the conditional parole, and the wheels were moving. He had called them for one last meeting before they left to join Gwilym and the other members of the Way. He wanted to be stern but not discouraging. They would get enough of that, he was certain, on the way to Oregon.

"You men are now officially conditionally paroled." He stressed the word *conditionally.* "I've told you all this before, but I've written it all up and have copies for all of you. Basically it says, if you get the wagon train through to Oregon and cause no trouble along the way, the parole will be made final. It also says that if you run or refuse to obey Tremayne's orders, you'll be given to a local sheriff and sent back to serve a life sentence."

The men listened as Casey's eyes ran over the faces of the men he would be bossing on the trip. He knew them fairly well and had already made up his mind he would be fair, but they would have to obey him instantly and without reservation. The only two he was really certain of were Elsworth Charterhouse and Billy Watson. Young Watson was excited at getting out of jail and had developed a severe case of hero worship for Tremayne. Casey couldn't move without finding Billy at his side, and that suited him very well. The young man was immature, but there was good stuff in him, and Casey was determined to bring it out. As for Elsworth, he would be of little use on the drive, but he'd persuaded Tremayne to take him along.

"I can quote Latin to the stock," he'd said.

"It's been scientifically proven that Latin has charms to soothe the savage beast." Tremayne had agreed, for the Englishman could make him laugh, and he knew he'd need humor on the journey.

Warden Bryce finished his brief speech and then said, "Come along with me." He moved quickly. Casey motioned with his hand, and the others followed as he brought up the rear. They left the building and walked into another one, and when they stepped inside a large room, Tremayne saw that it was a supply room. "This is where we keep all the clothing and supplies that men bring with them. I've also requisitioned a little from the local sheriff's office," Bryce said. He motioned toward a table. "There're some good firearms. Rifles and side arms. Tremayne, you go through them and see that each man is well armed."

A look of shock ran across the faces of most of the prisoners. This was the ultimate evidence that things were going to be different. They all watched closely as Tremayne began to examine the weapons. From time to time, he called out a name, and a man would go over and accept the pistol and the rifle.

"These are yours, of course, Tremayne, that you had when you were arrested."

Tremayne picked up the rifle the warden handed him and saw that Bryce was smiling. "Well, I wasn't sure I'd ever see these again."

"I've got some ammunition, not much, but I'm sure that the settlers will see that there is plenty of that. Now, there are quite a few bits of clothes here that incoming prisoners were wearing. You can't leave wearing these prison uniforms so go through these boots and clothing and see if you can get each man outfitted."

There was a hubbub, and Casey nearly smiled as he watched the men laughing and trying on different articles of clothing. Jack Canreen tried to get into a shirt and shook his head in disgust. "There ain't no man-sized clothing here."

"We may have to outfit you from a store, Jack. We need good boots, too, so find the best boots you can."

An hour later the men were outfitted and stood there holding their weapons. Most of them had found a holster and had belted the gun on, and there was a look of satisfaction on their faces.

"Well, it's time for you to leave," Bryce said. He stopped for a moment, and every prisoner gave him an intent look. Since most of the men were disillusioned about life, they would not have been totally taken aback if he had said, "We're calling the whole thing off." Instead Bryce stated, "I know most of you men are not Christians, but I am. You may not believe it, but I think God is in this. These people you'll be helping deserve a good life. It's been put into your hands to give it to them. You may not deserve a better life, but your slate is being wiped clean. This is a chance for each of you to be a different kind of man. I'm not going to preach a sermon, but I'm going to pray right now for you men to arrive safely at Oregon."

He bowed his head and said a brief prayer. Tremayne was shocked for the warden mentioned each man in the group by name. He heard his own name called with a fervent prayer that God would give him wisdom to make this journey, to arrive safely in Oregon, and to begin a new life.

Finally the warden ended the prayer by saying, "I ask this in the name of Jesus and claim these men and the entire party for God. Amen."

He looked at the men, then said, "Well, I've assigned Fred Orlin the job of taking you to your point of departure. The weather is nice, and they know you're coming so I'm sure you'll have a good meal when you get there." He approached Tremayne, stuck his hand out, and said, "God be with you, Casey."

"Thank you, Warden. Speaking for all the men, I wanted to say that we'll do the best we can for these people."

"That's all a man can do."

Bryce turned quickly and walked out of the room, and the men all followed. Outside, one of the guards, a slight man of thirty, stood beside the wagon. It was longer than usual and could carry as many as ten in the three seats. He was leaning against the wagon, eating an apple. He came to attention as the warden approached. "All ready, Warden," he said.

"Take them to my people," Bryce said. "They'll give you a good meal. I have a letter for you to give to Gwilym Morgan."

"Yes, sir. I'll see that he gets it."

Bryce stood back. "I guess this is goodbye. I'll be expecting great things from you men."

The men piled into the wagon; Casey sat in the front beside the guard. He turned, and as the wagon went through the gate in the wall that surrounded the prison, he suddenly felt like crying. It was something he had not done for many years. He could not even remember the last time, but he knew he couldn't show it. The rest of the men gave a cheer, and Orlin nudged Casey with his elbow.

"Time for celebrating, Casey. You're a free man."

"No, I won't be until we get these folks to Oregon."

"Ah, you know that country. It'll be easy for you."

"No, Fred, it won't be. Nobody ever had an easy time on the Oregon Trail. I'm not complaining though." He smiled at Orlin. "You've been a good friend to me and to the other inmates, Fred. I want you to know that I won't ever forget you."

Orlin was embarrassed. "Why, shoot, Casey, I wasn't all that good."

The wagon rumbled with the road, and as it did, Casey Tremayne wondered, not for the first time, why this was happening. He was not a man who believed in much, but it was plain to see this was not accidental. He stayed deep in thought all morning, and he finally shook off his contemplation and began to make plans for the trip ahead.

"The criminals are here!"

Meredith had run to the window and stared out. She saw the wagon and dashed toward the door. Charity was across the room, and she and Bronwen followed. The wagon pulled up, and Meredith ran right up to it. She looked into the faces of the men and said loudly, "Are you the criminals who are going to take us to Oregon?"

Tremayne was climbing from the wagon, and he couldn't restrain a smile. He looked down at the small girl from his great height. "We're the criminals. Are you afraid of me?"

"No, I ain't afraid of you."

"Well, that's good. My name's Casey. What's yours?"

"Meredith."

"Hello, Mr. Tremayne."

Tremayne looked up. "Hello, Miss Charity. No mister about it. Just Tremayne or Casey will be fine."

"I'm glad to see you." She hesitated, nearly offered her hand, and then thought better of it. She looked over the men and recognized some faces. "Hello, Billy," she said. "It's good to see you."

"Hello, Miss Charity," Billy grinned shyly. "Sure am glad to be here."

Charity greeted the rest of the men, determined to learn their names, and said, "I got a letter from my Uncle Paul. He told us what time you were leaving so I've got a big meal prepared. Are you hungry?"

A murmur of ascent went through the

men, and she said, "Come on in. This is my sister, Bronwen. My brother, Evan, isn't here nor my father, but they'll be coming in later. Come along."

Ringo Jukes glanced at Tremayne. "Bossy, ain't she, Casey?"

"Pretty much so."

"Well, I hope she's a good cook."

"Whatever we get," Frenchy Doucett said, "it'll be better than what we've been getting." His dark eyes were alight, and, like the others, when he entered the small house, he fell silent.

Casey knew what he was feeling. He had not been in a private home for years now, and there was a strange feeling to it. The smells of fresh-baked bread and meat cooking were in the air, and he turned to the young girl with the bandaged hand. "Your name is Bronwen?"

"Yes, sir."

"Did you help cook this meal?"

"Yes, I did. I'm not as good a cook as my sister, but I'm learning."

"Well, I'll bet you'll be just as good with a little experience."

"All of you, have a seat. It's all ready," Charity said. She opened the oven and began bringing food on platters and plates while Bronwen and Meredith brought coffee in large cups. The men all sat silently, and Charity said, "We'll have the blessing now."

Casey bowed his head but kept his eyes open. Some of the men, he saw, were struck dumb by this.

She prayed quickly and then said, "Now, I'm not the cook my mother was, but I hope you'll find something you like."

Indeed, there was little not to like — fresh beef steak, carrots, two kinds of beans, and bread. The men, somewhat self-consciously, began to eat, but soon Frenchy Doucett glanced toward Charity. "Miss Charity, this is very good. You are a fine cook."

"Thank you. I'm glad you like it."

Jack Canreen was stuffing his mouth and said, "I ain't had a good meal like this in four years, but you won't be able to cook this good out on the trail, I'll bet."

"I don't suppose so. There are no stores on the way, are there, Tremayne?"

"No. A few army posts and whatever we can shoot."

Meredith did not sit down but had filled her plate, stood up, and moved around, looking at each man in the face. It was disconcerting.

Finally Jack Canreen said, "What are you staring at?"

"At you."

"Why you looking at me like that?"

"I never saw any criminals before. Did you kill somebody?"

Frenchy Doucett laughed softly, and Ringo Jukes said, "Go on, Jack, tell her what a bad man you are."

"No worse than some others I see here," Canreen said. "Miss Charity, don't you teach this child any manners?"

"It doesn't seem to take, Canreen. We do the best we can."

Casey enjoyed the young girl. She stopped in front of Ringo Jukes and fixed her eyes on him. Jukes winked at her and said, "Well, do you like what you see?"

"You are a handsome man."

"Well, you're a handsome girl."

"Do you have a wife?"

"No."

"Why not?"

Charity spoke up. "Will you hush? Stop asking questions."

They were nearly finished with the meal when Gwilym came in. "Well, I see our pilot and his men are here."

"This is Casey Tremayne, Father. He'll tell you the rest of the names."

Gwilym studied them and then said, "When you finish your meal, everybody will be waiting at the meeting house. The people are all eager to hear what you have to say about the journey."

"Well, I'm not all that much of a talker."

"You're a talker enough to tell us what we'll be facing," Gwilym said. "Was the meal good?"

Every head nodded, and Ringo Jukes said, "Your daughter is a fine cook, sir."

"Yes, she is. Not as good as her mother, mind you, but she will be one day."

The meeting house was very full. Charity found a place close to the front and held firmly onto Meredith, trying to keep her quiet. Gwilym rose and went to the front of the room, and everyone instantly grew quiet. "I want to introduce Mr. Casey Tremayne who will be our scout on this trip. He's made the trip, I understand, before. Casey, come and tell us what we're to expect."

Feeling uneasy, Tremayne rose and stood beside Gwilym. "I'm not much of a speaker, but I want to say at the very beginning this is going to be a hard trip. Probably the hardest trip any of you will ever make." He described some of the difficulties, including Indians, disease, flooded rivers, and buffalo stampedes, and finally he said, "We're getting a late start. You're not ready to go yet, I

144

assume. We have to have wagons, good animals, everyone has to be well supplied. There are no stores along the way." Then he added, "We'll have trouble, sooner or later, over what you're going to take. I realize all of you have personal possessions that you treasure, but you can't take them for the most part. No furniture. I've seen trains start out loaded, but when the animals play out, good furniture gets abandoned because the animals can't handle it."

He hesitated. "I might as well say something about discipline. We will be going through dangerous country filled with hostiles — not at first but later. All of the men without exception will have to stand guard, and we'll all take turns herding the extra stock, which will trail the wagons." His face grew harder. "There'll be times when you question an order I give. Usually during those times there won't be any time for debate. I just want to assure you that I'm not going to give any order I don't think is necessary."

He shrugged and said, "You all know we're just out of prison. We were all put there because we committed crimes. I've warned the men that they'll treat you with respect. If they don't, you come to me, and I'll discipline them." He thought for a moment and added, "It would be good if we had a doctor. Lots of sickness and accidents on a trip like this."

"We have one, Tremayne," Gwilym said, "Dr. Wingate there is going along."

"That's good news. We'll have plenty to do. Are there any questions?"

Karl Studdart rose and said, "Can we make this journey, Tremayne?"

His question was as blunt as the man himself.

"It's always risky, Mr. Studdart. One company, the Donner family being the largest group, got trapped in the snow so they nearly all died. They even resorted to cannibalism. That's why I say we've got to get out of here as quickly as we can. I'll say this. I'm thankful to be out of prison, and I've given my word to Warden Bryce as I give it to you. I'll get you through or die trying." He answered several more questions.

Then Gwilym said, "We'll have more meetings, and we'll expect Tremayne to tell us about what we need."

When the meeting broke up, Helga Studdart, a very pretty sixteen-year-old, leaned against Charity. "How do you like our guide?"

"I think he's very capable."

"Don't be silly," Helga grinned. "He's not

handsome, but he looks like a real man."

"He looks well enough."

"You have no romance about you, Charity."

Charity gave Helga a disgusted look. "If he gets us to Oregon, I don't care what he looks like. I'll be satisfied."

CHAPTER EIGHT

The group of men gathered outside the corral attracted Charity's attention. Seeing Evan standing on the outside of the circle, she approached him.

"What's all this about, Evan?"

He grinned briefly at her. "A bit of an argument, it is, about whether to take oxen or mules or horses to get us to Oregon. Some of the men don't like what Tremayne is telling them."

"What's he saying?"

"He's saying, for one thing, that most of the horses we have in this country aren't sturdy enough to pull all the way across to Oregon."

Charity stood on her tiptoes to see Nelson Brand standing in front of Tremayne. His face was flushed, and he was obviously excited. He was an even-tempered man usually, but Charity could tell from his tone and from the set expression on his face that he wasn't happy.

"You may know how to get a train across the country, Tremayne, but I figure I know as much about horses as you do."

Tremayne shoved his hat back on his head and seemed untroubled by the argument. "In that, you're probably right, Nelson."

"These horses of mine" — Brand waved his hand at four fine-looking geldings, all of matched color — "they're the finest horses in the country. I'll match them against anyone's."

"They're fine-looking horses. I've already said that."

"What's wrong with my taking them on the trail?"

"I don't think it would be the best idea. For one thing, the fact that they're good-looking animals will make them real tempting to Indians. If they look good to us, they'll look better to them. They'd love to have some good-looking, spirited horses like that."

Karl Studdart was standing close by. He interrupted. "You mean an Indian would be more likely to steal a good-looking horse than he would a broken-down one. That makes sense."

But Nelson Brand loved his horses. "These horses can work all day. You're telling me they won't make it across the plain?"

"They might, but they're pretty light-weight for the wagons we're going to be pulling. You folks are like everyone else, I expect. You'll pile everything you can in the wagons, and these horses will wear out quicker than some other animals."

The argument went on for some time, and finally Brand said, "Well, I'm taking these horses no matter what you say."

"That's your privilege, Nelson."

Gwilym had been listening intently. "What kind of animals do you think we need? I know some take mules and some take oxen and some horses. What's your preference?"

"Well, there's some advantage in mules. They're tough, and they can keep going when horses will stop, but if I were choosing, I'd get me some prime young oxen. They live a long time, and they work pretty much until they die. Can't beat them for stamina or strength. Besides that, they're — well, they're sweet-natured beasts. Not like mules. Mules are hardy enough to pull a ton for a day and a night. They can eat rocks and go without water, but nobody ever called them an easygoing animal."

The men murmured among themselves, and then Charity said almost without thinking, "What do you mean they're sweet-natured? They look so fearsome."

"Well, they're the most loyal animal I've ever seen to their teammates and to their owners if you treat them right. You know, when they're teamed up, they form a bond for life. If one of them dies, it's real hard to team up the other again. Sometimes they kind of get sick, give up, and die."

Charity was struck by that. "That's sad. I had no idea."

"They're not cheap," Gwilym said.

"No, they're not. They don't cost as much as mules, but more than horses. Then you've got to have good oxbows. That's those big yokes around their necks. Those things weigh about two hundred pounds so you can't carry a spare on the trail. I've seen men make them out of thin reeds and cover them up with leather." Suddenly he slapped his hands together and said, "Well, anyway, I can't tell you what to do. I can just give you my opinion."

"What about those of us who have animals already?"

"There's probably a good place to sell them around here or maybe in Pittsburgh."

"That's right," Gwilym said, "and you can always buy oxen there too."

"I expect you'd better get busy and make up your mind. It's late in the season."

There was murmuring again among the men, and it was obvious that some weren't convinced by Tremayne's choice of oxen. "I've been wondering," Studdart said, stepping forward slightly. He had a pushy manner. "I'm not sure about this route you've chosen. Tell us about it again."

Tremayne studied Studdart, knowing he was a natural leader, but he thought he knew why the other members of the company looked to Gwilym Morgan. "I think it would be best to go by the old Mormon Trail."

"What's wrong with the Oregon Trail?"

"Nothing, but we've got a long way to go until we hit the Oregon Trail. I plan to go by Nauvoo, then hit Council Bluffs. We'll cross the river there, and then we hit the Platte River. We'll have good water for about a third of the way until we get to the South Pass. One good thing about the old Mormon Trail is that it won't be crowded, but the others will already have gone before us and gotten the best of the grass."

The meeting went on for some time, and finally Charity saw Tremayne shake his head as if in doubt. "Whatever you decide, you better decide quick. We're late as we are." He turned and walked away, and Charity left the group. She caught up with him as he was headed toward the general store.

"I wanted to talk to you for a minute, Tremayne. How do you feel about all this?" She was interested as were the rest because they were, in effect, putting their lives in the hands of this man. "You seem doubtful about everything."

"It's a doubtful trip." That enigmatic reply seemed even more uncertain, and he added quickly, "It's a hard trip, and I've never been on a journey to Oregon when someone didn't get hurt or killed. It's the nature of the trail."

"Well, I don't like it that you're so negative. God will take care of us."

Her words agitated Casey Tremayne, and he looked down at her. Her eyes were sharp and alert. She was in a gray dress that seemed to deepen the color of her eyes and turn her hair more golden red. "Were you ever married?" he asked abruptly.

The question caught Charity off guard, and she flushed. "No."

"Why not?"

"That's none of your business, but just so you know, if the Lord wants me to have a husband, he'll send one to me."

"You don't plan on having to catch one? Setting your cap, I think folks call it?"

"I'll have no man I'd have to run after

and catch," Charity said. She turned and walked away quickly and was aware he was smiling at her, which for some reason made her very angry.

The crew had been sleeping in the church, for the most part, but Tremayne had had enough of four walls pressing in on him. He had chosen a spot out underneath a huge hickory tree where he had built a fire and was sitting in front of it across from Elsworth Charterhouse. The Englishman was staring at him with curiosity, and now he leaned forward, picked up a stick, and stuck it into the fire. When it caught, he held it up like a small candle and stared at it fixedly. Tossing it into the fire, he said, "Well, how does it look, Casey?"

"It looks like it's going to be a lot of hard work, and a lot of trouble these folks don't even dream about."

"Well, as you know, Casey, *Nil sine magno vita labore dedit mortalibus.*"

Tremayne smiled across the fire. "I don't think those words mean anything. You're always spouting stuff in some language that you call Latin. I think you just make it up."

"No, indeed! Those are the words of Horace. It means, 'The prizes of life are never to be had without trouble'."

154

"Well, we'll be pretty well tested, you and me." The words were gloomy, but Tremayne seemed placid and even happy. "I'm so glad to get out of that prison nothing seems bad to me."

"Well, Horace may be wrong."

"I don't think he is. The Sioux believe that hard things make a man strong. Either that or they kill him." Elsworth smiled. "I expect the Sioux know as much about things like that as Horace did." The two men were quiet for a while.

Then Elsworth said, "That Charity is a good-looking woman, but she's pretty strong willed."

"That may not be the worst thing in the world, Elsworth. That's what it's going to take to get this bunch across the plains and through the mountains — strong-willed folks!"

"When are we leaving?"

"Day after tomorrow, and that's too late." He lay down, pulled the blanket over him, and stared up at the skies. Elsworth stared at his friend and wanted to talk more, but when Casey Tremayne grew silent, not even the Sioux, he figured, would be able to get a word out of him.

Two days later everything was ready for the

departure. Everyone, according to Tremayne's instructions, had gotten up before daylight. As he strolled among the houses, he saw some women crying, others biting their lips. He considered trying to make a speech encouraging them, but he decided against it. *They'll have to find out the hard way that going to Oregon is not like a Sunday picnic.*

Karl Studdart had given him a horse, at least for use on the trip. Tremayne had not asked for it, but Studdart had said, "You'll need a horse, won't you, since you'll be doing the riding ahead and hunting new grounds for the night?"

"That's right, Karl. Maybe I can bring in some grub too. Lots of antelope and deer, and buffalo later on."

"I'm worried about this trip, Tremayne. It's more than I bargained for."

"It'll be all right if we just keep our heads about us."

He lifted his voice and said, "All right. Get to your wagons, It's time to leave."

Jack Canreen was seated behind four mules he was driving for York Wingate. Frenchy Doucett walked by and grinned up at him. "Some of these women are not so bad looking, are they, Jack?"

"After being without a woman for three

years, any woman would look good."

Elsworth was standing close enough to overhear. "You better be careful. You know what Casey says about leaving the women alone," he said.

Canreen glared at the Englishman. "I'll do as I please. He's not so much."

"Better be careful. You know that he's a hard man to best in a fight."

"I'm a better man than Tremayne in any case," Canreen retorted. "Some of these women are not as holy as they look."

Elsworth shook his head but said no more. Canreen had been the man who had given him the most problems when he had first entered the penitentiary, and only Tremayne had saved him from disagreeable circumstances. "Don't get him stirred up, Canreen," he said and walked off, leaving the man cursing.

Charity was struggling to pick up a chair and lift it over the back of the wagon. Suddenly she felt it leave her grasp and gasped with surprise. She turned and saw Tremayne holding the chair easily.

"Just put it in the wagon, Tremayne."

"Can't take it, Miss Morgan. It's too heavy."

"It's my chair, and those are our animals.

If we want to take it, we can."

The small drama attracted several people who had gathered. All of them knew Charity Morgan as a willful woman who would have her own way, all other things being equal. But Elsworth was smiling slightly. *She'll be sorry she started this,* he thought, and he was exactly right.

"I'm sorry, but you'll just have to leave it."

"My grandfather made that chair for me."

"I'm sure he did, but you've got too much weight on this wagon already. Your animals will give out on you."

Charity's lips grew tight and her cheeks were flushed. "I'm taking the chair," she said.

"No, Miss Morgan, you're not taking the chair. That's what I'm here for, to keep you from doing foolish things."

Gwilym Morgan had been standing by the oxen, waiting to start. He came back now and listened for a moment. "Daughter, I expect Tremayne is right."

"But, Pa, it's Grandfather's chair. Your own father made it. You brought it all the way from Wales."

"It's just part of the cost, Charity," Gwilym said. "I'm sorry."

Furiously Charity stared at Tremayne, and

then she turned and walked away blindly.

"You shouldn't have argued with him, Sister." Charity turned to see Bronwen had joined her. "He's already told us we couldn't take any extra furniture."

Knowing that Bronwen was right did not help Charity's feelings. "He's just a tyrant."

"You don't like him because he's the boss. You never did like to be bossed."

"Go away, Bronwen."

Bronwen grinned impishly and then skipped away. Even as she did, the call came from Tremayne who was mounted now on his big roan gelding. "All right. We can start now. It's a long way to Oregon."

Gwilym, standing beside the oxen, said, "Hup, you beasties, come along now," and was gratified when the big beasts surged forward, and the wagon wheels creaked. Gwilym watched the wheels turn and whispered, "Just keep turning, wheels. You turn enough, and you'll get us to Oregon."

Nearly everyone walked except those who had mules to drive. The proper way to drive an oxen surprised Charity. Some of the men simply walked alongside the lead oxen, and others after a time, jumped on the broad backs. Charity relieved her father in midmorning and walked along. She was afraid of the big animals at first, but she had been surprised by their gentleness.

They stopped at noon for a cold lunch, which Tremayne called *nooning,* then Charity got in the wagon and rode for the next three hours. It was an uncomfortable ride for there was no padding on the hard seat. Once Tremayne came by and stopped the roan long enough to say, "Are you making it all right, Miss Morgan?"

"Oh, for heaven's sake, call me Charity!"

"That's a nice name. I've always liked it. Seems like there's a sweetness in it. I think that's the word for *love* in the Bible, isn't it?"

"Yes, it is."

"Well, you're doing fine."

Meredith, perched on the seat beside Charity, piped up. "Her bottom hurts, Tremayne."

Charity's face flamed. "Be quiet! Don't talk about things like that."

"Well, I expect everybody's got a bottom. What's wrong with mentioning it?"

Tremayne laughed aloud. "Going to be an interesting trip for you, Miss Meredith. You do know how to amuse a man." He touched his spurs to his horse and rode off.

"Don't talk about bottoms in front of a man," Charity said.

But all that did was start an argument, for Meredith could see nothing wrong with mentioning anything.

Two hours later they stopped beside a small creek. Tremayne led the first wagon around so that all the wagons formed a circle and evidently had measured well because there was precisely enough room for the last wagon to fit.

"Is this the way we'll camp every night?" Elsworth asked.

"Yeah, we'll sleep inside the circle. There are no Indians around here, but it's good practice."

The women got out, and the men started fires. A wood box was on the back of each wagon, and Tremayne had instructed the people to throw dead wood in it so that they wouldn't have to hunt for firewood. Soon the darkness was falling, but the campfires penetrated it with bright and cheerful dots.

Charity was cooking steaks, and when she called her family together, Evan took his plate with beans and steak and said, "You know, this isn't bad."

"It's a long way to Oregon," Gwilym said. He was not tired for he was used to hard work, but he knew others were tired. At that moment Tremayne walked by, and Gwilym said, "Stop and have a bite, Casey."

"All right, I think I will." He sat down and took a plate from Bronwen who smiled at him. "I cooked this steak myself."

"It'll be good then." He began to eat.

"Did we make good time today, Tremayne?" Evan asked.

"Very good for the day. Almost ten miles. But this was easy going. We'll have to do better on these easy stretches so when trouble comes and we have to hold up, they'll make up for it."

"You're expecting trouble, aren't you?" Charity asked. She still felt defensive about the big man.

"Well, man is born to trouble as the sparks fly upward."

"Ah, you know your Bible," Gwilym said, pleased to hear it.

"Know it. Don't do it. I guess that's my story."

Meredith had wolfed her supper, and then began, as usual, to pepper Tremayne with questions. He answered them easily, and finally she said, "Are you going to heaven when you die, Tremayne?"

Tremayne seemed unable to answer for a moment. "I don't think so," he said and studied the young girl's face. She was a beautiful child, and he had never seen one with such an inquisitive mind. She was, he thought, probably the smartest person on the train.

"Well, if you don't go to heaven, you'll go to the pit."

"I guess that's right."

"You shouldn't do that. Jesus died so that we could all go to heaven. Did you know that?"

"I believe I heard it a time or two." The rest of the family listened. They were accustomed to Meredith's straightforward questions. "Jesus died for our sins. That's what the Bible says, and it says that anybody who wants to can be saved."

"She's a good Calvinist," Gwilym said, "and she preaches a pretty good sermon too."

"Why don't you ask Jesus to come into your heart, Tremayne? Then you wouldn't have to go to the pit."

Tremayne could not remember a time when he felt as awkward. Everyone was looking at him, and finally he said, "I guess it just never come to me, Miss Meredith."

Charity had been listening. "Meredith, don't be so forward."

"Well, if I can get Tremayne to believe in Jesus, he'll go to heaven. That would be good, wouldn't it?"

"Yes, of course, but —"

Immediately Meredith turned and started quoting Scripture, and then, in the middle of a sentence, she saw one of her friends, jumped up, and ran off. Charity was still irritated with Tremayne over the chair, but she knew the conversation with her sister must have been painful for him.

"I'm sorry about that. You'll have to tell her to hush."

"She's a bright girl. Smart as a whip."

"Are you afraid to die?" Evan asked curiously.

"Well, when everything is still, I am."

"Still? What do you mean still?" Charity asked, tremendously interested.

"I mean when things are going fine, I don't think about things like that, but when I'm alone, maybe at night, then the thoughts come trooping in. And I know what Meredith says is true." A silence fell over the small group. The Morgans could hear the music of someone playing a guitar and singing in an off-key fashion. They were all interested in Casey Tremayne who seemed as foreign as someone from another planet to them. Finally he lifted his head and said, "I saw a bird die once."

"You mean you killed him?" Evan asked, not understanding the man.

"No, I was crossing a prairie, and this bird

164

flew across, and suddenly, right in the middle of his flight, he just dropped out of the sky. I don't mean anybody shot him. He just fell as if he were shot." Tremayne rubbed his chin thoughtfully, and the memory seemed to come flooding back to him. "I went over and picked him up. There wasn't a mark on him. You know what I thought? I thought that bird didn't have any idea when he woke up that morning he'd be dead before dark. For some reason that scared me because I knew I wasn't in any better shape than that bird." He smiled ruefully and stood up. "I didn't mean to tell you that."

Evan, who was a fine Christian himself, said, "Well, Jesus is the friend of sinners, Casey. He'll be your friend if you let Him."

The words surprised Tremayne, and he fastened his eyes on Evan Morgan. "I expect you're right," he said. Then he turned and left. Later that night he related the conversation to Elsworth. "I wonder why I told that story. I've never told it to anybody else."

"So you told them you were going to the pit, did you?"

"Yep, true enough."

"What did Charity Morgan say about it?"

"She was against it, I think."

The two were silent for a while, and finally

Tremayne said, "Don't you have a Latin saying for something like that?"

"I can't think of one offhand, but I remember my father told me once that *dead* is a long time."

"I expect he was right."

The two lay down in their blankets, and for a long time Casey Tremayne watched the stars as they made their silver spangle against the dark sky.

Chapter Nine

The sound of a rifle exploding close by brought Charity out of a sound sleep. She started and for an instant was tempted to throw the quilt over her head, but that was impossible. She reached over and shook Bronwen. "Time to get up."

Bronwen stirred and peered at Charity in the dim light of the canopy. "All right," she said, and then the two got up. They had formed a routine and set about cooking breakfast at once. From all over the camp came the sound of voices. A man was whistling, and Charity wished he would stop.

She first splashed tepid water into a pan from the water keg and washed her face. She felt gritty and dirty for the days on the trail from Pittsburgh had offered no opportunities for more bathing.

As she cooked breakfast, she heard Evan talking to her father as they yoked the oxen to the wagons. Evan's voice was cheerful, and Charity knew that he was far happier than she was herself. The fifteen miles a day that they had had to cover for what seemed like many weeks had drained her strength. She had tried not to let the strain show.

Now the daily routine began; young and old poured out of their tents and out of wagons. Slow spirals of smoke began to drift up in the sky from many campfires. Glancing across the way, Charity saw that in the wagon right behind her the oldest couple on the train, Konrad and Minna Dekker, was cooking, and their voices sounded cheerful. Charity shook her head, wondering if she would be that lively when she was in her seventies.

When the breakfast was ready, the men ate, and they threw down the bacon and eggs quickly. "I'll cook biscuits if we camp early enough tonight," Charity said. She was learning the cooking routine in a whole new way with no stove, and the change was unnerving.

She began cleaning up, noticing that the hunters were leaving. They always moved ahead early, and then the caravan began. She saw Casey Tremayne on his big roan watching carefully. He seemed to be everywhere, his eyes never pausing. She noticed when they began moving now that some of the stock was already weak. It had been a long trek from Pennsylvania, and they had not yet begun the longest part of the journey across the plains and through the mountains. *Tremayne was right,* she thought almost resentfully. *Some of the horses we started with have already played out, and people have had to trade them for oxen or mules.*

An hour later she was trudging along. The sky overhead was a pure azure. Large, fluffy clouds as white as cotton drifted lazily. As far as she could see in any direction were the bright gold black-eyed Susans, cheerful yellow dandelions, deep green wild henbane, and muted brown sagebrush and prairie grass. Far off to the south was a line of storm clouds. *It may rain. I hope not,* she thought. *It makes such a mess.* They had already had two storms, and Charity had enjoyed them, but now she was tired. Today was bright, however, warm and benevolent, and Charity, despite her aches, enjoyed the sounds of creaking leather and jingling harness and the scent of wild sage.

The morning passed, measured by the slow, sure tread of the oxen and the mules, and the sun began creeping up from behind low-lying hills. By the time the train halted

169

for lunch, everyone was hungry and ready to eat. The travelers did not cook at nooning but ate what was left over from breakfast. Charity had learned to cook more than was necessary for the morning meal.

After the nooning the train continued, and about mid afternoon Charity noticed something in the distance. She was walking beside the train, staying out of the dust, and she saw Tremayne riding back. He stopped beside her. "Well, we've made a start anyway. We can do some shopping tonight."

"Is that a town?"

"Yes. It's Nauvoo. It was settled by the Mormons. When they got run out of Missouri, they came here and built this town. They didn't stay long. They moved on. I hear they've gotten all the way to the big salt lakes now."

He stepped off his horse and walked along beside her, the big mount following him docilely. He told her a little bit about the Mormons, which she didn't know, and then he called to Elsworth, who was passing by.

"Elsworth, I'm going to ride on a little bit. Bring the train to the outskirts."

"Right."

Charity watched him swing into the saddle and thought, *What a physically able man he is.* He was tall and not heavily built, but his muscles seemed to be like steel springs. He mounted the horse easily and then galloped away toward the town.

"Well, you're going to get some town living, I understand, Miss Morgan."

"Yeah, I'm ready. You know what I miss, Elsworth? I miss a chair to sit down in. It's hard sitting on the ground or the wagon seat."

Elsworth smiled at her. He was very lean and short and was a mystery to the rest of the train. He was obviously highly educated. She asked, "What did you do before you went to prison?"

"I was a professor at a school called Harvard."

"What did you teach?"

"Oh, philosophy and whatever nobody else wanted." He shrugged. "It's a way to make a living."

"Why did you go to prison?" Charity hated to ask, but she was curious. Charterhouse was from a different stamp than the rest of the inmates, who were rough-hewn and ill-mannered.

"Embezzlement. My best friend took money from a business I was in and ran off with my fiancée. Left me nothing but a prison term."

"Do you hate them?"

"Not anymore. Life's too short for that sort of thing."

"I think that's a good way to think of it." She hesitated. "I suppose prison was worse for you since you were used to better things."

"It was pretty bad. If it weren't for Casey, I wouldn't have made it. Some of the men in the prison are pretty abusive. I was black and blue and bleeding before long, and then Casey stepped in and broke a few heads."

"Well, you two are great friends."

"Yes, we are." He stared at her, and she met his gaze. "Tell me, Miss Morgan, is there someone you love or someone you hate?"

"What a strange question!"

"Well, as Horace said, *Aut amat aut odit mulier; nihil est tertium.*"

"What in the world does that mean?"

"It means a woman either loves or hates — nothing in between."

Charity smiled. "I'm not sure that's true."

"I'm not sure either, but I quote Latin to make people think I'm wise." He looked ahead at the town and rubbed his face. "I think I'll get a shave and a bath if there's a barbershop there."

"I wish there were a barbershop for women."

"Maybe there will be someday in a more enlightened world."

Nauvoo was not much of a town after Pittsburgh, but at least it had a general store and a blacksmith shop so the travelers could buy supplies and get some of the animals shod. Charity took Bronwen and Meredith to the store and let them buy small things, mostly candy. Meredith saw a gun up on the wall and said, "I want that gun, Charity."

"You can't have a gun, silly," Bronwen snipped. "You're just a girl."

"When I grow up, I'm going to have a gun just like Casey does."

"You're not supposed to call him by his first name."

"He told me to, and besides, I like it. I may marry him when I grow up."

Charity had been listening. She smiled and said, "He'll be too old for you."

"Lots of older men marry younger women."

"Don't talk foolishly. Now pick out what you want."

They returned to the train and had time to wash clothes and resettle the loads in the wagons. But later that night a situation came up that Charity had been expecting for some time. A sheriff came to the camp and talked for a short while to Tremayne. As soon as he left, Tremayne turned and would have passed Charity by, but she stopped him.

"What did the sheriff want?"

"Just wanted to tell me most of the crew got drunk and created a ruckus. I'll have to pay their fines to get them out of jail."

"What will you do to them?"

Tremayne pushed his hat back and rubbed his jaw thoughtfully. "Nothing except give them a tongue-lashing."

"They need to be punished."

Tremayne considered her remark. He seemed both alert and relaxed at the same time. "Men are men, Charity," he said quietly. "They're going to do things like this."

"Well, you need to punish them."

"You think this is a schoolroom where I can take a paddle and bend them over my knee? These men are going to get us through some rough country. I know they're a wild bunch, but it takes something tough to get us to where we're going. If we get hit by a Sioux war party, you'll be glad enough."

"We think very differently about things like this."

"Yes, we do." He left her abruptly, and

she turned to where her father was standing with Evan. They were examining one of the wagon wheels, and she burst out, "That crew from the prison — they're all in jail."

Evan looked up, surprised, and grinned. "Drunk, I suppose."

"Yes, they're drunk, and they got into a fight. I told Tremayne he ought to punish them."

Gwilym Morgan stood up and gazed at his daughter. "You're like your mother, Charity. She always wanted everything done exactly right. The trouble is, girl, in this world it doesn't go like that. We'll be needing these men to get us across the plains."

Because this was exactly what Tremayne had said, Charity was upset. "Well, it's not decent."

"I've been expecting it. You can't expect men like these to behave like men in a Sunday school."

The next morning when they pulled out, some of the men were the worse for wear. Frenchy Doucett had a puffy red ear and a cut over his eye. Jack Canreen's knuckles were skinned, and some of the other men had minor injuries too.

Tremayne stopped at the Morgans' wagons and announced, "We'll go single file until we get out onto the prairie. We're going to throw ourselves into a wide horizontal line."

"Why would we do that?"

"It's going to be pretty dusty from here on. In a line the last wagon has to eat lots of dust. As it is, the men who bring the stock are going to get their share of it. You bring your wagon along first — your father behind you."

"All right," Charity said shortly. She was upset with Tremayne but knew it would do no good to say so. Instead, she went to stand by the big ox named Babe. "All right, Babe," she said. She was actually getting fond of the great creatures. Babe's mate was named Sampson. She slapped Babe on the shoulder as the signal, and the animals lurched forward, pulling the wagon that always made a creaking noise.

The wagons had reached the outskirts of town when she saw Tremayne suddenly move forward and turned to see what was attracting him. In front of a shack with a tin roof, a group of men was tying another man to a tree. One of them had a whip in his hand, and she could hear their laughter.

Tremayne shouted, "Hold the animals!"

"Whoa, Babe. Whoa, Sampson," she said. All the wagons lurched to a halt, and Charity moved to where she could see what was going on.

Tremayne stepped off his horse and faced the group of men. "What's going on, fellas?"

"We caught us a horse thief." The leader was a short, bulky man with gaps between his teeth. He had obviously been drinking. His face was flushed. He was the one with the whip. He let it out behind him and made it snap through the air. "We're going to teach him a lesson."

"Are you the law around here?" Tremayne asked almost idly.

"My name's Jake Finch. I'm law enough to take care of a horse thief."

Some of the crew had come closer, and Canreen stood there, grinning. He said to Doucett, "Let's see how tough Tremayne is to tackle five guys. He always thinks he's got to save everybody."

"They're a rough-looking bunch. Maybe we ought to help."

"No. Let him take care of it. I hope he gets his head knocked off."

"I didn't steal anything."

Charity could see the speaker who was already tied to the posts, his arms locked and his back to the group. "They wanted my horses so they stole them, and they want my sister."

"Your sister? Where is she?"

Charity moved to one side so she could see the man's face. He had an olive complexion and black, glossy hair. His eyes were dark, and he was a handsome young man of some twenty years. "They've been after her and she fought them off, and when I threatened to shoot them, that's when they said we stole some of their horses, but I never did."

"He's lying," Jake Finch said. "You sodbusters get on out of here and mind your own business, or maybe we'll give you a taste of the whip."

Tremayne noticed that Charterhouse and Billy Watson were standing beside him. They both had their guns on as he had cautioned them, but nobody else moved. There was silence until a woman appeared from behind the shack. She was dressed in colorful clothing, and her face was a dark olive. She had a brilliant yellow kerchief on, and her black eyes flashed. She was an old woman; the years had put wrinkles in her face.

"Make them turn my granddaughter loose if you are men!"

"Shut up, old woman," Finch said. "Henry, go shut her up."

A tall, bulky man started to turn, but Tremayne's voice hit him as cold as ice.

"Stay where you are, Henry."

The man called Henry turned, his eyes widening. "You're not telling me what to do."

"I guess I am. You fellas pull out of here, and things will be all right."

"Easy won't do it," Finch grinned. He looked at his crew and decided he had no problem. He dropped his hand to the butt of his gun. "Looks like to me we've got the best of the argument."

Tremayne suddenly moved forward and he whipped a knife from his pocket. He started toward the post, and Finch yelled out, "Cut that rope and I'll cut you down!"

Charity felt her breath seem to leave her body. She had never seen violence like this; the ruffians who faced Tremayne were obviously men who thought nothing of killing. She was too frightened to cry out.

Tremayne stopped beside the man tied to the post. "What's your name?"

"Stefan. Stefan Krisova."

"You didn't steal a horse?"

"No. They want my sister, and she wouldn't have anything to do with them."

Tremayne faced the group and said, "It's your last chance. I'll kill the man who goes for his gun."

Tremayne's words were like cold steel in

the air. Jake Finch glared at him, and suddenly slapped at his gun. It wasn't even out of his holster when an explosion rent the air, and a black hole appeared over Finch's left eyebrow. He took one step backward, his eyes rolling up, and then he fell over. "Who else wants to die?" Tremayne challenged.

The man called Henry held his hands up at once. "I ain't drawing," he said hoarsely.

"You fellas drop your guns and git. You can come back and get them later. Get out of my sight!"

Tremayne turned to see that both Billy and Elsworth had drawn their guns, but he didn't speak. They all watched until the men had dropped their guns and moved away as quickly as possible. Tremayne looked down at the dead man and said, "You would have it that way." He turned to the old woman and said, "Where is your granddaughter?"

"They got her locked in the house, sir."

"What's your name, Mother?"

"They call me Lareina."

"You're all right, ma'am." He cut the rope that held Stefan. "Maybe you'd better go get your sister out of that house."

Charity watched as Stefan ran like a deer to the door. He pulled the latch that held it shut, and at once a woman came out. She had the same olive skin and raven black hair. *The blackest thing in nature,* Charity thought. Her eyes were enormous and dark. Stefan caught her and said, "It's all right now, Zamora. These men, they help us."

He led his sister back, and her grandmother, the one called Lareina, said, "See. I told you the good God would help us." She turned and said, "This is my granddaughter, Zamora Krisova."

Tremayne took off his hat and nodded his head. "Glad to know you, Miss Krisova."

"I thank you for helping us." The woman's voice was lower than most women's. She was of medium height, and though she wore a colorful dress, it did not hide her splendid figure.

"They will come back as soon as you are gone," Lareina said. "Please take us with you out of this place."

"Why, we can't do that, ma'am. We're going all the way to Oregon."

"Just out of this place, please. We are Gypsies. People hate us everywhere we go, but my grandson is not a thief. He knows horses, and he buys and sells them."

"But I'm not the one to say."

"Then who is? I have asked the good God to get us out of here."

Charity stepped forward. "You're a Christian, Lareina?"

"Yes, I serve Jesus."

Gwilym was standing beside Charity. Confused, he said, "Ma'am, we would like to take you, but it's a long way, and you have no equipment."

"We have plenty of horses and a good sound wagon," Stefan said quickly. "At least let us go part of the way until we get out of this town."

"I'll have to call a meeting of the members of the group."

"Then please do it. We have nowhere to go, and these men will kill us when they come back. They will soil my granddaughter. You would not want that, sir."

"Of course not," Gwilym said quickly. He looked around and said, "You men come on. We'll meet on this."

The men quickly gathered next to a wagon and obviously started arguing. Tremayne, still holding his hat in his hand, put it on and said, "Where did you folks come from?"

"Hungary. We come ten years ago. The life was hard for Gypsies," Lareina said. "So God spoke and we came."

"We've done fine here in this country," Stefan said. He held his head up proudly. "I know horses, and I know how to breed them, but Gypsies are hated by everybody."

"Not by me," Tremayne grinned.

"I don't think we can take you." Charity did not intend to speak up. The three Gypsies turned to look at her and so did Tremayne.

"That'd be up to the men, wouldn't it, Charity?"

"Why do you not want us to go?" It was the young girl who spoke. *She's no more than twenty,* Charity thought, *and a real beauty.*

"We couldn't be responsible for you. It's a long way. You might die on the road."

"Any of us may die at any time."

Charity saw that Tremayne was in favor of taking the three, but she stubbornly said, "It can't be. I'm sorry."

But she was wrong. Her father came back and said, "There were a couple opposed, but at least you can go with us until we get to Council Bluffs. That's the next stop, isn't it, Tremayne?"

"Yes, not too far from here."

"We will be no trouble," Stefan said quickly. "I will help with your horse herd."

"And I will help, too," Zamora said. "I can cook."

Charity started to speak. She saw that Tremayne was waiting for her to do exactly that so she knew she could say nothing. She was aware, too, that the old woman was looking at her, and her eyes had a strange light in them.

"Why do you wish not to take us, lady?" Lareina asked.

"I am — afraid that something will happen to you. Something bad."

"We could but die, and that's what life is."

Watching the old woman carefully, Tremayne said, "You'll have to have enough supplies to make the trip."

"We have plenty," Zamora said. "Come. I'll show you our wagon and the horses."

Tremayne turned with the Gypsies but first directed a comment to Charity, "A woman should have gentleness."

Charity's face burned. She thought of a sharp answer, but Tremayne had already walked away.

Later, after the Gypsies' wagon and horses had been checked and approved, Zamora approached Charity. "Why do you not want me to go?"

"I've told you. You could be killed."

"So might you." Her eyes went to Tremayne. "Are you his woman?"

"No!"

"Which is your man?"

"None of them."

Zamora's dark eyes were fixed on Charity, and she said only, "We are grateful for what your people have done for me." She turned, walked away, and found Tremayne standing beside his horse, waiting to begin the trip. "How far is it to where you're going?"

"Well, a long way. We're going all the way to the ocean, but it's not that far to Council Bluffs."

"What sort of place is that?"

"Council Bluffs? Just a little town on the river."

"I wish we could go to the ocean. It's far away from all this."

"Well, Miss Zamora, I expect people are what they are, no matter here on the prairie or in the mountains or at the ocean."

She smiled at him, and he was aware of her beauty. "I thank you for your help." She put out her hand like a man. He shook it. It was firm and warm.

"Well, you're welcome, Zamora."

"What can I do to show my thanks?"

"Make me a pie of some kind."

"I will do that." She walked away.

Elsworth came up and said softly to Tremayne, "Beautiful young woman."

"I guess so."

Elsworth laughed. "You're a devious son

of a gun! Come on. Let's get started. I'm anxious to get to the big water."

Chapter Ten

The Missouri had been low when the Angel Train, as the travelers had started calling the caravan, reached its banks. It had taken half a day for Tremayne to find a place where a fording could be made without any trouble. The journey so far had been simple, with plenty of trees, springs, creeks, and fresh water available at all times. Tremayne had warned them that at some point in their journey all of these things would be hard to find.

The sun was high in the sky as Tremayne and Charterhouse crested a small rolling hill. To their left were wooded areas and to the right, hills sprawled against the horizon. A breeze was blowing, and Tremayne pulled off his hat. He wiped his brow, and his eyes moved from point to point, which Charterhouse noticed was his habit.

"He's always careful, always watching. I think that must be from his Indian days,"

Charterhouse had told Stefan. It was a habit that would come in handy.

Charterhouse said, "Look, there's a creek over there. We could pull up tonight maybe."

Tremayne's eyes narrowed, and he nodded. "I think there are deer in there."

"You see that far?" Charterhouse asked, astonished.

Tremayne didn't answer. He simply stepped off his horse and said, "You stay here with the horses. I'm going to get downwind from them. We can use some fresh meat."

Charterhouse watched as the tall man pulled his rifle from his saddle holster and began loping in the opposite direction Charterhouse had expected. Watching as the hunter circled, Charterhouse wondered if he would ever be able to hunt like his friend. He knew it was impossible, for a man had to be born in this kind of setting, and England didn't have this sort of hunting ground, nor was Harvard a place where one learned to shoot deer. Stepping off his horse, Charterhouse recalled the journey so far. He had been pleased, and he knew that Tremayne also was happy that there had been little friction between the rough crew and the saints of the train. The thing that held it all together was the scout. Everyone knew that any infraction of the rule would bring a sudden confrontation with Tremayne, and no one wanted that.

Fifteen minutes later Charterhouse straightened up, for two shots, very close together, had sounded. He remounted and galloped ahead, leading Tremayne's roan behind him. When he reached the edge of the woods, he paused and called out, "Where are you, Casey?" He heard a faint reply and then made his way through the brush. He called twice more and finally reached Tremayne.

"Had luck, Elsworth. Got two of them. A buck and a doe."

"We going to haul them back to camp?"

"I'll dress these out and we'll go back to the train."

Elsworth nodded at once and pulled a book from his inner pocket. "I'll just broaden my knowledge a little bit while you're busy."

Tremayne grinned at his friend. "You need to suffer more. Isn't there something in the Bible about that — 'whom the Lord loveth he chasteneth'?"

"Ah, that's true enough, but as Seneca said, *Plus dolet quam necesse est, qui ante dolet quam necesse sit.*" He added quickly, "He suffers more than is necessary, who suf-

189

fers before it is necessary."

"That doesn't make any sense."

"It sounds wise though. It's the secret of my success, Casey. Always sound wise, and people will think you are."

Tremayne laughed. "I'm glad I brought you on this trip. If you're going to ever get any education, you'll have to get it from me."

"I have an education."

"You haven't really been educated until you face a Sioux war party. That'll teach you a few things."

Tremayne went to work on the meat. Charterhouse sat down and put his back against a tree. He began to read and at once was lost in the world of Seneca.

The train was already drawn into a circle when Tremayne pulled up his horse in front of the Gypsies' wagon. He had been interested in the trio, and now he stepped down and said to Stefan, "Had good luck. Brought you a quarter of a deer."

"Thank you," Stefan said politely. He took the quarter and turned to Zamora. "Look, a gift from Mr. Tremayne."

Zamora was wearing a colorful scarf around her head, and her dress also caught the fading sunlight. She said, "That is good.

I will cook some of it for the crew if you would like."

"They're a pretty rough crew," Tremayne said.

Zamora gave him an odd look. "I'm used to rough treatment."

Her statement intrigued Tremayne, and he said quickly, "If any of them bother you, you let me know."

Zamora smiled. Her teeth looked very white against her olive skin and red lips. She reached deep into a hidden pocket in her skirt and came out quickly with a six-inch knife. "Tell them I'll cut their throat if any of them tries to touch me."

Tremayne grinned. "You got my permission. Just don't kill them. I need them to get this train through."

Putting away the knife, Zamora said, "I'll soak some of this venison in salt water. It makes it good and tender for our grandmother."

"I've got something better than that." Tremayne turned to the saddle bag and pulled out a piece of canvas that seemed soaked with blood. "I thought about your grandmother, and I took the livers. Let me cook her up something tender and delicious."

Zamora's eyes narrowed. She was suspicious of men, Tremayne saw, but there was nothing he could do about that. Nevertheless, he tried. "I'm going to just cook a little stew for your grandmother. You don't have to be afraid of me, Zamora."

"I'm not afraid of you. I'm not afraid of any man," she said, her eyes locked with his.

"That's good. Lareina is your grandmother's name. What does that mean?"

"It means 'the queen.' "

"Couldn't get a better name than that. Give me a pot, and we'll get started on this liver. You have to cook it until it falls apart. That's when it's really good."

Zamora turned to the wagon and came back, and the two of them got a fire going, and she watched as he sat in front and, from time to time, requested salt.

"I have some herbs that will make it tasty."

"Throw them in. Liver is pretty good by itself. When we get some buffalo, we'll eat the livers raw."

"Not me. I like my meat cooked."

Charterhouse also took a quarter of a deer to the Morgan wagon. "We had good luck. Here's a quarter. I'm not much good at dressing them, I'm afraid."

Meredith came forward and turned her

blue eyes firmly on him. "What are you good for?"

"Nothing much."

"Why do you talk so funny?"

"Don't be impolite," Charity admonished.

"I'm not impolite. He does talk funny."

"She's right, Miss Charity. I do talk funny. Well, Miss Meredith, I talk funny because I come from another country far away from here."

"Does everyone there talk funny like you?"

"Pretty much."

Evan was examining the venison. He nodded to Charterhouse and said, "You must have had good luck."

"Not me. Tremayne knocked them both down. He's a wonderful shot."

"I guess he sharpened his skills all those years on the frontier." Evan pulled him to one side and said, "Sit down. We'll have some coffee. I want to ask you about England. What kind of farms do you have there?"

"Oh, most of the farms are rather small. There are some large properties, but they're mostly for grazing sheep and cattle."

"Is it good farming country?"

"Oh yes. In the summertime the grass is so green it hurts your eyes." He went on talking about the fertile soil, and finally he said, "You want to be a farmer, do you, Evan?"

"Yes, I do. Why did you leave England?"

"Lack of good sense, I suppose."

"You could go back."

"There might be some objection to that."

Evan was curious about the Englishman. "Did you get in trouble with the law?"

"Not so serious with the law, but I displeased my father. I was a younger son, you know."

"Is that bad?"

"Well, in England the oldest son usually inherits everything. We younger boys have to root around and do the best we can." His eyes grew thoughtful. He reached down and drew a figure in the dust. "I wouldn't be too much of a welcome addition if I went back."

Charity had noticed Tremayne cooking at the Gypsies' wagon. She walked over and saw something in a pot. "What are you cooking, Tremayne?"

"It's liver for Lareina. Zamora has put more spices in. I don't know what it will taste like, but it'll be a lot easier to chew than that tough steak. Here try it." He carefully spooned some of the mixture out. He held it out and she tasted it.

"Why, that's very good."

"Liver is pretty good. When we get some buffalo, I'll let you have a chunk of the liver and a piece of the tongue. That's the best part, I think."

"Will we be seeing large herds?"

"Some of them so big you couldn't believe it. I got caught once in the middle of it, just me and my horse. It must have covered ten square miles."

"The Indians must like that."

Tremayne looked out over the plains. As always, he was alert. He seemed to be more aware of his surroundings than any man Charity had ever seen. "Well, they don't like it because we're coming in. Buffalo don't stay where they're hunted, not too often, so they're headed more into the north country now."

"Where are the Gypsies?"

"Lareina was here a moment ago. Stefan is helping guard the herd tonight, and Zamora is cooking for the crew."

"Isn't that a little bit dangerous?"

"What do you mean?"

"Well, these men, they've been without women for a long time."

"They won't bother her. They know what would happen if they did."

"Well, what would you do?"

He smiled at her. His alert form revealed his tough, resilient vigor and physical power. Discipline lay along the pressed lines of his broad mouth, but there was a rash and reckless will in his eyes that struggled against discipline. She saw it clearly. His cool reason would never betray that discipline but a latent storminess could make him dangerous to others.

"What was it like living with the Indians?" she asked abruptly.

Tremayne laughed. "You've got a mind like a grasshopper. Changes from one subject to another."

"Well, what was it like? It was hard, I suppose."

"Well, it's not so bad if you're very young. The older people who were captured couldn't adjust. Most of them died."

"What are they like? All I can think of is they're merciless and bloodthirsty."

"They're like us," he said.

Charity stared at Tremayne with surprise. "What do you mean like us?" she asked.

"They laugh at funny things."

"I never thought of them having a sense of humor."

"You'd have to live with them. They do though."

"But aren't they cruel?"

"They do things that we don't agree with. In war they're cruel, but they're very generous. If you admire something one of them has, he's likely to give it to you. It wasn't a bad life." His eyes grew cloudy. "I've had worse since I left the Indians."

"I hope we don't meet any."

"I expect we will. Some of them won't be any trouble. It's the Comanche or the Kiowa we have to watch out for, and maybe the Cheyenne if we go farther up north."

Suddenly a movement caught her eye, and Charity turned to see the old Gypsy woman. She was not tall, and she was thin, but she stood very straight. It was impossible to guess her age, but the wisdom in her eyes and a settled determination in her dark features were impressive.

"You have come to visit the Gypsy?"

"Well, yes," Charity said, a little flustered. Somehow the old woman's gaze seemed to look deeper than most. It did not merely examine things on the outside but scrutinized inner feelings.

"Mr. Casey Tremayne is fixing me a special meal. He is a very kind man."

"There, Charity, I got a good recommendation."

"You are kind. You want me to tell your fortune, Tremayne?"

197

Tremayne smiled. He held out his hand, but she ignored it. She came over to where he was sitting, knelt down, and stared at him full in the face.

"The fortune isn't in the hand. It's in the face, in the eyes," Lareina said.

Charity watched as the old woman stared into Tremayne's face. He was also caught by the intensity of Lareina's gaze. Something about her made him feel apprehensive. It was not a physical fear for she was old and frail, but her expression, her eyes, and her demeanor kept him very still. He heard the fire crackling and far off, a dog barked, but he was conscious mostly of the dark eyes that seemed to be boring into his.

"You have been alone too much, Tremayne."

"That's right."

There was a long silence, and then she smiled. "You will not always be alone."

"How many wives do you see? Three or four ought to do me." He smiled, but Lareina didn't return the smile.

"You will find one someday. There's an old Gypsy tale," she said. "It's a myth, of course, but I always liked it. Do you like stories, Tremayne?"

"Sure do."

"This is a story about how the great God

made a creature, and something very sad happened. It was torn in two so there were two where before there was only one. One was called man and one was called woman. They were scattered throughout the earth like two pieces of paper."

A silence fell over the three, and they seemed to be held together by a strange force. "The one called man and the one called woman had been torn in two, and where they were torn there was a jagged gap, but there were others that were torn in two, yet only the one she was separated from would suit this woman, and only the one that fit his torn side would fit this man. So they spent their lives looking throughout all the world — through the woods and through the forests and across the sea. They found many others who had been torn, but none of them fit, and then one day, the story goes" — Lareina smiled slightly — "they encountered each other in the deep woods. They came together and saw that the torn place on his side exactly fit the torn place on her side. So they found each other, and they were joined together and became one again as the good God had intended it."

Charity was moved. "That's a wonderful story, Lareina," she said.

"Do you believe that story?" Lareina

asked Charity. "Do you believe it, Tremayne?"

Charity offered, "Are you asking whether I believe that there's only one man who will be right for me in all the men in the world?"

"Yes. Do you believe that?"

"It may be so," Charity said. "The Bible says the steps of a good man, and I suppose a woman, are ordered by the Lord. So if God thinks on us, He may pick out one particular man for a woman."

"And what do you think, Tremayne?" she asked, and there was a sharpness in her birdlike eyes.

"I never think much about those things. Here, try this soup." Lareina allowed him to pull her down to sit on a box. He spooned some of the soup into a bowl. She tasted it.

"Is very good. You are a thoughtful man."

Charity found the contrast between the two interesting and fascinating — the tall, lithe, and muscular frontiersman, and the diminutive Gypsy woman. Her skin and eyes were much darker than his, but Charity saw that Tremayne liked the Gypsy woman, and she respected him for that. It soothed her to see him go to the trouble to fix a meal for this woman, and she knew that she would think of it often.

"I must get back and do my own cooking," Charity said.

She had walked only a few steps when Lareina called out, "Be watchful. Somewhere there is a man who will match you perfectly, Charity Morgan."

Charity looked back quickly and saw that the old woman was staring fixedly at her. "I'll be watching," she said. Then she turned and went back to her wagon.

CHAPTER ELEVEN

York Wingate sat limply on the seat of the wagon. The ground was bumpier than usual, and though he tried to avoid the deeper potholes, still the wagon lurched, dipped, and jolted. Nervously Wingate turned and looked at his wife lying on the bed he had made for her inside the wagon. Her eyes were closed, but her face was pale, and this troubled him. He turned back and tried to chase the thoughts from his mind, but they kept returning. *Shouldn't have brought her on this trip. She's not able to bear it. I may have to stop at one of the forts along the way and wait until she has the baby.* He had had these thoughts since they left Pennsylvania, and now the journey was less than one-fourth over, and Helen was not taking it well.

A white cloth caught his eye. This was how Tremayne marked the way for the wagons; he posted them on bushes across breaks and washes to show the lead teamster where to take the train. It was a help, but still driving across open country was not like driving along a street in Pittsburgh. Wingate saw a mustard-colored dog trotting back to the train with a frog in its mouth. He glanced to a line of trees that marked the small creek, and he wished they would stop there for the night, but it was too early for that.

He cast his eye along the line of wagons, gray and white in the sun and squirming in the haze of dust. It was nearly noon, and the train was broken into an uneven line of wagons. Behind the wagons came the loose horses and the other stock. He could see Stefan's bright green scarf. On the windward side, out of the dust, a group of people was walking, as always. The children were laughing and chattering, and some of the women were looking for wildflowers. Wingate realized that women often wanted the finer things of life, and flowers were all they could find on this journey. The land was covered with small yellow flowers he didn't recognize, and there were clumps of white daisies. Earlier that day he had seen a clump of wild roses next to a spring.

"I must be crazy thinking about flowers." He spoke the words aloud and shook his head, thinking he was the only man on the train who noticed such things. He glanced ahead, and the high sun made flashes through the dust. It was not a colorful land, and the white of the wagon covers, and the reds and browns of the oxen, mules, and horses brightened the landscape. Here and there a woman wore a blue dress; another, green.

Then he saw Tremayne riding back. He threw up his hand, which meant stop. Wingate liked nooning. The wagons pulled up, and no one bothered to build fires for they would not stop for long. Turning, he jumped out of the wagon and watered the stock, which took some time. Then he took a small bucket, put water in it, and found a clean cloth. Stepping to the back of the wagon, he hauled himself into it and saw that Helen was awake.

"How you feel, sweetheart?"

"All right."

"You always say that. Here, let me bathe your face. It's getting hot out there." Carefully he wet the rag with the tepid water, wrung it out, and began to wipe her face. She had delicate features and clear blue eyes, but an unhealthy pallor in her face disturbed him.

"How do you feel? Could you eat something?"

"I don't think so."

"I'll fix you something that's easy to digest. You need to keep your strength up." He left her for a moment, rummaged through the food box, and came up with a can of peaches. He opened it with his knife, grabbed a spoon, and returned to her.

"Look," he said, "peaches, just like back home." He broke off a small piece with the spoon and said, "Open up. I'll feed you just like you were a little bird."

"I'm not very hungry," Helen whispered, but she opened her mouth obediently. She chewed on a bit of peach and said, "That's good. You have some too."

To please her, he took small bites, and she managed to get down perhaps a fourth of the can. He finished it off. She reached out and took his hand, and he was somewhat shocked, as always, at how fragile it seemed. She had been strong when they had married, but expecting a baby did not agree with her. He had seen that situation before in women, strong until the baby seemed to drag the life from them.

She looked up at him. "How far is it, York?"

"Oh, quite a ways, but it will probably get cooler as we go on. You'll feel better."

She held onto his hand, and her eyes

searched his face. "What do you want? A boy or a girl? I'd like a boy."

"I'd like to have a girl, just like you." He sat beside her, and they listened to sounds of their fellow travelers. Someone was singing, and someone else was playing "Oh, Susannah" on a harmonica. He waited until she dropped off, then left the wagon. He dropped to the ground and leaned against one of the large wheels. He was standing there when Charity Morgan came by with a cloth-covered dish. She smiled.

"I brought you some pie, Doctor."

"What kind of pie?"

"I don't know. I found these berries. They were ripe. I hope they don't make you sick. Evan and Father liked them and so did the girls."

He took the dish and said, "It looks like gooseberries."

"I don't know what they are. They may not grow back home."

Charity watched him, noticing that he was not eating hungrily as had her father and her brother. "How is Helen?"

"Not too well. I shouldn't have let her come on this trip."

"She'll be fine, Doctor."

"I hope so. What about you?"

"Oh, I'm fine. We're all healthy so far."

He studied her and noted that she was round and mature and wore a brown dress trimmed with white at the neck and wrists. Her hair was pulled back, but the sun still caught its red hue, and her eyes were bright and full of health. She turned to look at someone walking by, and when she turned back to him, he asked abruptly, "How is it you've never married, Charity?"

"I don't know. It just never came my way."

"What about John Mund? He used to come calling on you."

"I wasn't interested."

"Well, there was Caleb Freeman. He courted you. He's a mighty good man."

"I wasn't interested."

"Maybe you're too choosy."

"I suppose I am, Dr. Wingate."

He glanced up and saw Stefan standing beside his grandmother, and both were smiling. "I wonder about those Gypsies. It was quite a shock to find them out here in the middle of nowhere. They're not going to do much fortune-telling with this group."

"I don't believe in fortune-tellers."

"Well, I don't know what I believe in."

She hesitated. "I wish you knew God, Dr. Wingate."

"So do I."

"Well, why don't you? You know Jesus

said, 'Come unto me,' and He meant every-body."

"It's just never happened, Charity. But I wish I were a Christian man, then I could pray for Helen to have this baby safely."

Compassion touched Charity. She saw the worry in his fine eyes and noted that he had lost weight. "I'll pray for Helen and for the baby."

"Thanks, Charity." He smiled at her. "That's like you." But she saw he was filled with doubt, which troubled her. She turned and walked away, and Wingate glanced back at the wagon, and the thought came to him, *Maybe I could pray anyway. God may even hear a sinner,* but he couldn't find any way to speak his thoughts, even to God.

The days wore on, and finally the scenery changed. Evan Morgan was in the second wagon, and when the oxen crested a slight ridge, his eyes widened. Far off, small hills, not big enough to be mountains, made a change in the terrain. The line of wagons was weaving through a set of badger holes, and the hills turned out to be piles of sand thirty or forty feet high, blown by the wind. A powder-like salt patched the ground with white.

Evan had heard about flat country, but as

they went along, he couldn't believe that any land could be so flat or that the distance would be so great. The sky was lifted high over a world that seemed totally empty.

"Some sight, isn't it, Evan?"

He turned to see Tremayne riding beside him and grinning.

"I never saw such a land. You can see forever."

"And there's plenty of nothing."

"You know, Casey, it seems like I've been living in some place that was always shut off. Couldn't see much for the trees or the mountains, and the distance wasn't anything. I never knew it would be like this."

"I remember the first time I saw the Platte Valley. I felt just like you do, Evan. It'll change though."

"What comes now?"

"We follow the Platte. Nothing much to see until we get to Fort Kearney. We can restock then."

"Are we doing pretty good, Casey?"

"Real good so far. Mighty proud of this bunch. No trouble at all. That's the way I like it."

"You think we'll see any Indians?"

"If we do, they'll be mostly tame Indians. Of course, sometimes the Comanche wander by on a raiding party. Hope we don't meet any of them. They're about the worst Indians on the plains."

He rode off, and an hour later they stopped for nooning. Charity fed the men leftovers from supper the night before, and then she and the girls ate. Like Evan, she was struck by the flatness of the plains, and she walked away toward a line of trees that marked a stream. The greenery made a splash of color on the grayness of the land. She found the stream, washed her face and hands, and, as always, wished she could get in for a bath, but that was out of the question.

A faint sound caught her ear. Through the saplings Charity could see Helga Studdart talking with Ringo Jukes. Instantly, Charity felt a warning. Helga was the daughter of Karl and Freida Studdart, probably the wealthiest people on the train. She was sixteen, a blonde with dark blue eyes, and very attractive. There had been some difficulty with her back in Pennsylvania. She had been freer in her manners with men than most of the women of the Pilgrim Way, and her parents had not been able to handle her.

For a time she stood there. Then Jukes reached out and touched Helga's hair, and Helga laughed, but the girl turned away and started toward the wagons.

Charity hurried to catch up with her, and when Helga turned, there was guilt in her face. "Were you spying on me, Charity?"

"I came to the stream to get fresh water. You shouldn't be meeting that man. You know the rules."

"I haven't done anything wrong." Helga held up her head, and there was a defiant look in her eyes. "He was telling me why he went to prison. He was innocent."

"Couldn't have been too innocent if he was in prison."

"Well, he was. He was in with the wrong crowd. He's going into business when he gets his parole. Going to San Francisco, he says. He's been there before. It sounds so exciting."

Several thoughts came to Charity, and she nearly spoke aloud, but Helga was in no mood to listen to her. *She wouldn't listen to her own parents, so why would she listen to me.* Instead, she said, "You could get him in trouble, you know."

"How could I do that?"

"You know what Casey Tremayne says about the men. They're supposed to stay away from us."

"You mind your own business, Charity," Helga said, and she ran away.

Charity saw Evan, who nodded at her and asked, "Is it a pretty good stream?"

"Yes, it's very clear."

"I'll fill the cask with fresh water. This is getting stale."

He grabbed two buckets and started toward the stream. He filled them and was turning to go when he saw Zamora approaching. Her bright clothing made a colorful picture, and he saw that she was watching him carefully. *She's standoffish with men,* Evan thought.

"Pretty good water here, Miss Zamora."

Zamora knelt down and put her hand in the water. "It is a nice stream."

He tried to think of a way to make conversation. She acted as if he were not there, and finally he said, "It must be a little lonely the way you are living now."

Zamora turned and faced him. "What do you mean?"

"Well, there are no other Gypsies around. Don't you miss them?"

"Yes, I do."

"What was it like in the old country?"

Zamora's eyes brightened. They were dark, and the blackness of her hair was a wonder. Her skin was as smooth as any Evan had ever seen, and he felt embarrassed staring at her.

"It was good back in the old country. We had a big band. I miss having them around — cousins, uncles, relatives. I miss all that."

"I don't know what that would be like, to be cut off from my people," Evan said. He spoke slowly and thoughtfully. "I've always been surrounded by my family and friends. What's it like being alone?"

"Lonely," she said and smiled. He noticed there was a slight dimple to the right of her full lips. She was looking at him in a strange way that made him nervous.

"Well, maybe you'll find other Gypsies when we get to the coast."

"I don't think so. Most of our people stay in the East. Easier to make a living there, but Stefan wants to start raising horses."

"Oregon ought to be good for that. What about you?"

"What do you mean?"

"Well, you're pretty. You'll get a husband and have a family."

"Who knows about things like that? Maybe I will, maybe not. What do you want, Evan?"

"Well, I worked in a mine, and I hated every day of it. It's like being buried alive. I want to be a farmer, be outdoors, and watch things grow." He continued to speak, and Zamora watched him carefully.

213

"I hope you get it, but not many of us get what we want in this life."

Evan was puzzled but still drawn to her. She saw him looking at her and recognized his shyness. Suddenly she laughed, "I can tell your fortune."

"I — I don't really believe in that."

"I can tell what you're thinking right now."

"No, you can't."

"Yes, I can. If I tell you, will you admit it if I'm right?"

"I suppose so."

"You're wondering what it would be like to kiss me." She laughed. "Look at your face. It's as red as those berries on that bush over there." She saw his embarrassment. "Don't be ashamed of being a man, Evan Morgan."

"I'm not. How did you know what I was thinking?"

"Not too hard to read that in a man. Most of them have loving on their minds. I've had to discourage enough of them."

"How do you do that?"

Zamora's hand plunged into the deep pocket in her dress, and she pulled out her knife. "I have to threaten to cut their ears off," she said.

It was Evan's turn to laugh, "Well, you won't have to cut my ears off, Zamora."

"You wouldn't try to force yourself on me?"

"Of course not!"

"That's good. I think I'll go get some fresh water."

"I'll help you with the buckets," he said.

"I may read your mind again."

"That'll be all right. I don't mind."

The train stopped early that day, and after Zamora had cooked for the crew, avoiding the men's attempts to get close to her, she looked for the Krisovas' goat, Ruzal.

"Grandmother, Ruzal's wandered off. I'll have to go find her."

"Don't get lost."

"Oh, she couldn't have gone far. Probably wandered down to the river."

She made her way to the river and found the goat eating the vegetation beside the small stream. She took off her shoes and waded into the water, holding her skirt high. The train was out of sight, and she longed to take a bath but dared not. She came out finally and sat down while the goat ate. The silence sank into her.

She began to sing an old song her grandmother had taught her. The land made her lonely. There was nothing here. It was flat, and it was truth she had spoken to Evan

Morgan. She did miss the band. Back in the old country when she was a very young girl, there had been singing every night. Most of the men played instruments, and life had been good. But it had become hard for Gypsies when the government cracked down on them, and they had to flee to the New World.

"You can't be this careless when we get into Kiowa territory, Zamora."

Zamora leaped to her feet and whirled to see Tremayne. He had a rifle in his hand, and when he stood before her, she had to look up at him. "You followed me!"

"Why, not really. I always look about at night. Not like there'd be any danger here from Indians, but a man can't get careless in this country."

Zamora was angry and suspicious of him, "Don't sneak up on me, Tremayne."

"Zamora, not every man you see is out to get you."

"Most of them are."

He held the rifle across his arm. "Zamora, I've got enough on my mind just getting this train to Oregon. You're safe enough with me."

"Maybe so, but I had to learn about men the hard way. They all think that a Gypsy girl is easy prey."

"That's too bad. It must be hard."

"It is hard. Hard being a Gypsy in the first place. Nobody likes us. They think we're all thieves."

Tremayne listened as she continued to speak. He was impressed by the girl's beauty as was every man in the train, and he was seeing a side of her he had never seen before.

"I wish I had a way to make it easy for you. All I can say now is that none of the crew will bother you."

Zamora was curious about the man. She felt safe with him, which was unusual for her. At the same time a thought came to her, *He's never tried to touch me, and he doesn't watch me in the sneaky way that most men do. I'll bet I can make him want me.*

She stepped closer and had to look up because he was so tall. She took his arm and said, "I appreciate your taking us on the train. I don't think we could have come if you hadn't been with us." She pressed herself lightly against him and knew that most men would take this as an invitation.

Tremayne didn't speak for a moment, but he moved back slightly and said, "Don't do that, Zamora."

"Don't do what?"

She was angry; she saw that Tremayne

hadn't been fooled. He had seen through her motives, and then she flung off without another word. Tremayne watched her go and chewed on his lower lip thoughtfully.

"I feel sorry for that girl," he muttered. "She's got a hard way to go, but then most of us have."

Chapter Twelve

July had come to the land, bringing with it hot weather. The sun beat down mercilessly on Charity as she walked beside Babe, the lead ox. She glanced ahead at the wagons in line, and it seemed they had been on the trail forever. It was hard to remember what it was like not to be caught up in the routine of the journey; it was always the same.

Usually at 4:00 a.m., the guards discharged their rifles signaling that sleep was over. The travelers began pouring out of the wagons, and soon smoke began to rise. Breakfast was eaten between six and seven; the wagons were loaded, the teams yoked, and then the trek began.

The lead wagon would move out, and Tremayne would soon disappear into the distance, looking for game to eat and for country to avoid. Hunters usually went with him. The Platte River made a shining body under the sun, and the wagons usually formed a horizontal line so no one would have to eat the dust. Following the train came the horses and the spare animals, and during nooning the teams were not unyoked but allowed to stand. The trek continued all day long until late afternoon when the train formed a circle at the spot Tremayne had chosen. Soon everyone began preparing the evening meal, and the sun went down, sometimes dropping like a plummet, so it seemed. At times there was music in the camp with some of the younger people organizing a dance. Finally, all was hushed as the fatigue of the day drained the life out of the travelers. Only the guards stayed awake as the night deepened, and the rest were deep in sleep — the sleep necessary to do the same thing on the following day.

Charity moved quickly to one side for a snake had appeared, a bright green length that caused her to jump away with fear. It was, she knew, a harmless snake. She had learned to recognize the deadly kind, but still a snake was a snake.

She looked up and down the line of wagons. *What will happen to all of us when we get to Oregon? Will we all make it?* So far they had had no deaths nor even accidents. At the head of the line she saw Karl Studdart. His wife, Freida, and Helga, their attractive daughter, walked alongside the wagon. Charity knew that Helga, a sly girl, was seeing Ringo Jukes, and she wondered what would come of it. It occurred to her that she ought to tell Tremayne about the situation, but she didn't want to add to his load of responsibilities. Besides, she had no proof of wrongdoing, only strong suspicions.

She noted the Novaks, the Dekkers, and the Brands with their wagons all bunched closely together. Right behind her was the Cole wagon, and last in the line were York Wingate and his wife, Helen. Helen was not doing well, and Wingate had a perpetual frown on his face.

She thought, as she walked alongside Babe, how she had learned to know the others so well. It could not be otherwise, tight as they were, living in a line of wagons that formed a circle with all of them inside every night. She thought she had known her neighbors well back in their village in Pennsylvania, but there everyone retreated into a house and who knew what went on behind the closed doors.

She looked to her right and saw some of the younger children, including Meredith and Bronwen. They were chasing a butterfly, it seemed, and their cries of laughter made a pleasing sound. Her father, Gwilym, and Evan were helping with the herd; the men all had to take turns. There was some complaining about this for the Studdarts had far more animals than anyone else, and the Studdarts' cattle were included in the herd. Studdart proved more amiable than anyone had thought, especially to Charity. She knew the big man had thought himself capable of being the master of any group, but so far he had not tried to force this on anyone.

For the next three hours they trooped on, and finally Tremayne appeared and led the wagons to the camping place he had selected. He led them into a circle a hundred yards across, and so accurate was his dead reckoning that the last wagon in line would always precisely close the gap so that there was a fort, of sorts, each night. Once Konrad Dekker had complained that it wasn't necessary since there were no Indians, but Tremayne had simply remarked, "Better to be safe than dead."

As soon as the circle was completed, the struggle began to fix a meal. Charity had been amazed at how hard it was to cook by campfire rather than in a kitchen with a stove waist high. Trail cooking involved muscles not previously used, and for the first days of the journey, she had been sore constantly from the difficulty this brought on. Now she went at it methodically.

Wood was so scarce that they had to use mostly buffalo chips. They were in buffalo country now, and the land was littered with the dried dung of the huge beast. There had been some apprehension at first. Recalling this, she smiled. Some of the men had objected to their wives picking up such items, and they had called a meeting of the council — a rather heated meeting — but finally it was decided there was no choice. There was little wood along the Platte, and buffalo chips did burn well when one learned how to create a draft for them. Charity had heard Tremayne say when the meeting broke up, "Mighty big doings for something so important." She had caught his eyes; he smiled and shook his head. She had found herself smiling back at him.

She began cooking, helped by Bronwen and somewhat by Meredith, and they worked quickly. It took too long to bake bread even though she had a small oven. It also took a lot of fuel. She did make fried cakes from flour and water mixed with rendered beef fat. When the cakes had browned on both sides in the skillet, she salted them. She made about twenty cakes.

She cooked buffalo steaks; Tremayne had killed one of the animals the day before. As he had promised, he had given her the liver and the tongue, and despite her reluctance, she found them delicious.

Knowing that everyone was tired of the same fare, she had also made an apple pie. She had been soaking two cups of dried apples in water for eight hours, then added sugar, allspice, and cinnamon. She decided to make two pies so that she had some to give away, and after the Morgans had eaten, she made her way to the Wingates' wagon.

"Doctor," she said, smiling, "I brought some pie for you and Helen."

York turned. His face was lined with worry. "I don't know as she can eat much. She's not well."

"Try to get her to eat a little bit. I think you'll like it too."

"You're good to us, Charity. Thank you."

"How is she, do you think?"

"She's afraid, and I can't blame her. She didn't realize how hard it would be and neither did I. We should never have made this trip, but it's too late to go back now. We may stay at Fort Laramie until the baby's born. I think that might be best."

"Let me know if I can do anything."

Charity walked to the Gypsies' wagon and

found the three of them seated around a fire, and with them was Casey Tremayne. The old lady said, "Here is our friend. Have some tea."

"Thanks. I believe I will, and I brought you all a pie, part of one. I gave some of it to the doctor and his wife."

"How is the lady?" Tremayne asked.

Charity bit her lower lip and shook her head nervously. "Not too well, I'm afraid, Tremayne. She's not strong. The doctor's sorry he brought her."

Zamora cut the pie into slices and passed it around. She tasted it and said, "This is good cooking."

"Anybody can make a pie."

"Not this good," Stefan said. He ate his pie quickly, washed it down with tea, and then picked up his fiddle. He began playing a sad tune.

"Why do you play such a sad tune?" Zamora said. "Play something happy."

"No, I'm a sad man. My heart is broken."

"If you don't stay away from Kirsten Dekker, Jacob will break your head."

"I'm teaching her some things she needs to know about life." Stefan was smiling; he winked at Tremayne and said, "You women just don't understand what it is to have a broken heart." He stopped playing long enough to put his hand over his heart and assumed a sad countenance. "You women folk just don't have it here. When we men suffer over love, we really suffer."

"You're going to suffer from a broken head if you don't leave that girl alone," Zamora said. Her eyes were sparkling, and she wiped a morsel of pie from her lips.

"I wish I had some idea of where we are, Casey. We should have some kind of a map."

"Why, I can take care of that. Have you got a piece of blank paper, Zamora?" He waited until she brought him a large piece of paper and a pencil. He laid it flat and began to sketch a rough map. The rest of them gathered around to watch, and finally he said, "I'm no mapmaker, but you can see Nauvoo here, and how we'll follow the Platte River to Fort Kearney. We're headed for Fort Laramie, and after that, we'll rest up at Fort Hall."

"But this isn't the end of the journey, is it?" Charity asked.

"No, just about halfway. But if you're a good child, I'll draw you a map of the last half when we get to Fort Hall."

Charity sniffed, then said, "I'm always a good child." She stayed long enough to drink a cup of tea and then left. Tremayne left shortly after that.

As soon as he was gone, Lareina turned to her granddaughter. "Zamora," she said, "it's better not to play games with men."

Zamora flushed. "Who's playing games?"

"You are with Tremayne. You'd better leave him alone."

"I do leave him alone. He's like all other men. He'll take what he wants from a woman and then throw her out."

"Not all men are like that," Lareina said. "Your grandfather wasn't."

"No, he wasn't, but there aren't many like him, if any, left." She kept her eye on the tall form of Tremayne, but she soon left and walked toward the men finishing their meal. They all greeted her.

Ringo Jukes said, "When are you going to fall in love with me, Zamora?"

Zamora liked Jukes. He was a big, good-looking man, and she turned to face him. "You don't want me. You're too busy thinking about the Studdart girl."

"Well, a man's got to try a few girls out, not settle on one," Jukes said. He grinned broadly and picked the plates up from the men.

She took them, saying, "I'll help you wash these." He went with her, and she enjoyed his company. She saw, as they passed the Studdart wagon, that Helga Studdart gave

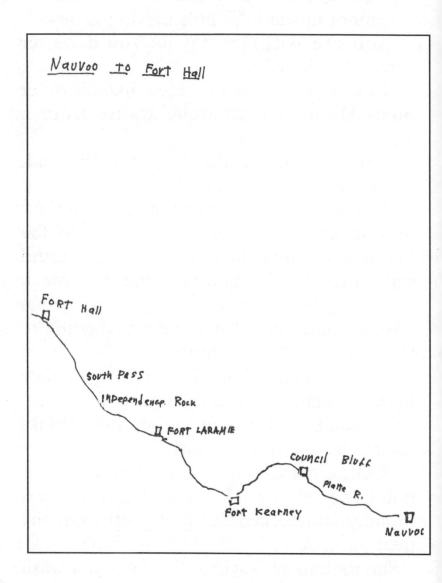

Nauvoo to Fort Hall

Fort Hall

South Pass

Independench. Rock

Fort Laramie

Council Bluff

Platte R.

Fort Kearney

Nauvoo

228

her a venomous look. "Helga may try to stick a knife in me. She's jealous."

"Nothing going on with us. She's just a nice young woman."

"Didn't Tremayne tell you to leave the women of the train alone?"

"I am leaving the women of the train alone, except for the good-looking ones like you," he said.

She laughed. "You stay away from me, or I'll poke your eye with my knife."

Actually she liked Ringo Jukes. He made no secret of his admiration for her, but neither did he make veiled suggestions, and he never tried to put his hands on her as most of the other crew had. The two of them washed the dishes.

"Frenchy Doucett brought some whiskey along," Jukes said. "I think we're all going to get a little bit drunk tonight."

"Don't let Tremayne catch you at it."

"He won't catch us. Man has a right to drink if he wants to."

The crew did indeed drink, but the next morning when Tremayne was checking the wagons, Ringo Jukes came to him with a worried look. "Got some bad news, Tremayne."

"What is it, Ringo?"

"It's Doucett. He's gone."

Tremayne turned to face him. "He didn't walk away?"

"No, he took one of the Studdarts' horses. We was all drinking last night. I guess you knew that, and I guess he didn't drink as much as the rest of us. We all passed out. When I went to get him this morning, he was gone."

"What horse did he take?"

"That tall gelding. He's shod, but one of the shoes came off."

"Then he'll be easy to track," Tremayne said.

"You going after him?"

"What do you think, Ringo?"

Ringo Jukes shoved his hat back and shook his head, "It makes it hard on the rest of us."

"I'll be leaving. You better tell the rest of the men that if any of them leave while I'm gone, they'll look up one day and see me behind them."

"Nobody's going anywhere. Are we not moving today?"

"No. I'll have him back soon enough."

The word spread quickly throughout the train, and everybody knew what had happened. Canreen studied Tremayne, who was saddling his horse. "You won't catch him.

That's a fast horse he stole."

"The fool will get lost, and there are Indian signs around here. If he runs into a Blackfoot or a Cheyenne, we won't have to worry about him." He turned then. "Jack, don't try to run."

"You think I'm afraid of you?"

"I think you should be. Remember what I said. Don't run."

He led his horse to the Morgan wagon and found Gwilym. "Gwilym," he said, "we'll stay here today. Be a good time for the women to wash down in the river and let the animals rest up."

"You're going after him then," Gwilym said. "What will you do if you catch him?"

"I'll make him wish he hadn't run."

"Will you shoot him?" asked Charity who had been standing close by.

"Not unless I have to. I need him too much."

Karl Studdart approached Tremayne and spoke up, "We don't have time to chase after him."

"If I don't stop him, the rest will run too. I'll have to make an example out of him."

Studdart studied the tall man for a moment and saw what a forceful man he was. "You want me to go with you?"

"No, you stay here, Karl. You and Gwilym

take care of things. I'll be back as soon as I can."

The camp was quiet that day. Everyone was talking about the situation. Lareina was not feeling well, and Zamora grew worried. She went to the Wingate wagon and found York Wingate sitting outside, smoking a pipe.

"Well, hello," he said.

"Doctor, my grandmother's sick. I wish you'd come and look to her."

"All right. Let me tell my wife." He went over to where his wife had been sitting in the shade of the wagon and said a few words to her. He picked up his black bag. "How long has she been sick?"

"Just since this morning."

"Is she sick often?"

"She's old but in good health." Zamora turned and looked back to York Wingate's wagon. "Your wife isn't well."

"No, she's not. I'm worried about her."

Zamora was curious about the doctor but made no comment. When they got to their wagon, Lareina was lying on a pallet where she could catch some of the breeze. York knelt down, felt her pulse, and asked her a few questions.

"There's nothing wrong with me that you can fix," Lareina said.

"Maybe I can."

"Can you stop someone from growing old?" Lareina asked and suddenly smiled. "You'd be a rich man if you could."

York asked her more questions. "I've got something that might make you feel better here."

He took a bottle from his bag, poured some medicine into an empty bottle, and gave it to Lareina.

"Thank you, Doctor."

Suddenly Stefan appeared, excitement on his face. "Tremayne is back," he said.

"Does he have Doucett with him?"

"Yes, come on, let's see what happens."

Everybody had seen Tremayne's approach, it seemed, and Charity saw that Doucett's face was swollen. At Tremayne's command he got off the horse, moving very slowly.

"Where did you catch up with him?" Frank Novak asked.

"Not too far from here." Charity waited for Tremayne to say more, but the situation spoke for itself. Tremayne suddenly turned to Frenchy, "Try it again, Frenchy, and I'll tie you to a wagon wheel and break a bullwhip on you. That goes for anybody else who tries to leave. We've been over this before."

Charity was not at all satisfied at what she

had heard, but she was relieved because she had feared that Tremayne might shoot Frenchy Doucett.

She did not see Tremayne for the rest of the day. He had told the travelers that they would leave early in the morning. Then after the darkness closed in, she saw him standing at the edge of the wagons. Everyone had gone to bed, but she was curious. She walked over, and he turned to face her.

"You're up late."

"I couldn't sleep." She stood beside him and was very much aware of his height. "I was afraid you might shoot Doucett."

"I can't afford to lose a man. We need him."

"Did he try to fight?"

"He tried, but he won't try it again, I don't think."

The two were silent for a time. Overhead, the moon was full and bright, and the stars seemed brighter than ever. Charity felt uncomfortable around Tremayne, and he noted that. She was not wise in the ways of men, but several had been interested in her.

Tremayne studied her carefully. He had studied her more than she knew. Small shades of expression softly darkened and then lightened her face, and her lips made elusive changes as her thinking varied. She was a well-shaped girl, and her features were quick to express her thoughts, and laughter and love of live seemed to lie impatiently behind her expressions, waiting for release. She had a calm manner, usually, but from time to time a liveliness had its sudden way and her lips mirrored the change. At times her face displayed a little-girl eagerness.

From far off came a lonely howl of a wolf, one of the many that followed the buffalo herd.

"That always makes me sad," he said, "the wolves. I don't know why."

Charity studied his face, and without warning he reached out and touched her hair. "You have beautiful hair," he said. "My grandmother had hair like this, as red as yours."

Charity stood very still. He had never touched her, and now she felt his light touch on her hair, and strong feelings shot through her. She smiled and said, "You loved your grandmother?"

"Yes."

Her nearness affected him, she saw that, and she waited, saying nothing. When he moved forward and put his arms around her, she was not completely shocked. She had been kissed before, and the big man had aroused her curiosity. He lowered his head. His lips fell on hers, and for a moment she gave herself up to his caress. She was shocked at her feelings, for she was not a woman to give herself to a man easily. Then, as never before, she was aware that they were close to a great mystery, and she knew this man attracted her more than any other man ever had. The attraction frightened her. She pulled back suddenly and stared up at him.

"You shouldn't have done that," she said. "You must never do it again."

"I probably will, Charity."

She tried to think of a way to answer him but found none. She was not cool and collected now for within her an emotion strongly worked and left its fugitive impression on her face. Tremayne saw it on her lips most clearly. It was always her lips that betrayed changes within her. For Tremayne she made a strong presence, and when she turned and walked away without another word, he watched her go.

As for Charity, she was shaken more by the kiss than she had ever been. "I must have lost my mind letting him kiss me like that," she whispered, but she knew even as she spoke that she wouldn't forget how he had held her.

CHAPTER THIRTEEN

"Fort Kearney's up ahead a few miles. We'll be able to make camp and maybe even look the place over."

Charity had been walking beside the lead oxen; her hand rested, from time to time, on Babe's rough coat. Casey Tremayne had ridden up and dismounted to walk alongside.

"Is it a big place?" she asked, more to make conversation than to seek information.

"No. You won't be impressed by it. It's more a trading post than it is an army camp — although a troop of cavalry is usually there."

Charity couldn't help but feel something near embarrassment mixed with anger, which surprised her. She had thought almost without ceasing about that moment when Tremayne had put his arms around her and kissed her. Her anger was not at him so much as at herself for permitting such a thing. She didn't know what to say to the tall man adjusting his stride to hers. She glanced covertly at him and wondered what kind of man he really was. His high, square torso made a trim shape as he strolled beside her. She was well aware of his physical strength and tough, resolute vigor. But what feelings and thoughts lay in the man — why had she permitted him to kiss her, and why had she responded the way she did? These questions troubled her as they walked along, the dust rising behind them.

"I know you're not a woman who is easy."

The remark startled Charity. "What do you mean? Why would you say a thing like that?"

"I think I took advantage of you last time we met. I caught you off guard. So I want to apologize. I know you're not a woman who gives herself easily to any man."

Confusion raced through Charity, for his apology was the last thing in the world she was expecting. She studied his features and saw that he was keeping his glance away from her. He was looking, as he always did, ahead, his eyes moving from point to point.

But suddenly he turned and added, "I don't like to do anything that makes a woman feel bad."

"It caught me off guard, and you're right. It's not the sort of thing I do easily."

A silence fell across the two, and Charity was aware of the creaking wagon wheels, the jingling harnesses, and from far off the high cry of a bird.

"I accept your apology," she said stiffly.

Tremayne seemed troubled. He stepped into his saddle, and before he rode away said softly, "A man gets urges sometimes, Charity, and it's hard to sort them out, but I know you're a woman who has strong convictions. I wouldn't want to upset those. As a matter of fact, I've been wanting to tell you I had a pretty low opinion of what you folks do in the Pilgrim Way, but knowing you and your father and some of the others has made a difference." His glance went up and down the line of wagons, and he seemed to be evaluating them. Finally he shook his head, "A man can make mistakes." He wheeled the gelding, touched its side with the spurs, and left, moving rapidly into the distance.

Charity watched him go, puzzled by his behavior. *I like him more than I should.* The thought startled her, and she almost wanted to argue with herself. Finally she set her jaw. *He's not a man I could admire. He's able, but he doesn't know God.* She continued to walk still troubled, for the memory of his caress and how he had gently held her had not left her. She had tried almost desperately to forget his kiss, but she recalled it repeatedly, and now she scolded herself for falling into such a situation.

Fort Kearney had been a disappointment to most of the travelers. There was no stockade, only a long barracks, a general store, a blacksmith shop, and several houses scattered seemingly at random on the open prairie.

"Not much, is it, Tremayne?" Gwilym remarked as the two of them met at sundown. "I was expecting more."

"It's really just a trading post, Mr. Morgan. Fort Laramie is a little bit better. We ought to get there in a week maybe."

Gwilym was studying the town, such as it was. He sighed and shook his head sadly. "Well, I see it has a saloon and no church."

"That's pretty standard for these posts."

Morgan was troubled. "Do you suppose you would be able to keep your men from getting drunk in that saloon tonight?"

"I could threaten them, but I don't know as it would do much good. They've done pretty well so far. Better than I expected.

They're not your kind of people. We're all of us a rough-hewn bunch."

"Why don't you try to talk to them?"

"I wouldn't care to do that. Maybe you could."

"They wouldn't pay any heed to me, but it saddens me to see men destroying themselves with things like liquor and bad women."

"Well, there won't be any bad women here. The post commander wouldn't permit it, but there'll be liquor, and I'm sure the men will find it. Probably already have."

"Well, it's the world. Men are sinners."

York looked up as the doctor came into the room. His name was Roberts, and he was old for such a post. His hair was salt-and-pepper, and his face was lined from years under the sun. He was a drinking man too. York could spot the signs — the redness of his eyes and a slight tremor in the hands. He was not the ideal doctor, but York had sought him out and asked him to look Helen over to get a second opinion. He had told Roberts, "I'm too close to the situation." Now he asked, "How is she in your opinion, Dr. Roberts?"

Roberts walked to a cabinet, opened it, and took out a bottle. He poured himself a drink and offered one to York, who declined. "It's not the best situation as you well know, Wingate."

"I wish I hadn't brought her. It was a mistake. Now it's too late to turn back, and there's nothing much to look forward to. The jolting of the wagon hasn't helped her any. She's had two miscarriages already."

"So she told me." Roberts drained the drink, capped the whiskey bottle, and returned it back to the cabinet. "I don't know if I can add anything to what you already know. If you care to stay here, we'll try to make arrangements until the baby comes."

"She would never do that." Wingate chewed on his lower lip thoughtfully. "I suppose we'll have to go on."

"Well, she's small and rather fragile, but with good luck she'll have this baby, and it'll be a healthy one." Roberts waved to a chair, but Wingate shook his head.

"No, I'd better get back."

"I'm curious. You probably had a pretty good practice where you were. Why would you leave it for a trip like this? It'll be a wilderness when you get to Oregon, from what I hear."

Wingate knew it was useless to explain because he didn't fully understand himself.

"A man makes the wrong decisions some-times. I wish I'd stayed in Pennsylvania now, but hindsight is pretty cheap. What I needed was foresight, and I didn't have it," he said.

Roberts said as cheerfully as he could, "Why, it'll be all right, I'm sure. Just be careful." The doctor realized as he spoke that this was feeble advice; no man could be careful on a wagon train going over rough ground. He said quickly, "I've got to go check on some of the men. Anybody else you'd like me to look at?"

"No. Thank you very much, Dr. Roberts."

"Wasn't much help, but I wish you good luck and your wife also."

As York Wingate left the office, he felt a sense of despair. There was a gloom in him that was not his usual mood, but now he knew there was nothing to do but grind out the miles and pray that Helen would be all right and the baby would be safe.

Charterhouse looked up and said, "There comes our relief, Billy."

Billy Watson, age seventeen, lifted his eyes. He had tow-colored hair, and his eyes were faded blue. He was small in stature and not as tough as the other members of the crew Tremayne had recruited. "You want to go into town, Elsworth?"

243

"Not much of a town, but I suppose we might as well." He nodded as their relief came to watch the herd on the early shift. "Come along, Billy. We'll see what Fort Kearney is like. Not much I'd say, from what I've seen so far."

The two left the wagons where they were circled and made their way to the fort. Darkness had closed on the town, and a few lanterns in front of buildings made yellow splashes in the night.

"Well, nothing much to see. Let's go into the saloon. Are you a drinking man, Billy?"

"No, not me. I don't like the taste of it, and the times I tried it, it made me so sick I wanted to die."

"Well, maybe they'll have lemonade. Come on."

The two men walked toward the saloon, and Elsworth noted that the music was from a tinny piano. It was off-key, and the voice that accompanied it was not much better.

As the two stepped inside, they saw it was one of the roughest of places. It was crowded, however, and smoke from cigarettes, cigars, and pipes made a thick haze. A poker game was going on at one table. A tall thin man with a fine mustache was dealing blackjack. The bar was across one end of the building, and a barkeep in a filthy white shirt with his sleeves rolled up to the elbows nodded at them.

"What'll it be, gents?"

"Whiskey for me, and something not quite so bad for this young fellow here. Lemonade if you've got it."

The barkeep grinned. He was missing several teeth and had a rough look. "Lemonade and whiskey it is. You come in with the train?"

"That we did."

"A long way to Oregon. I don't envy you."

Elsworth sipped the drink and made a face. "Strong stuff," he said. "You think the trail is pretty rough?"

"Yeah, it is. Some people get halfway there, turn around, and come back here. Not for everybody, but you two will probably make it all right."

The two stood at the bar. Elsworth had another drink, and Billy another lemonade. At least there was some noise and music although it was not as good as the music Stefan made with his fiddle.

"I'm glad we're out of that prison, Elsworth," Billy said abruptly. "I think I'd have died if I'd had to stay there much longer."

"Well, it's a hard place in a hard world. No place for you. I never did know why you

245

were there, Billy."

"I was hungry, and I broke into a store and stole some food."

"Doesn't seem like a prison offense to me."

"The judge was drunk at my trial. He sentenced everybody who came before him to prison that day."

"Well, we're out now. If we play our cards right, we'll never see the inside of a place like that again."

The two talked idly, and Elsworth saw a burly man wearing a strange fur hat like he had seen in pictures of trappers in the far West. "Who's he?" Elsworth asked the bartender.

"That's Wiley Tate. Better steer clear of him. He's a bad one."

The two were joined by Ringo Jukes who walked in the front door. "Hey, Charterhouse. Hi, Billy."

He was the best-looking man on the train with classic features, strong and very masculine. His teeth were very white against his tanned face, his neck was thick, and his shirt bulged with muscles and brawn. He kept himself looking neat, which was quite a feat on such a journey. The three stood at the bar. Suddenly the big man with the trapper's hat got up and started for the bar. It was crowded, and he simply shoved Billy aside and said loudly, "Give me another whiskey, Jake."

Jake got his whiskey, and then Wiley looked at Billy and laughed. "Well, ain't you a nice mama's boy." He slapped Billy on the shoulder. "Why aren't you home with your mama, boy?"

Billy Watson was the least offensive man in the room, but he said now, "I'm not a mama's boy."

"You calling me a liar?"

"No. I just —"

Tate slapped Billy in a sudden show of viciousness. His hand struck Billy on the neck and cheek and drove him down to one side. Tate was drunk and looking for trouble. His eyes were reddened, and there was a cruelty in all he did.

"You calling me a liar? I think I'll bust you up, son. Knock your teeth to snags and break a couple of them ribs of yours."

"Leave him alone, Tate," the bartender said.

"You keep out of this, Jake!"

Tate pushed Billy, who fell sprawling to the floor. Tate walked forward and began to curse. He kicked him, and Billy doubled up, crying out with pain.

Ringo Jukes had watched carefully. Now

he made two steps toward a table and picked up an empty chair. Tate's back was to him, and Elsworth was shocked to see Jukes raise the chair and bring it down with all of his might on Tate's head. It drove Tate to the floor; the blow would have rendered a smaller man unconscious, but Tate was not unconscious. His eyes were glazed, and he started uttering curses, but as he attempted to rise, Ringo raised the chair again. This blast caught Tate squarely on the head, knocked the fur cap off, and split his forehead over the eyebrow. This did put him out.

"I've ruined one of your chairs."

The barkeep stared down at Wiley Tate's still figure. "If I wuz you, I'd get out of here and hope he don't catch up with you."

"He better not." Jukes shrugged. "He might get worse next time. You fellas ready?"

"Yes," Elsworth said. He quickly helped Billy to his feet and saw that the boy was shaking. He had a cut in his scalp, and he said, "We have to get that cleaned up."

Ringo Jukes looked down at Tate. "Tell him he needs to mend his manners," he said, then turned and walked out of the saloon, accompanied by the two others.

"Better go have the doctor look at that cut."

"It's all right," Billy said quickly. "It don't hurt much."

"May need a stitch or two in it."

They started toward the camp and stopped at the doctor's wagon.

"Maybe I can patch it up myself," Elsworth said, "although I'm not handy with such." They continued toward their own wagon, but they had to pass the Gypsy wagon. A fire was going, and the old woman was sitting in front of it, eating something. Zamora saw them and came over.

"What's wrong?"

"Billy here has got a cut. The doctor's gone," Elsworth said.

"It doesn't look too bad." Zamora pulled Billy's head down toward the light. "Come on, I can help with this."

The three men followed the girl. She made Billy sit on a box. The old woman was watching him closely as her granddaughter began to gather something from a box in the wagon. Zamora came back with a cup. "Drink this."

"What is it?" Billy said.

"Don't ask questions. Just drink," Zamora said. Her lively dark eyes shone in the fire light. Billy drank the potion. "What happened?"

"A little trouble in the saloon." Ringo

249

shrugged. "I don't think he's hurt too bad, is he?"

"Not too bad."

"He will not die." The speaker was the old woman. "He has no shadow on him. He won't die — at least, not tonight."

"Nobody knows about things like that," Charterhouse said.

"My grandmother does," Zamora said firmly. "She can see a shadow on people who are close to death."

"Do you see one on me, madam?"

The old woman looked at Charterhouse. "Not yet," she said. "But someday."

Billy sat there, and finally, as the drink took its effect, Zamora put several stitches in his scalp. She was quick and adept.

"You've done that before," Charterhouse said.

"Yes. Not something I like, but things have to be done."

Ringo pulled Billy to his feet. "Come on. We'll put you to bed, son." He turned and faced the old lady. "What about me? See any shadow on me?"

"No." She suddenly smiled. "But sometimes I am wrong. All men need to walk carefully in this world. They only go through once."

Ringo Jukes was interested. His eyes took

in the old woman. "I guess you're right about that. Come on, fellas."

The three left. "I'm glad you didn't see any shadows on them, Grandmother," Zamora said.

"They had shadows, but not the shadow of death. All men have shadows. Women too. I have mine, and you have yours."

Zamora smiled. She was used to her grandmother's old ways. She hugged her and said, "Have some more soup."

The Fourth of July celebration was eventful for a small place like Fort Kearney. Tremayne had agreed to stay over and let the travelers take part. There had been a horse race, which Stefan won. A bad concert by a ragtag army band displayed more volume than skill, and there were speeches, barbecue, and beer.

Tremayne had heard about Billy's injury, and he had stopped by to ask him, "You feeling all right now, Billy?"

"Oh, sure. Just a cut."

"I hear the fellow was a pretty rough cob."

"That's what the bartender said." Billy swallowed hard. "He's over there. That big man with the fur cap."

Tremayne had already spotted Wiley Tate. He didn't know the man's name, but he could tell he was a born troublemaker. Tremayne wanted no trouble. "I guess I'd better keep an eye on him."

The trouble did come. Not ten minutes later Tate spotted Ringo Jukes. Evidently, someone pointed Jukes out as the man who had put him down. Tremayne saw Tate move until he stood squarely in front of Ringo and began to curse him. Moving easily and quickly, Tremayne put himself where he would be available if trouble started, but it came quicker than he anticipated.

Tate suddenly reached for the gun he kept in his belt, but he paused even as he grasped the handle, for a gun had appeared almost magically in the hand of Ringo Jukes. It was the fastest draw Tremayne had ever seen. The pistol was lined up on Tate's chest and the big man cried out, "I ain't drawing!"

Tremayne moved quickly. He stood beside Ringo, and his eyes bored into Tate. "Get out of here! We don't need you."

Quickly Major Simms, in charge of the military command, stepped forward. "Guards, arrest him. Take him to the stockade."

Two soldiers immediately were beside Tate. One of them pulled the gun from his belt, grinned, and said, "Come on, Wiley. We got a nice suite at a fine hotel for you."

Tate's eyes burned as they took in Jukes and Tremayne. "This ain't over," he said.

"It better be," Jukes said mildly as he replaced his gun in the holster.

"He's a rough one, Ringo."

"I've seen worse."

Tremayne would have said more, but Major Simms wanted to get past the ominous moment.

"All right," Simms announced, "we're going to have a dance now. Come, my dear, we'll start it." He turned to his wife, a heavy-set woman with a cheerful look, and the two began dancing to the music. The music was bad, but it was all they had.

Helga Studdart had dressed up, knowing there would be a dance, and her father stepped to her side. "I'll be watching you tonight, Helga. You're too free with some of these men."

Helga said impatiently, "Oh, Papa, there's nothing wrong. It's just a dance." She left, and Studdart noticed she went straight for Ringo Jukes, who had smiled at her, and the two began dancing.

"You need to be more gentle with her." Freida Studdart spoke quietly but with firmness.

"Freida, she's got it in her to get into trouble."

"We all have that in us."

"Not you," Studdart said, his eyes wide. "You were never in trouble."

"I came close a few times. Come along. We can watch her."

Charity danced with Major Simms and found that he was interested in the people of the Angel Train. He asked her several questions about their past. "It'll be a hard time for you. Nothing but a wilderness out there."

"But God is taking us that way. He's made the way clear."

"Well, I'm glad you feel that way." He observed Zamora dancing with one of his officers. "That's a beautiful young woman. A Gypsy, is she?"

"Yes. I've never known any Gypsies before, and, yes, she is very beautiful."

After she finished the dance, Charity started to return to her family, but Tremayne stopped her. "Could I have this dance, Charity?"

"Why, yes. I suppose you may."

"That's not a very good band," Tremayne said, "but it's better than nothing."

"Yes, it's a break in our journey. I guess we need to be a little foolish."

"I'm surprised you'd say that."

"Why should you be surprised?"

"Your people don't give themselves to foolishness."

"There's a great deal of joy among our people. We have our hard times, but people who know the Lord have a reservoir to grow on."

He was silent for a while, and after the dance he said gravely, "Thank you." She turned and said, "You're welcome." She hesitated and then walked to her family who had been watching.

"I wish I could dance with somebody," Bronwen said.

"Your turn will come," Gwilym said. "Now it's your turn for watching."

The family watched and the evening passed quickly. There was a new supply of food and drinks, and when the dance broke up, there was some disappointment that it was all over.

Zamora started back toward the wagons and looked up to see Tremayne slightly ahead of her. "Casey, walk me back to the wagons."

Tremayne paused and smiled at her. "You afraid you'll get lost? They're right over there."

"No." She took his arm, and they moved slowly. Others were moving in the darkness, and she pulled him to a stop beside her wagon. "It's a long way, isn't it, Casey, to Oregon?"

"Pretty far." The moon was silver and cast a glow over her features. Her dark eyes were fixed on him. Tremayne was attracted to her. "What will you do there, Zamora?"

"I don't know. What I've always done, I suppose. What will you do?"

"I guess I'll look at the ocean."

"You can't look at the ocean all your life."

Zamora found their conversation pleasant. She liked looking up at him because he was so tall. She asked, "Will you have a family and grow old there?"

"No man knows about things like that."

"Would you like to have a family?"

"Every man wants that. You know, sometimes back East when I was riding at night, and I saw a house and passed by it, there were lights and voices and the family was inside. Those people have everything, Zamora."

"I didn't know you thought like that. You seem so alone."

"I have been," he put his hand on her shoulder. "I wish you well, Zamora, you and Lareina and Stefan. It must be hard with none of your people around."

Zamora was very conscious of the strength

and warmth of Tremayne's hand, "I do get lonely sometimes." She waited, knowing that most men would have taken that as an invitation to touch her, to kiss her.

But he responded, "You'll find a man someday, and you'll have a family of your own."

"Not many men want a Gypsy woman, but I'll find one who does." She moved toward the wagon. Her grandmother was waiting there. Lareina saw at a glance that Zamora's eyes were filled with excitement.

"You've been with a man."

"Just talking, Grandmother."

"The tall man."

"Yes."

"Do you think he might be your man?"

Zamora didn't answer for a time. As a matter of fact, she didn't answer at all. "Go to bed, Grandmother. It's late." She helped her grandmother into the wagon, and she herself prepared for bed. She stood looking up, before going to bed, at the stars across the heaven and thought about her meeting with Tremayne. It stirred her. She was an honest young woman and knew she was interested in him. But whether he was interested in her she couldn't tell. With a sigh she got into her bed, closed her eyes, and went to sleep almost at once.

CHAPTER FOURTEEN

The days at Fort Kearney had been a break in the monotony of trail life. The Angel Train left the fort on the morning after the dance and had been steadily following the Platte River northwesterly. One morning Evan Morgan had gone out with the hunters and shot an antelope, which pleased him. Tremayne had praised his shot, and the words of the tall man were especially encouraging. Evan, now taking his turn in the rear where the dust rose, was glad the train was spread out horizontally instead of being in a straight line. The dust was still bad, but not as bad as it had been. Overhead the sun blazed white with nearly unbearable heat. After Pennsylvania, this was hot weather he had to learn to endure.

Suddenly he saw Zamora riding up on one of her brother's horses, a beautifully built mare of a blue steel color. She pulled up beside him, and her face was flushed, her dark eyes filled with excitement.

"This is my favorite horse. Her name is Princess," she said.

"Beautiful animal. You ride well too."

Zamora paced her horse next to Evan's mount. He liked the dark, beautiful young woman and her fiery spirit, which most women of the Way lacked. He had noticed that despite her self-sufficient nature, she was always on guard.

"Are you tired of the trip, Zamora?"

"No, I like it. I like that there's something new every day. I like a change."

Evan smiled. "Not much change. Same old flat country."

"Tremayne says it will be different when we get to the mountains. I like those too. What about you? You looking forward to getting to Oregon?"

"Yes, I am. I wanted to get away for a long time."

"Get away from what?"

"Get away from the coal mines. As I told you before, I hated it there, and it seemed like I spent all my life digging in the dark, waiting for the earth to cave in on me."

Zamora studied him more carefully. He was a lean young man with flaming red hair and the most amazing dark blue eyes. "How old are you, Evan?"

"Seventeen. How old are you?"

"I'm seventeen too. It's a good age, seventeen."

Evan grinned at her. "Not when you're in a coal mine, but out here it's all different."

"You have red hair."

"Why, yes, I do. Runs in my family as you have noticed."

"I've always heard that redheaded people have hot tempers. Is that so?"

"Why, no. It's foolishness. I don't have a hot temper. Neither does my father. He's the calmest man in the world."

"Well, I think I ought to tell your fortune."

"I told you I don't believe in such things."

"Sometimes it's true." She moved her mare closer, reached out, and took his hand. "Ah, I see you have a long lifeline." She was teasing him, and he knew, but the touch of her hand was stirring. "I see a dark woman in your future. You must beware of her."

"Maybe it's you."

"Maybe it is. I may be the temptress who's going to lead you away from your religious beliefs. Beware of dark-haired women, Evan Morgan."

He laughed. "You're making fun of me."

"I am a little bit, I suppose." She released his hand.

"I've never seen anyone like you."

"You never saw a Gypsy?"

"A few, but none as pretty as you."

She suddenly turned and laughed at him. Evan liked Zamora although he knew her bold, headlong qualities were enticing and could be dangerous, even forbidden.

"I think every man on the Angel Train has flattered me. All except you and Tremayne, of course."

"But I wasn't —"

"You weren't trying to flatter me so that you could kiss me? You've had sweethearts, Evan."

"I never have."

"Not one?"

"No, not one. Not really."

"Well, the next dance you can dance with me. That'll make some of the women in your train jealous. There must be some you've looked at in that group."

"No, never." Evan was out of his depth with this woman. He had done nothing but dig in the darkness of the earth, and she had had a life of sunshine and had traveled. He enjoyed her immensely, and after she rode off, he felt something was missing. "I don't care what she says, she's the prettiest woman I've ever seen," he said aloud. His horse tossed its head, and Evan muttered, "I'm talking to myself now. I guess the next stop is the insane asylum!"

"That fellow Tate. He's a dangerous man, isn't he?" Charity had not talked to Tremayne for three days. He left early with the hunters and usually came back late. This day he didn't go out, and she had mounted her horse and gone with him as he forged ahead. She had merely brought up Tate as an excuse to speak with him.

"Yes, he's a tough fellow."

"What about Ringo Jukes?"

"He's got something in him that most men don't. Did you see how quick he got his gun out?"

"Yes, I could hardly see his hand he moved so fast. He could have killed Tate."

"But he didn't. That's in his favor. Maybe he's learned something from his time in prison. Most of us did."

"You've had a hard life, haven't you?"

"No worse than some." He didn't want to talk about himself, and he pointed ahead. "Look, there's Fort Laramie."

"How long will we stay there?"

"We need to move on as quickly as possible."

"You're always in a hurry, Casey. Why is that?"

"I don't want the winter to catch us in the

mountains. That would be tougher than anything we've seen so far."

She wanted to continue talking with him, but he seemed to avoid any comments on his personal life. She fell back and watched as he put the wagons into a circle, and then she drifted to where her family was getting out of the wagon. She got ready to prepare the evening meal, but it was still early in the afternoon.

"Come on, Sister, let's go look at the town," Bronwen said.

"All right."

"I'm coming too." Meredith joined the others, and they moved toward Laramie.

"Look, there are Indians," Bronwen said.

The Indians had pitched their tepees — some of them white, some tan and aged — near the fort. There were men and women in the Indian camp and many children, it seemed. Their dogs moved about, and farther away their horses grazed as the afternoon cooled.

The Morgans encountered Tremayne and Charterhouse apparently on their way to the fort.

"This is a little better than Fort Kearney," Charity said.

"I guess so." Casey scanned the scene in front of him and murmured, "When I first saw this place, there wasn't a post on it. Weren't any tame Indians either. Buffalo and beaver. Beavers are all gone now. Buffalo too. One day all this country will be nothing but towns."

Charterhouse stared. "Does that bother you, Casey?"

"I guess it does."

"Well, some poet once said, 'God made the country, and man made the town.' "

"What other country will we see?" Charity asked.

"Further on, out of sight, is the Sweetwater," Casey said, "and farther still, there's the South Pass. You'll see that."

"Father says we're going to have a service tonight if the commanding officer will permit it."

"He probably will."

"Would you come, Casey?" She was slightly awkward using his first name, but there seemed a formality in always calling him *Tremayne,* although most people did.

He hesitated a long time, and then he nodded. "Yes, I will." He noticed the surprise in her face. "I'm not totally a lost cause, I hope, Charity."

"I don't like to think of anybody as a lost cause."

They entered the frontier fort, and he

mentioned again what it had been like when he had first seen it. Charity noticed it troubled him, and finally he said, "Every-thing changes."

"No, some things don't." She felt his gaze as he turned to look at her and added, "God never changes."

"I reckon that's so."

"Love doesn't change."

"I've not noticed that." There was surprise in his tone, and he shrugged slightly. "I've seen people stop loving each other."

"Then they never really loved," Charity said. "Shakespeare wrote a poem about that once."

"What did it say?"

"Oh, I can't quote it all, but one line of it has been with me for a long time. 'Love is not love, when it alteration finds. Oh, no, it is an ever fixed mark that looks on tempests and is not shaken.' "

As she spoke, Casey was staring at her. "You really believe that love never changes?"

"Yes, I do."

"I'm glad you feel like that," he smiled faintly and then shook his head as if in doubt. "I hope you always do, but I don't think I can handle it."

"Come to the service," she said. "You may like it."

The crew was getting ready to go to the fort. Jack Canreen had been appointed the spokesman by the crew, for he said, "How about a little money for us to have a drink or two, Tremayne?"

Tremayne had been sewing a rent in his shirt, and a fancy struck him. "Jack, you ought to go to church like me."

The others gathered around, and Doucett said, "You ain't a church man."

"Well, I am today."

"Come on, don't be that way," Canreen said. "We've worked hard, ain't we?"

"Well, as a matter of fact, you have." He put the shirt aside, and a glint of humor came into his eyes. "You a gambling man, Jack?"

"Sure."

"How about if we make a bet, you and me? If you win, I take you all to the saloon and buy all the drinks you can safely handle. If I win, you go to church with me."

Canreen was a gambling man; his eyes glittered with excitement. "Cut the cards?" he asked.

"No, I figure we might do a little arm wrestling."

Canreen stared at him in disbelief. He had beaten everybody in this old game. His bulky muscle spoke of tremendous strength in his arms.

"All right," he said. "That all right with you men?"

"Sure," Frenchy Doucett grinned. "You ain't never been beat, have you?"

"Never have. Don't intend to start now. Find us a table."

A table was located and two chairs. Canreen took his seat, and Tremayne sat opposite him. Word spread, and a crowd from the train and even a few soldiers gathered to see the contest.

"You know the rules," Tremayne said.

"There ain't no rules to this. We count three, and you try to put my hand down, and I try to put yours down. But you ain't gonna do it, Casey."

"All right. Turn your wolf loose on the count of three."

Casey started counting. "One — two and —" Suddenly, Canreen threw his strength into his arm. Tremayne was not ready, and his hand was driven nearly to the table, but then by a tremendous effort he withstood the pressure of the burly man's grasp. The two men were still, and seemingly not moving, but there was tremendous pressure

267

from both. Charterhouse was staring at both faces. Both showed strain, and there was shock in Canreen's face. *He expected to win by that trick,* Charterhouse thought. *I don't see how Casey can beat him.*

Charity had come to watch, too, feeling somewhat out of place. She saw that Canreen's arm was more muscular than Tremayne's, and the hands of the two men had turned white with exertion.

The struggle went on for what seemed like a long time. Slowly Tremayne's hand was able to move Canreen's arm back until finally they were straight up in their original position. Canreen gasped and half rose from his chair, but Ringo Jukes was behind him. He shoved him down.

"You know the rules, Jack," he grinned. "You can't move out of your chair."

The two men were locked in an immense struggle, and most of the crew was cheering Canreen on. "Come on, Jack, you can do it!" Doucett cried. "Don't let him get you!"

Finally Jack Canreen's arm began to move back toward the table. He moaned and tried to muster strength, but Tremayne's power was irresistible. He continued, and finally Canreen collapsed. The back of his hand slapped the table, and a groan went up from the crew. Tremayne released his hand and sat there, his eyes fixed on Canreen.

"I never knowed you could do that, Casey," Canreen said, staring at the tall man as if he had never seen him before.

"I almost didn't. You're a strong fellow."

"Me? I ain't nothing but a baby."

Tremayne looked around and saw disbelief on the faces of all the crew. He said, "I'm letting you fellows off on the bet. I don't believe in forcing anybody to have religion."

"I ain't no welsher!" Canreen snapped. "We'll be there."

"Good," Tremayne said. He got to his feet and rubbed his arm. "I'll see you fellas in church. May be too late for fellas like us, but you never know."

Zamora had watched the contest and found herself straining, trying to help Tremayne as he had fought the battle. She released her breath then and saw that Evan was standing next to her.

"That was really something, wasn't it, Zamora?"

"Yes, I didn't think he could do it."

"What about you? Won't you come to the service?"

"Me?"

"Sure. My father's a good preacher."

"You think I need God?" she challenged him.

"I think all of us do. I do anyway."

Zamora smiled as if she found something amusing. "I will come then."

The service was held on the parade ground. The major in charge had all the available chairs and benches brought out. They were all filled, and many of the soldiers came out of curiosity. Gwilym started the service with a prayer, and he said, "Now we'll have some good singing, will we?" He began singing a hymn, and those who knew it joined in. They sang several hymns, the volume growing, and finally Gwilym said, "Now, my daughter Charity will sing my favorite hymn." He continued, "It was written by a man called John Newton who was a slave trader, an evil, wicked man, but God's grace saved him, and he wrote this song. It's called 'Amazing Grace.' "

Charity lifted her head and began to sing.

> Amazing grace, how sweet the sound,
> That saved a wretch like me!
> I once was lost but now am found,
> Was blind but now I see.

Her voice was sweet and clear, and those who watched couldn't miss the joy in her face. Casey Tremayne had his eyes fixed on her and thought, *I've never seen such in-nocence and such joy in a woman.*

After she finished, many cried out, "Praise God!" and "Amen!," not all of them from the Pilgrim Way. Some of the soldiers even called out.

Gwilym Morgan rose. "I could speak of no other thing this afternoon than the amazing grace of the Lord Jesus Christ who died to save us from sin. Let me remind you of a story in the Old Testament in the book of Numbers. The Bible says this occurred after God had delivered His people Israel from slavery and bondage. He brought them across the Red Sea on dry land and worked mighty miracles to deliver them, but the Bible says in Numbers 21 that 'the soul of the people was much discouraged because of the way. And the people spake against God, and against Moses.' And because the people sinned and doubted God, the sixth verse says, 'And the LORD sent fiery serpents among the people, and they bit the people; and much people of Israel died.'

"This is one of those pictures that show us what we are. Then when God is gracious to us, even then we complain about Him, and we do not believe Him.

"If you can picture these people out in the middle of the desert bitten by serpents and dying, you get a picture of our world. We've all been bitten by a serpent. We're all dying. So says the entire Old Testament and the New Testament." His voice lifted. "But then the people came to Moses and said, 'We have sinned,' and Moses prayed for the people. And verse 8 says, 'And the LORD said unto Moses, Make thee a fiery serpent, and set it upon a pole: and it shall come to pass, that every one that is bitten, when he looketh upon it, shall live.' And that's what Moses did. He made a serpent of brass. He put it up on a pole. This was God's cure for man's terrible problem. It was life instead of death. Can you see it? A man is out in the field. He feels a fiery pain in his leg and looks down to see a serpent and knows that he's a dead man, and then he remembers that God said, If any man will look at the brass serpent, he will live. Oh, with what eagerness he turned to look, and there in the sunlight was the brass serpent! Even as he looked, he felt the poison leave him, and he felt health and strength. Then surely he must have cried out, 'Praise thee to Jehovah who saves His people.' "

Silence had fallen over the congregation, and Gwilym paused. Finally, he said, "I weep every time I read that story because it is so much my own story. I was bitten by the serpent. I was a sinner until I found the Lord Jesus Christ. Let me read you from the most famous book, perhaps, in the Bible, the most famous chapter, John, chapter 3. Jesus was explaining why He had come to this world to save men. In verse 14 we find these words that Jesus spoke of His own reason for coming to earth: 'As Moses lifted up the serpent in the wilderness, even so must the Son of man be lifted up: That whosever believeth in him should not perish, but have eternal life.' And then the most famous verse in the Bible, 'For God so loved the world, that he gave his only begotten Son, that whosoever believeth in him should not perish, but have everlasting life.' "

Gwilym lifted his head, and tears glittered in his eyes and ran down his cheeks. "Do you hear that? Even as Moses lifted up a serpent, so when anyone was bitten by a deadly serpent and looked at it, they did not die but felt the healing touch of God. And that's what Jesus said of Himself, that He would be lifted up. Lifted up how? On a cross bleeding, His body broken, suffering unimaginable torment, but He said, 'If I'm lifted up, and a man or a woman or a young person looks to My death and knows that I am the Savior, he or she will not perish but will have everlasting life.' "

As Gwilym said this, Casey Tremayne felt something he had never felt before. It began deep down in his heart, and fear seemed to grip him. He knew he was a man who did not know God, but the story and the verses that Gwilym Morgan had read seemed to run through his veins, and he found that his hands were unsteady, a rare thing indeed for Casey Tremayne! He knew something was happening. Despite his fear, he felt hope, and he continued to listen as Gwilym preached.

"In the story in the Old Testament, it didn't matter whether a man had just been bitten or whether he had been bitten and was dying, all he had to do was look. This was God's way of saying that He would save His people. And that's what Jesus meant, and God's great love provided that. The Lord Jesus left heaven and donned human flesh and suffered humiliation and pain and finally death. For God had said, 'Without shedding of blood [there] is no remission' of sin, but it had to be innocent blood. An angel's blood would not do. A man must die, but one who was innocent enough to pay for the sins of the world. No one but Jesus Christ, the Son of God could do that."

The sermon was not long, and he closed by saying, "I know two things. One, I was a guilty man, a sinner doomed to hell. I was like those bitten by the fiery serpent. My friends, I tried every way I could to change that. I tried being good. I tried going to church. I tried to cut off my bad habits, but I was still a sinner. The other thing I know is that in my grief and despair I looked to Jesus on the cross. I remember to this day, and I will remember it throughout eternity; I was doomed and in despair, but I saw Jesus dying on the cross and then I cried out, 'Save me, Lord,' and He did! No man or woman will perish if they look to the Savior, the Lord Jesus Christ.

"You say, 'I'm a sinner.' I say, 'That's good!' Jesus is the friend of sinners. He's the best friend you will ever have. He will be with you in life. He'll be with you in death. He will be with you when you stand before the Father in judgment, and He will say, 'This is my own. He's bought with my blood. He's free. He has My life in him.' "

Gwilym Morgan closed the service with another hymn, but Tremayne didn't hear it. He tore himself away, but he didn't know that Charity was watching him. She saw the movement of his body almost as if he were enduring a wound and the torment in his face as he whirled and left the grounds.

His eyes met hers, and she saw his pain

and fear, something she had never thought to see in Casey Tremayne. And she thought, *God has touched him.*

CHAPTER FIFTEEN

Marzina Cole had lived most of her life in the mountains of North Carolina, and she missed those mountains, but the Platte Valley had its own fascination for her. She walked steadily, keeping one ear tuned to a cry from six-month-old Benjamin or the call from five-year-old Rose. She was a tall woman, well formed, with dark hair and startling blue eyes. She wore, as did all the other women, a cotton bonnet to keep the hot sun off and a plain, unembroidered brown dress. The trip had turned her skin a summer darkness, and her smooth, beautiful complexion was attractive.

The plains on either side of the river were bare of trees. She missed the trees a great deal, and the short grass and the wide-open spaces made the landscape look like the regions of Africa, or, at least, pictures she had seen. About three miles on both sides of the valley, the land rose in sandstone cliffs, higher and more broken as the trail moved west.

Marzina was delighted with the prairie wildlife. She had seen antelope, coyote, grizzly and black bears, buffalo, and the strange prairie dog villages that covered sometimes five hundred acres. To her right she saw a herd of buffalo and hoped they stayed away. The buffalo sometimes were a nuisance. They ruined streams that would turn dark and muddy, but Marzina didn't know what the travelers would do for fires if it were not for the enormous herds that left buffalo chips scattered over the plains. She had learned to make a blaze by drafting a fire pit, and cooking had been a new adventure.

Her attention was caught by a rider, and she saw it was her husband, Nolan. Purely as a reflex action she stiffened herself, for she could see even at this distance his face was flushed from drinking. He had been a drinking man before their marriage, arranged by her father. She had been only sixteen and had had little choice.

As Nolan pulled beside her, Marzina thought how few knew a happy married life. She certainly didn't! Nolan was a short man, well built and strong, but no taller than Marzina herself. He could be amiable, but drink always turned him vicious, and she had borne the marks of his blows many times.

She had so few happy memories; her past was grim and her future uncertain. Nolan had decided to go to Oregon without consulting her. The first she had known of it was when he had come in drunk and said, "We're going to Oregon." At least she had some stability in the cabin and the home she had made since her marriage. But that was all lost, and she keenly remembered her sense of loss when they left the mountains. And now on these flat plains, she felt alien and saw nothing in the future but grim days, hard work, and abuse at the hands of her husband.

Finally the train stopped for the night, and she led the oxen into the circle. Nolan was not there, so she started unyoking the animals. She was interrupted when a voice said, "Let me help you with that, Mrs. Cole." She turned around to see York Wingate, whose wagon was right behind hers.

"I can do it, Doctor."

"No trouble." Wingate at once began unyoking and loosing the oxen. Benjamin began crying, and Marzina went to the wagon and pulled him from the pallet. Rose was waking up.

"I'm hungry, Mama."

"We'll have supper soon." Marzina pulled her dress back and began nursing the baby. When York had finished unyoking the oxen, he started to leave, but she turned to one side and said, "Thank you very much, Doctor."

"No trouble at all. How's that fat baby of yours?"

"He's fine, Dr. Wingate. How's your wife?" Marzina saw a shadow pass over Wingate's face.

"She's not making it too well."

"Maybe it'll get cooler up ahead, and she'll feel better. Could I sit with her awhile?"

"That's a kind heart speaking, but I know you have plenty to do. Thank you anyway. I'll tell her you offered. Maybe you could come over after supper and visit with her a little bit. I know she's lonesome."

"I'll do that."

Tremayne and Charterhouse returned to the train. They had looked for game but had killed only a single buffalo. Charterhouse noticed that Tremayne had spoken little for several days. He dated it from the time they had left Fort Laramie, and he was correct.

The sermon had affected Tremayne tremendously. He had not spoken of it to anyone, but the words of Gwilym Morgan seemed to echo in his mind. He had quoted many Scriptures, and now it seemed to Tremayne that he could remember every bit of that sermon. He slept poorly, and once the startling thought came to him, *Maybe I'm losing my mind. I can't get away from that preaching.*

Charterhouse slipped off his horse and watched as Tremayne did the same. "What's the matter with you, Casey? You haven't said a dozen words all day."

"Nothing."

"Must be something. You've clammed up for several days now. Are you worried about Indians?"

"No, there won't be trouble with Indians here. The Platte Valley here is kind of a no-man's-land. Sioux are up to the north, and the Cheyenne to the south. But they're not likely to give us any trouble."

Suddenly Charterhouse was astonished to hear Tremayne ask, "What do you think of God, Elsworth?"

Elsworth stared at his friend. It was the first time Tremayne had voluntarily mentioned such a thing as religion. "Well," he said, "there is a God. I'm sure of that. All of this" — his gesture took in the river, the skies, the mountains, and the sun falling to the west — "all this didn't make itself. There's got to be a world maker."

"Are you a Christian man then?"

"I'm afraid not. I was reared in the Church of England, but it never touched me, and I don't see much hope for myself."

Tremayne unsaddled his horse, as did Charterhouse, and as he put the saddle down, he said, "That sermon by Gwilym Morgan at Fort Laramie, I can't stop thinking about it."

"Well, the man's in earnest. He believes in God. I'm sure of that much. All these people pretty much seem to be that way. That girl, Charity, when she sings, you can see the love of God in her face."

"Can't help but envy that. At least, I can't."

"So do I. I've met a lot of church people I had little confidence in, but I think the Morgans and some others on this train are the real goods." His curiosity was aroused, and he said, "You never had any religion?"

"Not of the right kind, I'm afraid. I always trusted in myself. Didn't think I needed God, but Morgan's sermon was a powerful thing. That man has something."

Charterhouse wanted to pursue the matter, but when he tried to speak of something new about religion, Tremayne cut him off.

"I'm hungry," he said. "Let's cook us up some of this buffalo hump. I'm going to cook the tongue and the liver for that old Gypsy woman. It's hard for anyone her age to digest all this tough antelope we've been having."

"Thank you, Mr. Tremayne. You're a kind man." Lareina spoke to Tremayne who had offered to cook the buffalo liver and tongue. "No," she said, "I can do that much at least."

She looked around and asked, "What is that big rock there?"

"They call it Independence Rock, ma'am. Quite a spectacle, isn't it?"

Zamora was standing beside her grandmother. "It looks impressive. Have you ever climbed it?"

"Once. Lots of people do," Tremayne said, turning to face her. "They carve their names up on the top of it. Must be hundreds of names up there."

"Are you going up?"

"I might. Would you like to see it?"

"Yes. I'd like to leave my name there."

"Let me borrow a chisel. After you cook your grandmother's liver, I'll take you."

"I can cook the liver," Stefan said. "Nothing much to that. You two go on."

Zamora and Tremayne left at once, and Stefan began making soup out of the liver and roasting the tongue. He studied his grandmother for a moment: "What are you thinking? About those two?"

"She has something in her eye for that tall man."

"You're not thinking anything will come of it. He would never marry a Gypsy."

"You can never tell about things like that. He's a good man. Better than some in this train. Now, you let me fix that soup, and you roast this tongue."

From the top of Independence Rock, they could see the flat valley. Zamora's cheeks were brightened by the sun and by the brisk wind.

"This is beautiful, Casey."

"It is. Let's see if I can find my name." He had to hunt for a while. "It's kind of weathered, but there I am. C. Tremayne." He studied the name. "I think I'll dig it out a little bit. Make it last a little longer."

Zamora watched as he deepened the letters, and then she said, "Put my name there under yours, or let me do it."

"Let me." He began banging at the chisel with the hammer he had brought, and soon he had inscribed her name — Zamora

Krisova. "I think I'll put the date between them here. August the thirtieth, 1854." When he finished, the two looked down on it.

"It's almost like a grave, isn't it?" she said.

Startled, Tremayne asked, "What do you mean, Zamora?"

"Well, that's what happens. We put people in the ground, sometimes we put a stone over it with their name on it and something about them. I saw some very old tombstones in the old country. Some of them three hundred years old."

"Would you like to go back over there?"

"No, there's nothing for me there."

Finally Tremayne shook his head almost sadly, "There should be more to a man than a few scratches on a rock."

"There is more."

She moved closer to him so that her arm was brushing his. Startled, he turned and looked down at her. She was dark and exotic, unlike any woman Tremayne had seen before. Her lips were full at the center. Her hair was dark as the night itself. She wore a crimson kerchief, as she usually did, and from her ears two pearl pendants gracefully dangled. A blend of qualities in this woman attracted Casey almost each time he saw her — pride, honesty, and her deep, mysterious grace of heart and body. And he realized these elements stirred his hunger for the things a woman brought to a man. Her eyes were on his.

He said huskily, "A man wants something out of life, and I'm not sure what it is."

Zamora whispered, "We have to take what pleasure we can from life."

Her words seemed to echo his thoughts. He possessed all the hungers a strong individual can have, and suddenly she was there, and he read the invitation in her eyes. He reached forward, pulled her to him, and kissed her, and as he did, he felt her response and knew that Zamora's loneliness equaled his own. He released her and started to speak, but he heard a sound and turned to see Charity Morgan who had followed the same path up the rock. Awkwardly, Tremayne stepped back, for there was something in Charity's face like contempt, and he knew she had seen him embracing Zamora.

"Helen Wingate is having her baby," Charity said. "Her husband says she's not doing well. You might go see if there's anything you can do."

"You're right. I'll go now."

He turned to Zamora, who shrugged and said, "Go on, Casey. I can get back."

He left at once, and Zamora turned to Charity. She saw distaste in the other woman's eyes and something else she couldn't identify. "You didn't like what you saw?" she demanded.

"It's not my affair."

"I think it might be. You have eyes for him. I'm not blind."

"You're wrong, Zamora."

"He's not for you."

"What are you talking about?"

"He's a man of flesh and blood."

"Of course he is. What do you mean by that?" Charity demanded.

"You want a holy man."

Charity was startled by her words. "Well, I want a man who knows God. I wouldn't have any other kind."

The two women stared at each other, and then Zamora smiled a bitter, cynical smile. There was triumph in it though. "You'll never have him, Charity. You're not woman enough for him."

"And you are?"

Zamora didn't answer. She merely laughed and started down the trail. Charity watched her go and then saw the letters carved in the stone — "C. Tremayne and Zamora Krisova." Something about the names carved into the rock disturbed her, but she couldn't think why. Slowly she turned and made her way down the mountainside.

"How is she?" Tremayne demanded when Gwilym met him.

"Her husband says she's not doing well."

Neither of them knew what to say. Finally Tremayne muttered, "It's bad to be helpless, isn't it, Gwilym?"

Gwilym Morgan didn't answer for a moment, then he lifted his head. "God's not helpless," he said finally. "I'll get the men to pray."

The train's attention was centered on the one wagon where Wingate was trying to help his wife. The cries of the woman seemed to go through Tremayne. He had heard cries of agony before, but these cries were weak and feeble, and Tremayne had a dark picture in his mind of what was happening. Marzina Cole appeared with her husband, Nolan. Nolan was half drunk, as usual, and he gave one look at the wagon, snorted, and walked away. Nolan's callousness always incensed Tremayne. *The woman is too good for him,* he always thought.

"I hope Helen makes it," he said quietly.

Marzina Cole was holding her baby, a healthy, rosy-cheeked boy with the long name of Benjamin. "It frightens me, Trem-ayne."

"It's awful being helpless. If we could only do something."

But there was nothing to do, and finally Marzina said, "My husband has no sympathy for weakness. You know what he said when he heard Helen Wingate was having trouble? He said, 'If it's her time, she'll die.' "

Tremayne bristled. He had never heard the woman speak against her husband, although everyone on the train knew she had just cause. Everyone was aware he abused her. Tremayne had seen the marks on her face where Cole had struck her. It infuriated him, but he had had to suppress his anger, knowing their relationship was not his business. He couldn't think of any response, and then he asked, "How did you happen to marry him, Marzina?"

"My father arranged it."

That was not uncommon, Tremayne knew, but something in the weariness of her voice pulled at Tremayne's sympathy. *She's left so much unsaid.* He reached out and touched the silky hair of the baby, who had dark hair like his mother. "You've got two fine children."

"Yes, I do."

She would have said more, perhaps, but at that moment Wingate stepped out of the wagon. Tremayne took one look at his face and knew everything. He saw York's hopelessness, grief, and absolute futility.

"She's gone," Wingate said.

"The baby?" Marzina asked quickly.

"It's a boy. I think he'll be all right, but how in God's name will I take care of him?"

Marzina stepped forward and put her hand on York Wingate's arm. "I will care for him, Dr. Wingate. I'll nurse him along with Benjamin. God will take care of him."

Wingate's eyes went to the woman, and the tears suddenly ran down his cheeks. "That's — that's kind of you."

Wanting to help, Casey Tremayne said, "I'll take care of your wife, Dr. Wingate. I know a place beside the river where she can rest. We'll put a stone there and carve her name in it."

"Thank you, Tremayne." He returned to the wagon and came back, bearing the child. Holding him out, he said nothing as Marzina Cole took him.

"What will your husband say?"

"It doesn't matter. I promise you your son will be cared for. I don't suppose he has a name?"

"His name will be David. That was her

choice. Almost her last words."

"Come, David. I'll care for you."

The two men watched Marzina turn away, "Anything else I can do for you, Dr. Wingate?" Tremayne asked.

Wingate stared at Tremayne with tears running unheeded down his cheeks. "There's very little any one of us can do for another, but you're kind. And that woman, Mrs. Cole, is kind." He tried to say something else, shook his head, and turned away.

Eager to have something to do, Tremayne found Charterhouse and Billy Watson.

"Get some shovels, Billy. We've got to dig a grave for Mrs. Wingate."

CHAPTER SIXTEEN

Gwilym Morgan stood with his Bible in his hand. A silence fell over the crowd that had gathered for the funeral of Helen Wingate. A rough coffin had been built with spare lumber, and it stood beside the stark hole the men had dug.

Tremayne had helped to dig the grave, and he stood at the back of the crowd. He kept his eyes on York Wingate, but, for the most part, he was listening intently to Morgan.

Morgan said quietly, "You've read the story of how Jairus, the ruler of a synagogue, came to beg Jesus to come and heal his daughter. Jesus agreed, and when they reached the house of Jairus, he was met by servants who told him that his daughter had already died. I wonder how many of us would have given up at that moment? Death is so final to some but not to Jesus. Jesus said, 'Be not afraid, only believe.' "

Gwilym looked out over the crowd with sorrow in his eyes. "That, my dear friends, is always the Word of God to any whose heart is broken. 'Be not afraid, only believe.' And then the story goes on as I will read for you:"

And he cometh to the house of the ruler of the synagogue, and seeth the tumult, and them that wept and wailed greatly.

And when he was come in, he saith unto them, Why make ye this ado, and weep? the damsel is not dead, but sleepeth.

And they laughed him to scorn. But when he had put them all out, he taketh the father and the mother of the damsel, and them that were with him, and entereth in where the damsel was lying.

And he took the damsel by the hand, and said unto her, Tal-i-tha cu-mi; which is, being interpreted, Damsel, I say unto thee, arise.

And straightway the damsel arose, and walked; for she was of the age of twelve years. And they were astonished with a great astonishment.

Morgan lifted his eyes from the Bible, and

his voice was strong, "In this case the damsel came back from the dead at once. That, of course, is what we always would like to see. That's what we'd like to see for this dear sister. We want that for those who cross over, but God's timing is not ours. Sometimes, in His infinite wisdom, He takes from us that which we love best. We will know why someday, I believe. But in this life we cannot know. But I believe that Jesus gave us the truth about all death when He said, 'Be not afraid, only believe.'

"Helen Wingate will rise again. All who have taken Jesus Christ into their hearts will rise again."

Tremayne felt a stirring in his spirit — the same sort of stirring he had felt when Morgan preached the sermon that had so moved him. He kept his eyes fixed on the faces of the believers. He saw a victory there that most men would miss, and he knew, somehow, that the word from the Scripture had entered into his own heart. He felt the presence of God, and at that moment he knew that somewhere soon, perhaps, he would meet God.

The funeral ceremonies were short. Scriptures were read, and then the body was lowered into the earth. The grave was filled in, and York Wingate turned and walked away. He was joined by Gwilym Morgan who put his arm around the man and was murmuring as they left.

For some reason Casey Tremayne felt chained to the spot. Everyone was gone, or so he thought, and he began to walk around the clearing. Hearing a sound, he turned and found Charity approaching him. She stopped in front of him, and he saw tears in her eyes.

"I feel so sorry for Dr. Wingate."

"So do I, but your father said, if he's right, this woman is in a better place than she had here."

"Do you believe that, Casey?"

"Yes, I do. I don't understand it," he said in a low tone, "but I believe it."

The two walked on silently. Finally Tremayne said, "Look, there's another grave." The two moved forward, and they saw a board sticking up out of the ground. It had been carved, but the weather had nearly destroyed it. Tremayne saw the outline of what had been the grave, but it was almost gone. He began to trace the outline digging a crease in the earth with the toe of his boot. Charity watched and was somehow moved at the sight.

"We do that, don't we? Try to keep death from being final." Her voice was gentle, he

295

looked up, and she added, "I don't know what I would do if I didn't have God to look to."

Tremayne gave her a straight look, nodded, and said, "I envy you, Charity." He turned away. "Well, life has to go on. Come on, let's get back to the train."

Two nights later after setting up camp, Tremayne ate supper with the Morgans. Later he asked, "How many of you would like to have some ice-cold lemonade?"

Meredith, sitting next to him, gave him a direct look. "We don't have any ice here. We've got some lemons, but that won't make them cold."

"Meredith, do you believe I can get ice for you out here in this desert?" His eyes were filled with fun, for he was always amused by the youngest Morgan girl.

"I don't know, but if you say so, I'll believe you, Casey."

"Mr. Tremayne," Gwilym Morgan smiled. "Learn some manners, girl."

"That's all right. I was called that a long time before I even knew my last name," Tremayne said. "Come along." He rose, walked to the wagon, and found a pick. Walking a few feet away, he began to dig at the ground. They all gathered around him.

Bronwen asked, "What are you digging a hole for?"

"That's the way I make lemonade."

"That's foolish!" Bronwen said. "You can't do that."

As she spoke, the tip of the pick hit something, and Evan said, "I believe you've hit ground or rock there."

They all watched as Tremayne swung the pickax and then he reached down and brought something up. "Look at this." They all gathered around.

Charity reached out and touched it. "Why," she exclaimed, "it's cold!"

They all had to touch, and Casey said, "This is called the Ice Trough. We're up high here. Don't know why, but there's always ice only a few feet down. Why don't we wash this off and make some lemonade?"

The next few minutes were filled with excitement as Casey and Evan dug up plenty of ice. It had to be washed off carefully, but when water, lemons, and sugar were added, they all sat by their campfire, sipping lemonade.

Casey winked at Meredith, "There. You see? No one ever went broke betting on Casey Tremayne and his famous lemonade trick."

"What comes next?" Evan asked.

"A big decision, Evan. We've got to decide whether to take the shortcut that lies up ahead of us. It's called the Sublette Cutoff. We'll have to have everybody vote on this." He got up and disappeared into the night.

When he was gone, Meredith said, "I bet you didn't think he could do it, did you, Charity?"

"No, I doubted him, but he did."

"I may marry him when I grow up," Meredith said.

"Don't be foolish!" Bronwen snapped. "He's too old for you."

"I don't care. By the time I'm old enough to get married, he won't be much older than me."

The vote was taken the next day, and Casey answered quite a few questions. "It's shorter," he said finally, "and we'll save a few days, but it's rough going. Not much water. We may lose a few of the weaker stock." He hesitated, then added, "Let me show you what lies ahead of us." He located a sheet of paper and quickly drew a crude map.

"Here we are, and we'll be in Fort Hall soon, then Fort Boise, which will be the last settlement before we get to the Dalles — except for Fort Walla Walla. We'll take a

298

vote, but I'd say we take the shortcut. I think we can make it." The consensus was to take the shortcut, for people were tired of the trail.

After the meeting was over, Nolan Cole made his way back to his wagon. As soon as he got there, he saw Dr. York Wingate talking to Marzina. "What are you doing here?" he snapped.

"He just stopped by to see how David is."

Nolan Cole had always been jealous. He hadn't much true affection for his wife, but he was a man who liked to own things completely. He also had a considerable temper, and he snapped, "Stay away from my wife, Wingate!"

"Don't be foolish," Marzina said. "We're taking care of his baby, and someone has to help."

"You shut up, Marzina! You chase after every man you see." He saw that his words cut her, and it pleased him. He turned to face Wingate. "I'm telling you now to stop seeing my wife!" He grabbed Wingate by the front of his shirt and said, "If I see you around here again, I'll break your neck."

"Let him go, Nolan. He's not —" Cole suddenly turned and backhanded Marzina. She was holding the infant in her arms, and she fell backward, shielding him.

"Don't take it out on her. It's not her fault."

"Get out of here!"

Wingate hesitated but knew Nolan couldn't be reasoned with. He turned and walked away.

"Get up!" Nolan snapped. "If you're going to take care of that brat, do it, but stay away from that man!"

Marzina knew her husband well. He had a dog-in-the-manger attitude toward her and always had. She did not argue with him. Her face stung from the blow, and she simply turned and got into the wagon where she put the baby down. Then the tears began to run down her face.

It didn't take the members of the train long to feel the strain of Sublette Cutoff. The sun overhead grew as hot as a woodstove, throwing pale dry beams down on the oxen and cattle. The dogs even seemed to feel the strain, for they no longer dashed along, barking and chasing each other.

At times they'd travel far into the night, bumping over sagebrush and following the beds of old lakes that were now as dry as the dust itself that composed them. Each day they stopped and doled out water for the animals and turned them loose to graze

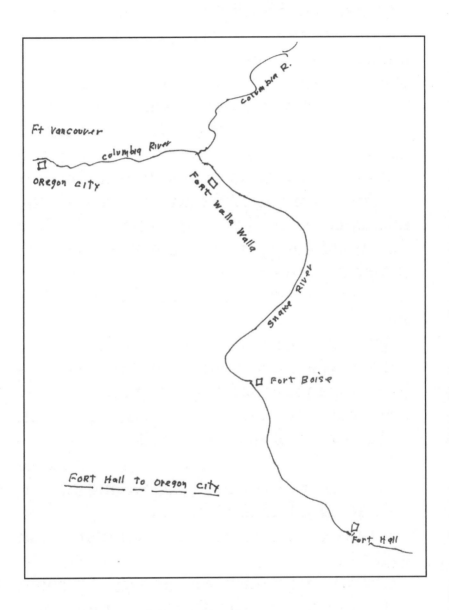

Ft Vancouver

Columbia R.

Columbia River

Oregon City

Fort Walla Walla

Snake River

Fort Boise

FORT Hall to Oregon City

Fort Hall

301

on the sparsely covered floor of the desert. They breakfasted on dry meat and drank water so alkaline that when one had drunk his fill, his stomach seemed to swell. It was a hard time for all.

Charity and nearly everyone else knew the hard time Nolan Cole was giving his wife. She made it a point to go by at least once a day and help with the new baby. She also found time, whenever possible, to encourage York Wingate. "I know it's hard," she said once when they had stopped beside a thin trickle of a stream, "but it will be over someday."

"I don't know what to do, Charity," York said. "He's cruel to Marzina, but the baby needs her. I guess I need her too."

Charity laid her hand on his arm. "She's a fine woman married to a bad man."

He gave her an intense look and said, "That's kind of final, isn't it?"

"It's bad, but the Lord will take care of your son. He's a healthy baby, and Marzina's doing a fine job."

Wingate shrugged his shoulders and walked away.

Charity knew there was no way she could help him except to offer encouragement, and she was determined to do that.

"Well, there it is. Fort Hall. What's the

date?" Tremayne asked.

Charterhouse seemed to add up in his head, "I think it's September the nineteenth."

The two led the train in, and Tremayne stepped off his horse and watered him in a trough. He saw Wingate walking wearily along and said, "Doc, if you need anything, this is one place you can buy it."

"Not much, is it, Casey?"

"No. Built by a man named Nathaniel Wyeth — owned by the Hudson's Bay Company. Not far up there, the trail turns off and winds its way down to California. A lot of people give up here and just go on there."

"You think any of our group will?"

"Some of them are pretty tired. Yes, and the animals are tired too. I'd like to rest them, but we're late. We're liable to get caught in snow or ice if we don't get out of here."

Tremayne went to the store, bought a few supplies, and when he came out, he saw Charity. "Hello, Charity. Here to buy a few things?"

"Yes. Where are you going?"

"The Indian camp over there. I want to see what they know about how the trail is, on down the way."

"Could I go with you? I've never seen any

303

Indians up close."

"Come along."

The two made their way out of the trading post, and he spoke of the Indian problem. "We've been lucky," he said. "All we had to do was meet a Cheyenne war party. There wouldn't be as many of us now."

Charity listened until they got to the Indian camp, and she stared at it with disgust. The camp stank to high heaven, and she had never seen such dirty people in all of her life. They were friendly and talkative but apparently also rather slow minded, dirty, and almost naked.

Finally they left, and she said, "Well, there goes all the romantic notions I had about Indians."

"What's that?"

"Well, I've been reading books about how noble the savages are. I had an idea they were tall, brawny, strong people with piercing eyes. These don't look like that at all."

"You're talking about the plains Indians, Charity, like the Blackfeet or the Sioux. These fish eaters are something different." He grinned. "You ought to see what they eat besides fish — lizards, grasshoppers, stuff you would think would choke a man."

They moved back, and Charity was amazed at how at ease she felt with Tremayne. It hadn't been that way earlier. She nearly commented about it, but they were interrupted by York Wingate. He came hurrying with a worried frown on his face.

"We've got a problem, Casey. We got three people down sick."

"What is it?" Tremayne demanded quickly.

York shook his head. "I think," he said regretfully, "it may be cholera."

"I hope not. That could be bad."

The cholera hit the train suddenly. The first victim was Nolan Cole. He died a hard death. Marzina stayed with him, and Dr. Wingate did all he could. When the man drew his last breath, Wingate looked with sadness at Marzina, "I'm sorry I couldn't save him, Marzina."

"He was an unhappy man," she whispered. "He would never look to God, and now he's gone to give account." Tears came to her eyes, and Wingate wanted to put his arms around her and comfort her but knew that was not the thing to do.

"You'll have lots of help, Marzina," he said gently. "We'll all help you."

"I feel so alone, Dr. Wingate!"

"I know. I feel the same way." He touched her arm. "We've both lost something, but we'll help each other."

■ ■ ■ ■

Cholera also claimed Elizabeth Douglas, ten years old, and Tom Brand, age fifteen. It also took Konrad Dekker and his wife, Minna. Several others had it, including Jack Canreen, but lived through it.

Helga Studdart, daughter of Karl and Freida, died the second day after getting sick. Charity was with her when she died. She had been bathing her face with cool water, and Helga began crying. "I never had anything. I never had a husband. I never had babies. My whole life is gone, and I've never done anything."

Charity felt tears in her eyes. Later she told Tremayne, "She was so sad. Crying out because she had missed out on everything. I think she liked Ringo Jukes."

"Poor girl," Tremayne murmured. "So pretty."

"She wanted so much and got so little."

"Well, there are people who say eat, drink, and be merry for tomorrow you may die, but I don't think that's any way to live."

"No, it's not. Helga's parents were afraid that she was going wild, but she was like all young girls. She was interested in young men and in marriage, courtship, and things like that." She found her eyes filling up with tears. They were at the edge of the camp now, and it was dark. There was a bright moon but no stars. Suddenly, the thought of the young girl full of life only two days earlier but now cold and dead moved her. She began to weep.

Casey stared at her for a moment and saw the depth of her suffering. He knew she was a woman of intense compassion. He simply stepped forward and put his arms around her. "I know it's hard. Life is hard." He held her until she stopped crying.

When she looked up, she said, "Don't — don't take advantage of me, Casey."

"I'd never do that. I think you're the best woman I ever knew. I wouldn't do anything to hurt you."

Charity was very much aware of his arms around her. She knew her will was weak and that if he held her tighter, and even if he kissed her, she wouldn't be able to resist. His words comforted her, but she was unprepared for his question.

"Do you think you could ever consider me as a man you might learn to care for and want to marry?"

Charity couldn't answer. She looked up, and his face was coated with the silver light of the moon. His eyes were piercing, and there was a gentle expression on his face, "I know you won't give yourself to a man who doesn't know God."

"No, I couldn't."

"I can't hunt for God just to get you. That would be like trying to trade with God. I can't do that. It would be a lie."

"No, you can't do that, but you need to seek God no matter what happens with me or any other woman. Seek Him, Casey, please."

She turned and walked blindly away, and when she got to the wagon, she undressed and went to bed, but she lay awake, looking up at the canvas overhead and thinking of what Casey had said. And the question burned in her mind: *Could you consider me a man you might learn to care for?* She suddenly knew that had already happened, but she saw no good ending to this situation.

CHAPTER SEVENTEEN

The Angel Train reached Fort Boise, and the animals were in such poor shape that Tremayne decided to rest them. There were livestock traders at the post, and many of the Way traded their sore-footed animals for fresh ones. It was a common practice on the trail, for many trains arrived there in poor condition.

Later that afternoon, Tremayne started into the fort to buy a new knife because he had broken his. He paid for one he liked, and when he stepped outside, he saw Charity accompanied by Bronwen and Meredith.

"Well, ladies, it's good to see you. Have you been shopping?"

"Just for a few things." Charity smiled. She feared Casey would reveal something about their last encounter — when she had wept and he had embraced her — but he said nothing, and she drew a deep sigh of relief.

Meredith piped up, "You know what, Tremayne? You ought to get married."

"Why should I do that?"

"Because you need a little girl just like me."

Meredith's answer delighted Casey as most of her remarks did. "Why would I need a little girl just like you?"

"Because little girls like me are pretty and smart."

Charity laughed. "Well, you're not broke out with modesty."

"No, you're not!" Bronwen snapped. "Why don't you be nice?"

Meredith hit Bronwen on the arm. "I am nice. You're the one that's always causing trouble."

"Wait a minute. Let's not fight about it," Tremayne said.

"Why don't you get married?" Meredith insisted.

"Why, I don't think I could find a woman who would marry an ugly fellow like me."

"You ain't ugly," Meredith said. She looked at Tremayne carefully and shook her head. "You're not very pretty, but you're not ugly."

"Thank you. I appreciate that."

Meredith glanced at Charity. "I know. You can marry Charity. She don't think you're ugly, do you, Charity?"

Tremayne was amused, and Charity was flustered. "Well, come on, out with it. Am I ugly?"

"Don't be silly and don't listen to this foolish girl!" she said.

"I'll tell you what. Suppose we go in that restaurant over there and get us some store-bought food?"

"I want some store-bought food," Meredith said.

"Come along then." He led them into the café, which was fairly rough, but the food was good. They had beef stew, boiled potatoes, and green beans along with biscuits and apple pie.

During the meal Meredith had been talking about things she wanted to do when she got to Oregon. "Are there any bears in Oregon, Tremayne?"

"You mustn't call him Tremayne. Call him Mr. Tremayne."

"All right. Mr. Tremayne, are there bears in Oregon?"

"I think so. Black bears and grizzly bears. Why?"

"I'm going to shoot one. I had a storybook about a girl who shot a bear so I'm going to shoot one. Will you let me use your gun?"

"Well, Miss Charity or your father will have to talk to you about that. Maybe you can start shooting something easier like a porcupine."

Charity listened, amazed that anyone as hardened and as tough as Casey Tremayne could make himself at home with a six-year-old. Meredith doted on him and so did Bronwen. Finally she said, "Well, it's getting late. When will we be leaving, Casey?"

"Probably day after tomorrow. This is the last chance if you want to buy anything."

"No, I guess we've got everything. What's at Walla Walla?"

"Just another military post, but we're not going there. I decided to skip that and go on for the Dalles."

"The Dalles? What's that?"

"It's a little settlement on the Columbia River. We'll have to camp out there while we build rafts."

"Why do we need rafts?" Bronwen asked. "Are we going to fish off of them?"

"No, I don't think so. You see, Bronwen, there's no way to get to Oregon City except down the river. The mountains are too steep, and there are no trails for wagons. So we'll build rafts. We'll put the animals and the wagons on them, and we'll float down."

"Won't that be fun!" Bronwen said.

"Well, if the river is low, it will be. If it's high, might be a little bit too much fun."

"Is it dangerous?" Charity inquired.

"It can be. Depends on how high the river is."

He paid for the meal and they left. When they returned to the wagon, Charity said, "You girls get on to bed. I'm going to get ready for breakfast."

Meredith came over and said, "You can kiss me good night, Tremayne."

"Well, I'll just do that." He leaned over, kissed her cheek, and then said, "What about you, Bronwen?"

"No, I'm too old for that."

"I guess you are. Well, I missed my chance. Good night, girls."

"There's some coffee left," Charity said. "Let's heat it up on the fire. I hate to go to bed this early. I'm afraid I might miss something."

"Not likely to miss anything out here."

She heated the coffee, and he sipped his while she prepared the elements for breakfast. Then she sat on a box next to him. "That was so good for my sisters, and for me too."

"A store-bought meal is good after cooking on a campfire."

"No, I mean it was good for them to

313

spend time with you."

"They're fine girls. All you Morgan girls are fine. Are you like your mother?"

"They say so. She died when Meredith was born, but I remember her. She had a good singing voice, and she was always ready to listen to my troubles."

They sat quietly for a time, and finally, she said, "Have you thought about God since my father's sermon?"

"Yes, I have. It got to me."

"I think God is after you, Casey."

"You make me sound like a varmint somebody's trailing with a dog."

"Well, in a way that's true. Jesus said, 'I've come to seek and to save that which was lost.' So, Jesus is on your trail, I think."

"Well, I'm ready to be caught."

Their silence continued. She thought with amazement, *It's like we were an old married couple.* "You asked me if I thought of you as a man I might care for and marry. What kind of woman are you looking for, Casey?"

"Well, a man gets pictures in his head, Charity. He sees one woman who is beautiful, another who is sweet, another who is smart, another who is clever. He sees all these things in different women, and out of all of them, he makes a woman up in his head. That's what he's looking for."

"That's not very fair to the woman," Charity said in a sprightly tone.

"Well, most of us take what we can get, the good with the bad." He rose and said, "It was a good evening. You looking forward to getting to Oregon?"

"I suppose so. It's what we set out to do."

"It'll be hard. Hard getting down the river. Hard finding a place, building cabins, putting in crops, clearing land — a lifetime of work."

"I know that's so, but I'm just glad to be this far along."

He leaned over and put his hand on her cheek. He didn't say a word, but she saw something in his eyes that kept her quiet. His touch thrilled her, and then he said, "Good night, Charity," straightened up, and left quickly.

She watched him go and wondered what sort of mental picture he had about her.

York was walking alongside the oxen and daydreaming when he heard the call come out for nooning. "Whoa, Jesse!" and the oxen obediently stopped. He began to water them and feed them. Then he heard his name called. He turned to see Marzina approaching quickly, holding David in her arms. "What's wrong?" he said.

"It's Benjamin. He's got a fever." She was frightened and she whispered, "It can't be cholera. It just can't be."

"Let me have a look." He walked to her wagon and stepped inside. Benjamin was lying on his back, and his face was flushed. York felt his pulse and his forehead and then jumped down from the wagon. "It's not cholera. I'm almost sure of it."

Relief washed across Marzina's features, and she said, "Thank God. I thought —"

"I know. We always think the worst about our children. I'm already the same way about David. I worry about him when there's nothing really to worry about. I'll tell you what. Let me get my bag. I've got a tonic that might help Benjamin a little bit, and then you need to keep his fever down with cool cloths. I'll show you how."

Ten minutes later the two were back in the wagon, and York gave the tonic to the boy. He then began to show her how to wet the cloth in the coolest water available and put them on the boy.

"I think he'll be fine," he said.

Wingate covered her hand for a moment, and when she withdrew it, he tried to smile. "You're a wonderful woman, Marzina. Your husband doesn't know what a treasure he had." Marzina watched him walk away. His

words had given her hope. She picked up
David and held him close to her heart.

CHAPTER EIGHTEEN

Tremayne and Jack Canreen were riding ahead of the train. They had seen no game, and for most of the time, the two had hardly spoken. From time to time, Tremayne glanced at his companion's expression. Canreen's face was blunt, brutal, and battle scarred around his eyes from barroom fights and other quarrels. Tremayne was somewhat surprised at the behavior of the big man. He'd had him pegged from the first as a troublemaker, and there had been trouble between them at the beginning of the journey. But especially since Canreen had overcome cholera, a silence had fallen over him almost like a curtain. Tremayne never asked him about it, but now as their horses moved ahead at a slow walk, Canreen suddenly began speaking.

"You know, Casey, I nearly died with that cholera."

"You came pretty close, Jack."

"I've heard stories that I thought were lies about people dying who looked over and saw something on the other side. I never put no stock in that sort of stuff. I never had any reason to." He fell silent and then turned to face Tremayne. "I ain't saying I had any kind of a vision like that, but I was so weak, I couldn't even lift my head, and I thought I was going to die. And the one thing I thought of was how I lived my whole life, and I've not done one good thing."

"Don't be too hard on yourself."

"Well, why shouldn't I? God was going to be hard on me. At least, that's the way I felt. I wouldn't want you to know some of the things I've done."

"The same here."

Canreen studied Tremayne carefully and said, "Well, not as bad as me, I reckon. Anyway, while I was lying on that bed as weak as a sick cat, expecting to be before the judgment any minute, I got scared. Never was scared of much, Casey. Too dumb to be scared, I guess."

"I know the feeling. I've done things that looking back on them give me the shivers. I wouldn't do them now. It's funny how the less life we have in front of us, the more we seem to value it. You take when I was a young buck, seventeen, eighteen — nothing scared me. Why, I'd put myself in situations where there wasn't any way to get out, and I didn't think anything about it."

Canreen laughed shortly, "I know what you mean."

"Well, I don't need the cholera to cause me to be afraid of God, Jack. I've always been afraid of God. I've tried to cover it up, of course, but you know, lately I've been thinking a lot, the more I look around me and see the way the world is. Those mountains over there, those clouds, the way the world turns around every twenty-four hours, night and day, seasons coming and going. It's all like a big clock, and all I can think is clocks don't make themselves. God had to have made all of this."

"I figure you're right about that."

The two men felt an unusual camaraderie. Canreen's openness surprised Casey. He hadn't expected Jack to have any thoughts of God, judgment, or salvation, but it seemed he did. Maybe all men did.

"We're going to make it, aren't we?"

Canreen's remark broke into Tremayne's thoughts, and he took his eyes off the horizon. "Yes, we're almost to the Dalles. I've got hopes."

"The warden will be surprised, won't he?" Canreen grinned suddenly. "I bet he thought you'd have to shoot me and some of the others before this was over."

"I never thought that."

"Yeah, well, I planned to run away."

"I thought maybe you would. It surprised me when you stayed put."

"Funny thing, Casey. I don't dream much, but I had a dream about running away. It was way back about the second week we were out, I think. I dreamed I got up, took a horse, left camp, and rode away, and I rode until the horse couldn't go no more, and I lay down and went to sleep. And then when I woke up, there you were, standing over me with a gun at my head."

Tremayne laughed. "I didn't know I was a boogeyman like that."

"It was a pretty real dream. Kind of knocked running away out of my head because I know you would have done exactly that. You'd have followed any one of us to the end of the world rather than let us get away."

"I guess I would."

The two turned and headed back toward the caravan. "Well, we'll be in the Dalles in a couple of days. Then we float the river, land in Fort Vancouver, and move on to Oregon City."

"What then, Casey?"

"Why, everybody will split up. These folks want homesteads. Free land!"

"You gonna do that?"

"Why, I don't know, Jack. I doubt it. I don't know what I'm going to do. What about you?"

"I haven't got an idea in my head except I'm not going back to that prison. They'll have to shoot me first."

"Good idea to stay away from that place," Tremayne said.

"I just don't know what to do with myself, I guess."

There was such a plaintive note to the big man's voice that Tremayne realized that under the toughness there was loneliness. Maybe all men had a loneliness like that, men like him and Canreen, wandering around without roots. He said without thinking, "File a claim, Jack, then find you a good woman. Marry her and have kids."

Canreen's eyes opened wide. "Me?"

"Why not you? You're not all that old. You got a lot of life left in you. You remember old Abe Cartwright?"

"Yeah, I knew him in the mountains."

"I ran across him a few years ago. He wasn't but about fifty years old. Didn't have any teeth. He was weak, eating his meat raw because he was too lazy to cook it. He was

322

a good mountain man at one time, but he was alone. That's a bad thing for anybody. I think I knew from the time I saw him I wasn't going to wind up like that."

"That's what you got on your mind? Finding a woman? Getting a claim?"

Tremayne didn't answer for a long time. He straightened in the saddle, looked out over the distance, and then faced Canreen. "I've always wanted that, Jack."

"Well, I hope you get it, Casey."

Evan was excited about being a farmer, but he was wondering if he could handle it. He knew little about farming, only enough to raise a garden perhaps. He knew mining, but he vowed he'd never set foot underground again. He walked beside the oxen; the creaking wagon wheels and the yelping dogs made a symphony. He saw Zamora, who had been riding her horse. She tied the mare to the back of her wagon, turned, and saw him.

She smiled, "Hello, Evan."

"Hello, Zamora. Been riding?"

"Yes, I get tired of walking and tired of riding in the wagon, don't you?"

"I guess so."

Zamora didn't say more, but she moved closer and rubbed her shoulder against him.

"Tell me something, Evan. Why do you never come around me?"

"Why, I see you every day."

She shrugged impatiently. The afternoon sun caught the blackness of her hair, and it made her dark eyes seem brighter. "I mean, you never try to put your hands on me. Why, you've never even kissed me or tried to."

Evan blinked and turned to face her. "Why, there are too many fellows after you, Zamora. I guess I wouldn't have a chance."

"You're too shy, Evan. You're a good-looking fellow. Besides, no one can tell what a woman may do." Amusement showed in her expression, and her lips broadened in a smile. "No telling what I'd do. Why, I might fall in love with you, marry you, and become a farm woman." The thought amused her, and she laughed aloud. "We could have ten children and grow old together until we didn't have any teeth and our hair was falling out."

Evan laughed too. "I can't see you like that."

"Would you like it?"

"Why, sure."

Suddenly Zamora realized she was not accustomed to Evan Morgan's seriousness. There was goodness in him too. She realized he didn't understand her teasing. "Well," she said quickly, "it's just as well you don't come around after me."

"Why's that?"

"What would you do with a Gypsy woman? You need a woman who can skin squirrels. All I can do is tell fortunes, dance, and sing."

"Wouldn't be bad having a good-looking woman like you dancing and singing."

Zamora laughed again. "Why, I declare, I think you're about to propose. But while I was doing all that dancing and singing, who would cook your meals and wash your clothes?"

"I guess I would."

"You know you ought to pay more attention to Alice Brand. She likes you, and Kirsten Dekker too. They're both good-looking girls."

"Which one should I pick? I wouldn't know how to start."

She pushed his hat down over his eyes. When he shoved it back, she laughed and said, "I'll pick one for you, and I'll put a Gypsy spell on her, and you can marry her."

"You like any man in the train?"

"Sure. I like Tremayne, but he doesn't need a Gypsy woman either. He's a strong man. I like that, but he's got a little bit too much of a Puritan in him."

"What does that mean?"

"Why, he's almost as backward as you are where I'm concerned. Can't figure that man out, but I'm going to keep trying. So long. Remember I'll be thinking about which girl you should marry."

Evan laughed. "I'll pick my own bride, Zamora. Don't fret yourself."

The days rolled on, and the wagons were close enough to reach the Dalles within the day, but two of the wagons broke down. The wheels had become dry, and the spokes fell out. The whole train had to stop while they were repaired.

Tremayne approached Gwilym Morgan and said, "I think I'll ride on and see what it's like up ahead."

"I need to get some exercise," Charity said. "Could I ride with you?"

"Sure. That all right with you, Gwilym?"

"That's fine. You take care of her, Tremayne. I can't afford to lose this girl."

"I'll do my best."

The two rode away, and Charity enjoyed the scenery. Tremayne started telling her how Canreen had changed. She listened intently. "I'm glad to hear it. He was a pretty bad man, wasn't he?"

"Pretty bad. I think he's ready for a change though."

"Are you, Casey?"

He looked at her and grew serious. "Yes, I told you I am. I don't know how it will happen though."

They rode along for some time, and then abruptly she asked, "Do you have any feelings about Zamora, Casey?"

He laughed. "Why would you ask me a thing like that?"

"Well, I saw you kissing her that time at Independence Rock."

"She's a pretty girl. She wanted to be kissed. I wouldn't have been considerate if I hadn't helped her out."

"Do you have feelings for her?"

"No, not the kind you mean."

"I can see how you would. She's one of the most beautiful women I've ever seen."

"Yes, she is, but she would never make a farmer's wife."

"Why not?"

"Well, the Gypsy life is hard, but she's told me — and so has Stefan — how it's exciting too. Always new places, new scenes, new people. A farmer's life is not like that. Maybe he sees some old friends at church on Sunday, or a stranger comes by, and he meets somebody new. But mostly it's pretty dull."

"Is that what you want to do, be a farmer?"

"No, I want to do something else."

"What is it?"

"I don't want to tell you. It's a secret."

She reached out and pinched his arm, and he yelped, "Don't do that! It'll leave a blue mark."

"Tell me what you want to do."

"I worked in a sawmill for two years. I liked it. I learned a lot about it. I'd like to find a place with a good stream, with a nice fall, and build a sawmill. I like the smell of wood, the sound of the saws biting into it. I don't know why. I just liked it."

"That would be different from what you have done. You've been a wanderer, haven't you?"

"Most of my life. Even when I was with the Indians, we wandered. I never had any roots."

She was quiet for a while, until both stopped their mounts. He turned in the saddle, reached out, and touched her hair. "You've got the prettiest hair I've ever seen," he said.

"I hated it when I was younger. Other children always made silly songs about my red hair."

"They were jealous."

She laughed. "I don't think so."

He let his hand drop to her shoulder. He squeezed it and said, "Did your mother have red hair?"

"Just like mine. It didn't get dull even when she got older."

"Yours won't either."

"You don't know that." She gave him a direct look. "Would you like to have roots?"

"I never had any. It's hard to say."

"Well, I hope you find what you want."

He grew very serious, and his hand tightened. "I know what I want. I want you, but you're not for me."

"Why would you say that?"

He had trouble answering. "I'm one of the rough ones, Charity. You deserve better." He turned away quickly and called out, "Come on. Let's get back to the train." She kicked her horse in the sides, and the mare picked up a gallop. She knew he was running away from her, and she understood why. The feelings between them were mysterious and still unexpressed. She couldn't explain it but knew their mutual attraction went below the surface.

The next afternoon Gwilym saw Tremayne

and Charterhouse come back from a scout. They drew up the horses, and Tremayne could barely contain his excitement.

"There it is, Gwilym, the Dalles."

"The Dalles," Gwilym breathed. "We made it, Casey. We made it."

"Yes, we did. Some didn't get here, but most of us did." His eyes went to Charity who was beside her father.

She smiled at him. "You still thinking about that sawmill?"

"More than ever. I'll let you help me run the first log through." He let out a yelp, turned and spurred his horse down the line, shouting, "We made it, folks! We made it!"

"What's that about a sawmill?" Gwilym asked curiously.

"That's what he wants to do, build a sawmill."

"And he wants you to help him?"

"He was just being foolish."

Gwilym Morgan looked at his daughter. She was the image of his dead wife, and it gave him a pang to look at her, but he only said, "A sawmill isn't a bad thing for a man to have."

CHAPTER NINETEEN

The days were fair with no hint of snowfall, at least not yet. As Charity walked toward the Dalles, the small town that was the end of this part of their journey, she could feel the approaching winter. She saw it in the dead grass and the leaves fallen to the cold ground. Memories of the hard trail they had traveled came to her, and she knew that for the rest of her life she would remember the journey from Pennsylvania to Oregon with the sharpest detail. But now it was nearly done. There was no question whether they would reach Oregon. They had conquered the desert, rivers, and mountains, and only one obstacle lay ahead — the Columbia River.

An eagerness seized her as the travelers approached the town they had been seeking for so long. She saw the Methodist mission Tremayne had said was there. It was merely a small log building nearly hidden in a mountain notch, a secure place between the heights and the river. The buildings gave the look of a settlement, but she saw that the missionaries, the schools, and the church hadn't changed the Indians much. They were as primitive, dirty, and dull looking as those she had seen earlier.

The wagons halted, and most of the people were fixing a noon meal, but Gwilym wanted to find someone in town who could tell him more about the journey on the river.

"I suppose we'll be breaking up now," he said, his voice breaking the silence. "Everyone taking their own way, but I hope we can stay close to each other and have a church as we did back home."

"Not home anymore," Charity murmured, and that was true. The only home she had ever known, she found to her amazement, was growing dim in her mind. All of the memories from there, she supposed, were hidden deep and would return later, but now it was what lay ahead that mattered — a cabin not yet built, fields not yet cleared, marriages not yet performed, and children not yet born. The future occupied her mind.

Gwilym had been watching Charity sharply all morning, and he asked abruptly, "Something bothering you, Daughter?"

"Not really. We've made it through safely. I guess I'm just tired."

"Not like you to be so quiet. Your mother was quiet now, but you've always been a talking woman. Can't you tell me what's troubling you?"

Charity hesitated, and her father turned to face her. For a moment she sorted through the thoughts she had kept within her breast, but now they seemed to beg to be told.

"It's something that happened that's bothering me. I've meant to tell you, but I wasn't sure it was right." She hesitated again, and an uncommon soberness came over her. She had a way of holding her lips together when she was deep in thought, oftentimes on the edge of a smile. She often observed her life, events, and people, absorbing them but seeming not to pass judgment. Finally, she said, "It's something about Casey."

Surprise, for a moment, showed in Gwilym's face, but then he asked quickly, "Tremayne is bothering you?"

"He — he asked me if I thought he was a man I might marry." Now it was out. She had said it, and she saw her father's thoughtful eyes fastened on her. She knew him so well, exactly what he was thinking. *What kind of a man is Tremayne? Was he a man of God? Would he be good to a wife? Would he make a good father?* He would be mulling all these over in his mind; however, he surprised her not by speaking of Tremayne.

"What about you, Daughter? How do you feel about him? What have you told him?"

"I haven't told him anything. I couldn't, Pa. He's not a man who knows the Lord, and the Bible is very plain on that."

"Yes, it is. A woman needs a Christian husband. There are decent men who aren't Christians, but the Bible says, 'Be ye not unequally yoked together with unbelievers.' And I can vouch for the fact that no yoke brings two human beings closer than the yoke of marriage. How do you feel about him?"

"I don't know. I do feel something for him, but how can I answer him when he's not the kind of man I've always vowed to marry?"

For a long moment Gwilym Morgan stood there, and his compassion, deep love, and respect for his daughter were obvious in his face. She was so much like her mother! He finally said, "I'm going to tell you something, Charity. You probably don't know this, but when I asked your mother to marry me, I wasn't a Christian."

"Why, Pa, I thought you were saved long before you met Ma."

"No, I went to church all my life, and I suppose people got the idea that I was a believer, but I wasn't. It wasn't until after I got to know her, and she began to witness to me of the inner life of Christ that I found Him. All I had known was the outer elements of religion. I knew what was right, and I could quote Scripture, but at one point she finally came to me, and she talked to me about giving my life over to Jesus completely. I still remember that day clearly. She had tears in her eyes, Daughter, and she was beautiful to me. She asked me to call on the Lord, and I did, confessing my sins, and that was the beginning of my Christian life."

"I'm glad you told me, Pa. I didn't know that."

"I hope it helps you. Of course, the man can't become a Christian just to get a wife, but when God wants to do so, He can convict someone. He wanted the apostle Paul so bad He knocked him to the ground to get his attention, so you and I will pray that Casey Tremayne will find his way to God. Then he can talk to you about marriage, and if you love him, you'll know what to say."

■ ■ ■ ■

Seeing what there was of the Dalles did not take long, for it was, indeed, a small place. Its main claim to existence was its location on the Columbia River. Beyond there, those who wanted to get to Oregon City had to pass dangerous rapids, for the mountains barred the way, forbidding travel by wagon, though individual animals could make it.

The travelers had spent the night resting and talking about what lay before them, but early the next morning Gwilym and several of the other elders met. Tremayne waited while they prayed for guidance, and then he accompanied them to the river. They stood on the banks and looked across it, and all of them fell silent. After a time Gwilym said, "Well, the river is bigger than I'd like, but it doesn't look too bad."

Karl Studdart shook his head. "I never did like boats or water, but I'm going to have to put up with it. Do you know how to build a raft, Tremayne?"

"No, I'm not a river man. We'll have to find someone."

"What about that fellow over there?" Nelson Brand, one of the elders, pointed to a man trimming lumber that lay in a neat stack. "Looks like he's building a raft right now. Let's ask him."

They moved across the open broken ground, and when the man saw them, he laid his ax down and approached. "Howdy. Just get in from on the trail?"

"Just yesterday," Gwilym said. "My name's Gwilym Morgan." He introduced the others. "We're wondering about how to build a raft."

"My name's Bob Crutchfield, Mr. Morgan. I've been here for about a month."

"Where did you come in from, Crutchfield?" Tremayne asked. He liked the looks of the man for the fellow was tall and strong. His hands were toughened, and he looked like a worker.

"We came from St. Joe, Missouri, with a train, but my wife got sick just before we got to the Dalles. She wasn't able to make such a rough trip."

"Sorry to hear that," Gwilym said. "How is she now?"

"She's doing much better. I'm building this raft for myself."

"We'd appreciate it if you could teach us how to do that. None of us know how to build a raft."

"Be proud to help you all I can. Some people abandon their wagons here and pack what they can on a horse and go over the mountains. But you have to leave every-thing."

"I don't think we'd care to do that," Stud-dart said. "Is it hard to build a raft?"

"It takes a lot of work. See those logs? That's about the size you need. You just cut 'em, and using your animals, drag them up here and fasten them together. That's about it."

"How do you carry the animals on a raft?"

"Well, most people don't. They put their wagon on the raft, take the wheels off, and tie it down, and then they have some of their menfolk take the herd through the gap. Rough going, but you can make it with animals like that. Then they're waiting there when the raft floats down and gets to Fort Vancouver. Be proud to show you how to build them."

"We'd be mighty obliged to you."

"You can talk to some of the other men around here who've watched a lot of raft building. They know the river too. It can get a might dangerous when it's high, but it ain't too bad right now. I figure you can get your rafts made in a week or maybe two, and the river is falling so it ought to be fairly safe." He laughed, showing his white teeth against his bronzed skin. "I can't swim a

lick so I'm going to carry a barrel or something to hang on to if I fall off. Here, let me
show you how this raft building goes."

Building rafts kept the men busy from early
morning until dark. The women were busy
with their chores, but since there was no
traveling, they had time to wash clothes,
sort out their foodstuffs, and cook better
meals. There was time for talk, too, and, of
course, plenty of that went on.

Marzina was washing clothes when York
Wingate approached her. "It's getting
colder," he said.

"I don't mind. I like the cold."

York smiled abruptly. "You better like the
rain. From what I hear from the folks
around here they had a drought in Oregon
that lasted nearly all day."

Marzina laughed. It made a pleasant
sound. "I'm dreading that trip on that raft.
It looks dangerous."

"Crutchfield says it's not really so bad at
this time of the year. It's a good time we got
here when we did. If it were snowing and
freezing, it would be a different story."

"I'll have to hire someone to build my
raft," she said.

"I already done that. I hired Crutchfield
to build us two rafts. He's done it before,

and he said he'd hire some help. I'm not much good with my hands like that — building things, carpenter work."

"Well, your hands are for other things like healing people, York. And you use them for that, which is important."

"Well, I want to do some good for people here."

"What are you going to do when we get there?"

"I'll open an office in Oregon City."

A faint line of worry creased Marzina's forehead, and she said at once, "We won't be having a doctor then."

"Yes, you will. I'll have a buggy and a team, and I'll make rounds regularly."

Relief came to Marzina's face, and she smiled. "That's good, York. The men have agreed to build me a cabin. Isn't that nice of them?"

"Well, you can't stay by yourself."

"I can if I have to."

Wingate looked embarrassed and then troubled. "What's wrong?" Marzina asked.

"Well, I've been thinking. I've got to have an office, and I've got to have a place to live. I'm no housekeeper, and I need somebody to work in the office to be there when I'm not. I was hoping you would stay in Oregon City. You could do my housekeep-

340

ing for me, take care of the office, clean it up, and, of course, you need to be close for David. There might be a nursing mother available, but David's used to you, and you're so good with him."

"I'm not sure that would be the right thing to do."

"Why not? What's wrong with it?" he asked.

"Are you talking about living in the same house? That would cause gossiping tongues to wag."

"We could have different places. I want you to be close. I'd like to help you, Marzina. We're tied together. We both lost someone, and we each have a baby to rear, and I don't know the first thing about it. That's another thing you could do — keep David while I'm working. We're yoked together like a pair of oxen, I guess."

For a moment Marzina hesitated, then she said, "We're not exactly the same, you and I. We both lost someone, but you loved your wife. I'm ashamed to say it, but I never cared for Nolan the way a woman should care for a husband."

"I guess I knew that."

"Marriage wasn't my choice, and I never felt really like a wife. I felt more like a servant. That's an awful thing to say."

The two were silent for a moment, and then York said, "You think on it, Marzina. I need you, and David needs you. We can help each other."

Marzina smiled. "It's like you to think of me that way, of my good and of my children's. I will think on it."

He took her hand and held it in both of his. "I'll be hoping you will stay because I need you something fierce."

The words soothed Marzina. They were words she had never heard from her husband. He had never told her he needed her, and now this man — such a good man! — was saying words she had hungered for. She was aware of his strong hands holding hers, and then York suddenly turned and left. Marzina knew that she would think about what he said. And in her heart that was what she had longed for.

The crew was gathered by the river, ready to cut logs. The men had brought saws, and all of them had axes. Now as Tremayne looked at them, he was surprised to find he had almost a fondness for them.

He laughed suddenly and said, "You know. I hate to tell you this, but you men have done a good job. I don't think anyone could have done better." He saw their pleased expressions and added, "One more chore here. Build these rafts. Float down the river to Fort Vancouver. It's a short way from there to Oregon City, and as soon as we get to Oregon City, all you men are free."

"We don't know how to build rafts," Jack Canreen said.

"Well, I don't either, but this is Bob Crutchfield. He's built plenty of rafts, and he's willing to boss the job. So you just listen to him. Bob, give us the outline of what we need to do."

Crutchfield had been standing slightly to the side of Casey, and now he said, "Well, you men may not have built rafts, but I imagine you've felled trees. All we do is fell the right-sized tree, trim it up, cut it to length, and have the oxen pull it down to the river. We use some pieces of timber or else short lengths of smaller trees to fasten it together. You use mostly pegs and cables." He explained how the wagons were placed on the rafts, and the wheels removed to lower it and give it more stability. Finally, he asked for questions.

"How do you steer the things, Crutchfield?"

"Put sort of a sweep on the back, a rudder. The river is slow right now so it's not much trouble. A couple of men in the front

343

can push off from the banks if you get too close, but a good man at the sweep can dodge most obstacles. It's like driving a wagon down a road. Stay in the middle of it. We won't have any trouble this time of the year."

After several more questions, Bob said, "You fellows come with me and bring your animals. We can get a bunch of trees down today. We'll have one crew hauling, another crew cutting, and another one trimming. You'll be in Oregon City before you know it."

Cold weather began as the last of the rafts was assembled. It had been hard work, but there were plenty of hands, and some like York Wingate had hired local help. In all, it had taken no more than two weeks. Crutchfield had given Ringo Jukes the directions on how to take the stock through the mountains.

"You can't get lost, Ringo. It's a narrow trail so the animals will have to go through one at a time in places. Pretty steep, but you can make it."

Ringo left almost immediately with instructions from Crutchfield on where to go. Crutchfield also identified the best landing spot, drew a rough map, and said, "When we come down the river, we'll steer for this place. You and the rest of the crew that are taking the cattle be ready. We'll throw you a rope, you drag the nose in, and we can take them down and put the wheels back on. You can't get lost. You'll find the landing spot easy."

That night Evan looked over the meal Charity had cooked. "This looks good."

"Well, Mr. Studdart slaughtered a cow, and he shared it with the whole train."

Gwilym was smiling. "Studdart's a different kind of fellow. Losing that girl took something out of him, but I think it put something in him too. A loss like that can strengthen a man if he takes it right."

"Pa, say a prayer and then we'll eat," Charity said. "Everybody's hungry."

"All right. Everybody gather round and hold hands."

Tremayne moved forward, and he was between Meredith and Charity. Meredith offered her hand. He took it, and then he turned to face Charity. He smiled at her, and when she put her hand in his, he felt the strength of her grip.

Gwilym said in a voice filled with emotion, "Lord, we can do no other than thank You from our hearts for bringing us over this long journey. Surely You've guided us even as You guided Moses and the children of Israel. We thank You for that, for the blessings of life. We thank You for this food, and, Lord, we pray that You will go before us and guide the way, and put us on the homestead where You would have us. And, Lord, we ask this in Jesus' name."

Evan laughed. "I'm glad that was a short prayer, Pa."

"Don't be irreligious," Gwilym said fondly. "You're eating fast enough to choke."

Indeed Evan did eat more quickly than the rest. Meredith said, "Why you eating so fast, Evan?"

"Because I'm hungry."

But everyone knew it was more than hunger, for when Evan finished, he said, "I guess I'll go walk around awhile."

He left and went directly to the raft where the Gypsies had their wagon tied down. They had fixed a fire, and Zamora was cooking steaks. She said, "We have plenty for everyone."

"Just ate," Evan said. "Nice of Mr. Studdart to slaughter one of his cattle for us."

Stefan said, "I'm going to raise some beef critters when we get our place. Don't want to be a rancher, but always good to have your own beef."

Zamora fed them all, and finally, she

346

whispered to Evan, "Grandmother is in a strange mood."

"Is she sick?"

Trouble came into Zamora's dark eyes. "I think she is. She never will say she is, but she hasn't been feeling well for several days. Come along. She'll want to talk to you. She's always liked you, Evan."

Evan moved to the raft where the bed was made up inside. He and Zamora climbed in and sat, one on each side, of the old woman who was lying flat on her back on a pallet. She reached up her hand, and her dark eyes took in Evan. "So, young Evan, you've come to see the old woman?"

"Yes, I have. Don't you feel well, Lareina?"

Lareina didn't answer him. Instead she reached both hands up, one on each side. Evan was surprised by it. He took one, and he was shocked at the thinness and the fragility of the bones. It was like a bird's bone. Zamora was holding the other hand, and he didn't know what to say.

"This is a dark world. Gypsies have a hard time, but the good God has taken care of us. I'm glad, Daughter, that you are in a new land."

"I'm glad too. You'll like it here, Lareina," Evan said.

The old woman didn't answer. She seemed to be withholding a secret. Zamora could recognize this. The young woman's face was inclined toward the old woman, and she was staring into her grandmother's eyes. The old woman suddenly began to speak in a foreign language. Evan couldn't understand a word, and her voice was strong for a time, then it began to grow faint.

Lareina turned her face and said, "You are a good man, young Evan. God be with you and give you many children and a family. It's good for a man to be surrounded by his children."

The old woman closed her eyes, and Zamora nodded to Evan. The two crawled out of the wagon, and Zamora walked toward the fire. They were alone, for Stefan had left on an errand.

"I'm worried about her. She's very ill. I've never seen her this weak."

"She'll be better when we get settled," he said.

"We won't be settled for a time."

"What do you mean, Zamora?"

"There's so much to do, and she's so tired. She can't go through this, Evan." Zamora turned to face him. "You didn't understand what she said, did you?"

"No. What was it?"

"It's her native language. Mine, too, but I couldn't believe what she was saying. She talked about me."

The silence surrounded them, except for the calling of a night bird in the woods. The voices of others came faintly from where the rafts were anchored.

"She's worried about me," Zamora said.

"Why is she worried?"

"She's always been on the move except when she was a very young girl. She talked about that. Then she lived with her parents, and they had a house. She never told me much about that, but she said it's good to have roots. She talked about how sad it was always to be living in a world of change, which is what Gypsies know, many of them. She wanted me —" Zamora broke off, and suddenly he saw tears glittering in her eyes.

"Why, Zamora," he said, "she'll be all right."

"I don't think she will. There's a shadow on her. She could always see it on people who didn't have long to live, and I have the same gift at times. She won't live long, and then I'll be alone."

"You'll have Stefan."

"Yes, I'll have Stefan."

Evan reached out and pulled her close.

She laid her head against his chest, and he whispered huskily, "And you'll always have me. As long as I'm around, you'll never be alone, Zamora." He felt her body tremble, and then the tears came. She was not a crying woman, he knew, but as he held her, he knew that this was a woman a man could tie to. He would never understand the depth of her gifts, but she had fire and beauty and wisdom, and what else could a man want?

Tremayne had only a moment for Charity before the rafts shoved off. They were going in the first raft, and he would handle the tiller. He said, "Are you afraid, Charity?"

"No, not really. God didn't bring us this far to lose us." She gave him a smile. "Besides, I've got a good man steering the raft."

"I'm glad you feel that way. If you got some prayers, you'd better say them."

"I've already started."

Tremayne turned to the men on shore and said, "Give us fifteen minutes and then the next raft shove off. Come at fifteen-minute intervals. That'll give Ringo a chance to pull us all in."

"God go with you, my boy," someone called out.

And at that, with Gwilym at the bow of

350

the boat with Evan, began to push it out. Casey felt the boat tremble with the power of the river. He steered easily, and the raft floated out to the center. He found it easy enough to steer, and the sun made its bright reflection on the waters. He glanced back and waved to Canreen, who was riding with York, and Canreen waved back. It occurred to him that Canreen had changed on this journey for the better. Then he turned and put his whole attention on steering the raft. They had been afloat for twenty minutes.

He called out to Charity, "This is easy. If it doesn't get any worse than this, we'll be there before you know it."

The trip was over so quickly that they were all caught by surprise. Evan called out, "Look, there's Ringo!"

Quickly Tremayne turned and saw Ringo and the others who had brought the cattle, waiting on the shore. He pushed at the tiller, and the raft obediently veered toward the bank. He brought it in smoothly, and Evan and Gwilym threw ropes in, and the oxen were quickly employed to pull the rafts up on dry land. They were there, and everyone gave a cheer that echoed across the open places.

One by one the rafts landed, and Evan waited as the current brought the Krisova raft into shore. He caught the rope Stefan threw, and Canreen and Ringo Jukes grabbed the rope. He was aware that Zamora was steering while Stefan was in the bow. As soon as the heavy craft nosed into shore, he snubbed the rope to a stump.

"Zamora, you made it!"

He scrambled on board and dashed past Stefan, halting in front of the young woman. He started to speak, but the sight of her face stopped his greeting. Her face was pale and her eyes were pools of grief.

"What's wrong, Zamora?"

"My grandmother — she is dead."

For a moment Evan couldn't speak. He saw Zamora glance toward the wagon, turned, and looked inside. Lareina was lying under a colorful silk coverlet, her eyes closed and her features relaxed in the way of the dead. Wheeling, Evan moved to Zamora, took her hands, and asked quietly, "When did this happen?"

"I don't know. She was all right when we shoved off from shore. She smiled at me and wished me a happy voyage. But when we were halfway here, I went to see how she was — and she was gone."

Evan pulled her close and she put her head on his chest. Her voice was faint and thin as she whispered, "I feel so alone, Evan!"

Evan Morgan tried to think of words of comfort, but none came. Zamora clung to him in desperation, and he could only say, "I'll be here, Zamora."

CHAPTER TWENTY

A light rain was falling as a crowd gathered around the grave the men had dug for Lareina Krisova. A small cemetery was already in place there, and tombstones, all carved by family members, dotted the ground. The old woman's death had surprised Tremayne. He had spoken with her often on the journey, and now it seemed unfitting that she had survived the hardships of the trail, only to simply pass away in her sleep.

A group of men was carrying the casket, which had been hastily made by a local carpenter. Their faces were sober, and since they wore no hats, their hair was plastered down by the cold rain.

"It's such a bad day," Charity murmured. "I wish it wasn't."

Looking down at her, Tremayne saw that the bonnet she had brought all the way from Pennsylvania kept some of the rain off, but her clothing was as sodden as his own. They stood together silently.

Tremayne said finally, "People come to this place for free land, Charity, but it isn't free, is it?"

"What do you mean, Casey?"

"Well, the Studdarts have lost a daughter. Konrad and Minna Dekker are dead. Mary Tomkins lost her baby, and Marzina lost her husband. Now Stefan and Zamora have lost their grandmother. Nobody thought this would happen when they were getting ready to come."

"No," she said quietly. "Everyone was excited. You never know what's going to come. The Bible says that no man knows the day nor the hour of his death."

"I've thought about that often."

They waited as Zamora and Stefan appeared, accompanied by Charity's father. Both of them wore dark clothing that differed greatly from the colorful dress they usually wore. Zamora wore no veil, and she had a dark black handkerchief over her head. The three took their places close to the casket placed on sawhorses.

But even from where he stood, Tremayne could see Zamora's eyes were filled with grief. "She was very close to her grandmother."

"Yes, so was Stefan. It hurts them badly."

She added, "You know, Casey, we all lose things. We have to hold on to the good things the Lord lets us keep for a while, but sooner or later we turn loose of everything."

"I reckon that's right, Charity. For everyone there's the last meal, the last sight of those who are family, the last kiss. The last of everything comes. That's a grievous thought, isn't it?"

"Not for those who know the Lord, not really."

She fell silent for her father had stepped forward. He had a Bible in his hand, but in the rain he didn't open it. He simply held it close to his body under his dark brown coat. His expression was set, but his voice was clear and even. He kept his eyes fixed on Zamora and Stefan.

"The Bible is very clear on one thing," Gwilym said, "and that is that this life is not all that a man or a woman can expect. After this life there is another one, and those who are in Christ Jesus are safe when they pass from the darkness of this world to the light in the other world.

"You will remember that in the fifteenth chapter in the book of First Corinthians, Paul devoted a long sermon on this very subject. He began by saying, 'I delivered unto you first of all that which I also received, how that Christ died for our sins according to the scriptures; And that he was buried, and that he rose again the third day according to the Scriptures.' "

Gwilym continued to read, and the words for Tremayne had a special impact. Ever since he had heard Gwilym Morgan preach, he had been thinking about his soul, and particularly during these recent days about what he faced after death. And now as the words rolled forth, they seemed to strike him with a particular force.

"The book of Hebrews tells us, 'It is appointed unto men once to die, but after this the judgment.' That verse is no threat to a believer. It was no threat to our dear sister here. I spoke to her many times as we made our journey here, and one thing was clear: She was a believer in Jesus Christ. She has crossed the line that we all must cross. Jesus rose from the dead and ascended to His Father. We who put our trust in Jesus will do the same. The patriarch Job said plainly, 'I know that my redeemer liveth, and that he shall stand at the latter day upon the earth: And though after my skin worms destroy this body, yet in my flesh shall I see God: Whom I shall see for myself, and mine eyes shall behold, and not another.' "

The sermon was composed of reading

Scripture and encouraging testimony from the preacher who spoke almost longingly of a desire to depart from this life and be with Christ. It was this latter that struck Tremayne so hard. He had known men to die before, most of them wild, reckless, unredeemed men, and most of them had died hard. None that he could remember went out praising God, but Gwilym made it appear there was another way to die.

He said in closing, "Sometimes we see our friends off on a ship, and we stand on the shore and see them as they get on board. Then the ship begins to move, and it turns away into the open sea. We stand there, and we watch it leave until finally it becomes a mere shadow and then a dot and then nothing. And often we say, 'He's gone.' "

Gwilym held his hand high in the air. "But think of where that ship is going. Someone will be standing there waiting for that soul, and the cry will not be that he's gone, but heavenly angels and the redeemed of God and Jesus Himself will say, 'He's come!'

"I would close this brief tribute to this dear woman by wishing and hoping and praying that every man, every woman, and every child in our world here were united with Jesus in such a way that one day when they die, it will be the Lord God Himself who will welcome them." He bowed his head and prayed a simple prayer.

"Let's go," Charity said quickly. "I never could stand to see a grave filled in."

Tremayne followed her, glad to get away from the sight. When they had walked several steps, they heard the first clods of dirt hit the casket, and a shiver went through Charity. She reached up and took his arm.

"I can't stand that sound." She began to walk quickly, and he followed her. When they were back at her wagon, she stood under the tarpaulin Evan had made to keep the rain off. Once she glanced in the direction where the burial was taking place. Nearly everyone else had stayed.

"I need to say something comforting to Zamora and Stefan, but I can do that later."

"She was a fine lady. It was a privilege to know her," he looked down at Charity. Something in his lean face was troubled.

"What is it, Casey?"

"Your father. He's right in what he says about being ready to die. I've always known it."

Charity put her hand on his chest and let it rest there. He covered it with his own, and she said, "Jesus said once to a man, 'You are not far from the kingdom of God.' Somehow I feel that applies to you, Casey."

"I hope so," he said soberly. "A man's a fool to live this life without ever thinking about the one to come." He wheeled suddenly and walked away, keeping his head down. Charity watched him go and uttered a prayer, "God, stay with him! Don't let him get away from this conviction he feels. Bring him home to Your house, Lord!"

Two days after the funeral, the wagons pulled into Oregon City. It was a rough-looking place as they had expected — raw and unfinished — and yet this was the closest thing to a city for miles along the coast. They pulled into a circle out of habit, and as soon as the beasts stopped, York hurried to Marzina. She was sitting on the wagon seat, holding David.

"I'll unyoke your oxen, and then mine. We'll go take a look at the town, Marzina."

"All right, York."

Glad to be at last at the end of the journey, he quickly removed the heavy yokes and staked the oxen. Returning to Marzina's wagon, he took David and then Benjamin and Rose.

"Well, this is it," York said. "Let's go see the wonders of Oregon City."

It didn't take long to walk down the main street. There were more saloons, it seemed, than anything else. The only church, an unpainted structure, had a small steeple on top. There were livery stables, a hardware store, a blacksmith shop, and a two-story hotel.

"Look at that!" Marzina exclaimed quickly.

York turned to see a sign, "Dr. William Jamison." "Well, it looks like somebody staked out this town. I don't know if they'll need two doctors or not. Let's go call on him and let him know we're here." But the door was locked and apparently had been for quite a while. "No one here," York said. "I wonder where Dr. Jamison went."

"Howdy, folks. You just get in with the train?" A man had come up beside them. He was a tall individual with sparkling blue eyes and a pleasant look. "I'm Caleb Davis. I own the general store down the way."

"Glad to know you, sir. I'm York Wingate."

"You need to see the doctor, but I've got sad news. Dr. Jamison left and went to a practice in San Francisco."

"Well, I'm a physician myself and had intended to set up a practice here in Oregon City."

An expression of pure delight came to Davis's eyes, "Do you tell me that! Well, that's good news, indeed! We're sore in need of a doctor here. We have one that comes over once in a while from a neighboring town, but that ain't like having your own. Let me greet you, sir, and you, Mrs. Wingate."

"This is not Mrs. Wingate, Mr. Davis. This is Mrs. Cole. She lost her husband on the trip."

"Oh, I'm plumb sorry to hear that, ma'am, I purely am. Look, you must be worn out and tired of eating off a campfire. It's nigh unto supper time. My intention is to take you to my house and introduce you to my dear wife. She plumb loves babies, and these two you got will be a delight to her."

"We wouldn't want to be any trouble," Marzina said.

"No trouble, no trouble at all! You just come along with me. There will be some more folks wanting to meet you. We intend to make it so enticing here in Oregon City that you wouldn't even think about leaving us to go anywhere else!"

A group of men from the Pilgrim Way were standing inside the church. The pastor had gone to a neighboring town to perform a funeral, but Tom Anderson, the town mayor, was helpful.

"We don't know which way to go, Mr.

Anderson," Gwilym said. "We thought you could help us — tell us a little bit about the land."

"Just Tom's all right, Reverend. I've been here for ten years now, and I know most of the land hereabout. Now some of it over toward the east there is low. It's good land, but it's underwater part of the time."

"I don't want anything like that," Evan spoke up.

"Well, most people don't. It's good for something but not for homesteading." Anderson spoke quickly and outlined the possibilities. "I think your best bet, if you want to stay close together, as you tell me, is the Tulatin Valley. Plenty of unclaimed land there for all of you. It's high ground, good soil, and you'll find it to your liking, I'm thinking."

"Does it ever stop raining around here?" Stefan Krisova asked.

"Well, not so much as stops. Certain times of the year you'll just kind of go around carrying your own atmosphere, but you'll like it. It's fine country — Oregon. Tomorrow I'll take you over to the valley and show you some choice sights, and you can take your pick."

"That will be most generous of you, sir," Gwilym said. "We'll be ready to leave whenever you say."

Tremayne left the meeting and found the crew at a local saloon. "It looks like you fellows have found your place."

Ringo Jukes was standing at the bar, a glass in his fist. "This is good-looking country, ain't it now, Casey?"

"It looks good to me, but I wanted to tell you fellows that, as far as I'm concerned, you're all free men. I'll send a letter back to the warden in Pennsylvania. It'll take awhile to get there, but he and I had an agreement that when we got to Oregon City, any man who wanted to go off on his own was free to leave. You've done a good job, and I wish you all well."

Jack Canreen was leaning against the bar. "You know, I reckon I've lost my mind, Casey."

"How's that, Jack?"

"I've done everything in the world except live a good life. I wouldn't want you to know all the stuff I've done, but if I could get me a piece of land here and find a good woman, I think I could make a pretty good citizen."

"Have at it, Jack. We're leaving in the morning to find homesteads. I'm going to do that myself."

"You're staying here?" Frenchy Doucett said. "I thought you was a mountain man."

"Oh, that's all gone, Frenchy. Beavers all gone, and it was good while she lasted, but a man has to change with the times."

"Not me. I ain't changing a bit," Frenchy said. "I'm going to head for San Francisco. They tell me there's big doings at that place."

"What are you going to do, Elsworth?" Tremayne asked. He saw that the Englishman seemed uneasy.

"I bloody well don't know."

"You ever think of going home to England?"

"Oh, I could someday, I guess, but not now. My elder brother's not too taken with me, and he'll be the earl when my father dies."

"What if he died?"

"Then I'd be Earl of Chatworth. Wouldn't that be something?"

"Sounds good to me."

Elsworth mused, "I don't know what I'll do. I don't want to be a farmer. I guess I'll just look around."

"Well, let's stay together as long as we can."

"That's right, old bean, we'll do that."

The next few days were spent in finding homesteads. Caleb Davis and Mayor Anderson led the people to the Tulatin Valley, and many from the train began to split off. York approached Anderson.

"I need two homesteads, Tom. One for me and one for Mrs. Cole."

"You want them adjoining?"

"Well, I'm going to be in town so they need to be as close to town as possible."

"Well, you can claim those now, and later on, if you decide you don't want them, Doctor, you can sell them."

"I'll depend on you to find us two good places."

York left Anderson and hurried to find Marzina at the hotel. He knocked on the door, and she opened it at once. "Well, I've got us some homesteads."

"Where are they, York?"

"I don't rightly know. The mayor is going to take me out and show me some."

He studied her for a moment and liked what he saw. In a way, her feelings were unfathomable because her features were always the same. Her character would accept hard times and good with equal calmness and resilience. No change of circumstances could disturb her. York vaguely comprehended this steadfastness and was impressed by her strength. During the latter part of the journey, he had become more conscious of her attractiveness — her supple shape; shiny, black hair; firm, round arms; and the graceful movements of her hands. He wondered why his awareness of her beauty had developed so slowly.

"I found something else, but I don't know if you'll like it."

"What is it, York?"

"You remember the doctor's office?"

"Yes, of course. Dr. Jamison."

"Yes. Well, Mr. Davis owns that building. It's big for one thing, but there are living quarters upstairs and downstairs. My thought is that you can live upstairs with David, Ben, and Rose, and I'll take the downstairs quarters. That way we could do what I said. You could help me with my practice, take care of the children, and we could make it fine."

"Would you really like it, York?"

"I would indeed. Is it a bargain then?" he asked eagerly.

"I think that would be wonderful. I need to be of use to somebody, and taking care of David is a good thing for me."

"Well, you'll be taking care of me too. I'm hoping we'll take our meals together. There's a fine kitchen. It could be a good way to live."

A secret thought occurred to her, but York

couldn't read her feelings. At the moment he felt he had come into a safe harbor. He had dreaded trying to raise a baby alone and dreaded the thought of finding another housekeeper and nurse who might be unsuitable. He put his hand out and she took it.

"All right, it's a bargain then."

"I'm glad, York. I felt so lost and lonely, but I've felt that way a long time."

"Well, you won't be lost anymore. Come along. Let me show you where we'll be living."

Tremayne had gone riding over some of the territory and had wound up at Stefan Krisova's claim. He saw the Gypsy wagon and horses behind a stream that intersected the property.

He stepped down, and Stefan met him with a smile. "Well, you've come to see our new home."

"Fine-looking claim, Stefan. Do you like it, Zamora?"

"Yes, it's nice." A sadness lay over the girl, and Tremayne knew that it was the loss of her grandmother. "I'll stay here. No more wandering Gypsy for me."

"You won't be alone long. I expect you'll have lots of men coming to court you."

"Perhaps." She smiled and her eyes brightened. "Where are you going, Casey?"

"I'm going to pick Charity up and take her to see my claim."

"Where is it?" she asked.

"Over there toward the river. We'll start building cabins pretty soon. We'll all pitch in and help. You better be finding yourself a good spot."

"I've already got it picked out," Zamora said. "Right over there in the middle of those trees."

"She's bossy, isn't she?" Stefan said. "But that is a good place. I've got to build corrals for these horses before we do anything."

"Plenty of good sturdy wood here. There's something called ironwood. It lasts like iron. I've seen some here. I'll show you when I come back."

"Thanks, Casey."

Tremayne nodded to them, stepped into the saddle, and rode on to the Morgan claim. He found the Morgans all busy, but he asked, "Would you like to go see where I'm going to put my sawmill, Charity?"

"Yes, I would. Let me get my horse."

Tremayne saddled her mare, and the two of them rode out. There was a happiness now in Charity, or a freedom, he hadn't noticed before. It was a long ride, nearly an hour and a half, and finally when they came to the spot Tremayne had found, he pushed his hat back and said, "Well, there she is. What do you think?"

He didn't look at the scene before him but at her face. He saw her taking in the sight of the river that lay at the bottom of a steep slope. "Your place goes all the way to the river?"

"Yes. Look at this timber behind and surrounding it. All kinds of cedar. The best thing you can find for shakes. A good market for it always. Doesn't take much of a mill either, so I can get started quickly."

The two walked over the property; thick timber rose up to a sharp rim two thousand feet above. Long meadows lay between, good for raising hay, he informed her. And there was a high-frame, half-log house, which someone had built and then left. It wasn't a spot for the mill, but he wasn't sure that a woman would ever like it.

"Lonely, I think, around here," he said.

"It's a beautiful place, Casey."

She faced him, and he saw that her face was a mirror that changed with her feelings. Her smile revealed pleasure. Tremayne thought, *She's got a beautifully fashioned face — graceful — more so than any woman's I've ever seen.* A small dimple appeared at the left side of her mouth. A light danced in her eyes.

"You'll be a hermit out here," she said.

"Not for long. People will be coming to pick up shakes. There'll be a road coming right by here sooner or later. In the meanwhile, I could take the shakes down to the river. Boats can pick them up."

She listened and watched the excitement in his face. She knew he was a man who would be good and honest although he'd wasted a great deal of his life. She sensed his subdued capacity for terrific gusts of feelings. As he spoke, she took in his intent eyes, high cheekbones, the minute weathered lines at the corners of his eyes, and his smooth and bronzed skin. She noticed that he was looking at her, and, indeed, he was.

Tremayne suddenly reached forward and put his hand on her arm. A silence fell on them, but she showed him a glance, half-startled, and a quicker breath stirred her breast. Her eyes widened, and color came to her cheeks. She leaned toward him, and he drew her forward. Her hand uncertainly touched his shoulder, and he brought her to him with a quick sweep of his arm. When he kissed her and felt a gentle hunger in her lips, he knew she would have this power over him, a way of lifting him to a height.

He felt vague hints of a glory that a man and woman could know. When she stepped back, her glance gave him hope.

"I'm tired of wandering," he murmured. "I want to put roots down in this place, and I want to do it with you."

During a powerful, poignant silence, he saw thoughts go through her mind by the look in her eyes. He waited hopefully for her to speak.

"You will put roots down, Casey."

"Will it be with you?"

She hesitated, and he saw an impulse in her, and for one brief moment thought with a sudden gust of joy she was going to say yes. But she didn't.

"We'll have to see," she said.

He didn't argue, for he knew what lay between them was the matter of God.

"We'll see," he said. "I don't think I've come this far and found you for nothing. Come along. I'll take you back to your claim."

CHAPTER
TWENTY-ONE

All through September of 1855, the building of cabins went on. It was a tiring business, but the men had become specialists. They had learned to cut the proper-sized trees. One crew trimmed them, and another crew hauled them to the cabin sites.

Raising the cabin was a quick affair. All the men would arrive and start early in the morning. The best of the axmen made the notches, and it was amazing how only by sight they could place the notches so the logs slipped nearly into the joints. When the walls grew too high to lift the logs, they were rolled up on two smaller trees that made a ramp.

All the cabins were the same, with one door and one window. This would be a temporary place to live. Later, these cabins would become a storehouse or a small room added to the main house. There were no floors except for the hard-packed earth, and the final shakes were made of split cedar. For the roof a crew first laid small saplings across the opening, then nailed boards to these. The chimneys were primitive, for the most part, made of mud and sticks with a minimum of stone.

When November came and the weather was growing cold, all the cabins were built and occupied. It was too late to plant, but there was plenty to do, for the land had to be cleared for crops. This was hard, grueling labor. The stumps were simply left in place, and for the first year those tilling the land would simply plow around them. Later, they would learn to build fires and burn them until the fields were perfectly cleared.

When the last of the cabins was finished, the members of the Pilgrim Way met for a time of Thanksgiving. Everyone came, and the hunters had been busy bringing in deer, squirrel, coons, and wild turkeys. They were thankful, and during the service Gwilym conducted there was special mention of those buried along the Oregon Trail — people who had begun the journey but had not finished it.

"We're here now in Oregon," Gwilym said, "and life continues. But as Tremayne has often remarked, the land is not really free. It has to be paid for in sweat, grueling labor, and dangers."

A week after the Thanksgiving celebration Elsworth Charterhouse was at loose ends. He was not a farmer and knew he would never be successful at raising livestock; his only knowledge was of fast horses, which he knew well. He had helped with the cabin raising, doing what he could, and had become good at splitting shakes, the extent of his carpentry skills. After the cabins were completed, he felt alone. Tremayne was putting his mill together, going to distant towns to get the blades, pulleys, and various parts, so their companionship grew dim. He visited several of the settlers, but except for Dr. York Wingate and Marzina Cole, he had no close friends.

York and Marzina had invited him to eat with them several times, and one cold Wednesday evening he arrived at the doctor's office. It was empty of patients for it was late, and York met him at the door smiling, "Come on in, Elsworth. We've got a treat for you."

"Something to eat?"

"Not exactly. Come on back." He led Elsworth through the offices — two large rooms and a reception room — opened the door, and passed into the living quarters. This consisted of one very large room with a kitchen, table, and various pieces of furniture. The other room was a bedroom.

Elsworth halted abruptly when he saw a woman in the room, and he took her in in one swift glance. She was not tall but extremely well formed. She had a wealth of light brown hair and warm, brown eyes. Her dress was more stylish than most he had seen here in Oregon; green silk seemed to change colors as she moved under the lamplight. He saw streaks of gold thread on the bodice and sleeves of her dress. Jade earrings moved slightly as her head turned, and she was watching him with a slight smile.

"Miss Russom, may I present Elsworth Charterhouse, a countryman of yours. Elsworth, this is Miss Emily Russom."

"I'm happy to know you, Miss Russom."

"And I you, Mr. Charterhouse. What part of England are you from?"

"From the southern coast. Hastings was my birthplace, and I grew up very close by. And you?"

"Cornwall."

"I know it well. A beautiful spot. They say that that's where King Arthur had his Round Table. I don't suppose you ever saw any knights there?"

Her smile came quickly. "No, I didn't, but it's rather a wild place, and I miss those towering cliffs and the ocean."

"Miss Russom is our schoolteacher," Marzina said.

"I'll have to watch my grammar then."

"I doubt that," Miss Russom said.

"Did you come over here to teach school?"

"No, I didn't. I was engaged to marry a man, and we were going to become missionaries to the Indians here in the West. He came first, and a year later I sailed to be with him. We were to be married, but when I arrived, I found he had died of cholera."

"I'm so sorry."

"It was a very hard time for me."

"Here, come and sit, you two," York said, "while I help Marzina with the meal." He drew the two to the fireplace, and they each took a chair.

Elsworth asked, "How do you like it here in this country? Quite different from Cornwall."

"Altogether different. There's a real wildness here. The forests — mile after mile after mile of nothing but trees. Nothing like that in England, not anymore."

"I suppose there was once. I'm at loose ends myself."

"I understand you came in the wagon

train with the group called the Pilgrim Way. I was very interested in that."

"They're interesting people. I was not a part of their original group."

"Oh, what did you do before you came?"

Elsworth thought for a moment, and then he spread his hands in a gesture of futility, "Well, murder will out and so will truth. I was in prison."

His announcement caused the woman to open her eyes wide. "Really? Why were you there?"

"Well, the charge was embezzlement. I went into partnership with a man, and I had a fiancée. The two of them took the money and ran, and I was left to answer for it."

"That must have been very hard."

"It wasn't easy, but I'm glad to say I was fortunate enough to be set free."

"How did that come about?" she asked.

Elsworth told her of the need to have inmates take the people over the trail to Oregon, and he ended by saying, "I really was not a candidate, but the fellow who led us all, his name is Casey Tremayne. We became friends in prison, and he dragged me along. I'm afraid I was mostly dead weight."

"No, that's not so. You've become a real pioneer," Wingate commented. "You two come now. Marzina's a wonderful cook. I'm actually getting fat. Here, you sit here, Miss Russom, and you over there, Elsworth."

"Really, Emily is my name, so unless you're in my classroom, in a situation like this I'd prefer it."

"I always liked that name — Emily," Elsworth said. "It was my grandmother's name."

"Where is your family in England?"

"Still in Hastings."

They all seated themselves, and there was an awkward silence, and then York said, "I'm afraid we ask the blessing."

"Quite all right," Emily smiled. "I like that very much." They bowed their heads, and York pronounced a quick blessing.

Then Marzina said, "It's so good to have real food again. Cooking over a campfire for two thousand miles became quite a chore."

They began to eat, and Elsworth found his interest completely taken by Emily Russom. They kept asking each other questions: "Have you ever been in Dover?" "Have you been to the Lake Country?" Both of them were hungry for memories that linked them.

"Is your family in business in England?" Emily asked.

For a moment Elsworth hesitated, "Actually not. My father is the Earl of Chat-worth."

Everyone suddenly looked at him. "I didn't know that!" York exclaimed. "Will you be the earl when he dies?"

"I suppose so. I have an older brother, but his health is very bad. It doesn't mean much. My family is one of the impoverished nobility. They have the title and some land and what used to be a castle, but now it's mostly memories."

"What will I call you?" Marzina smiled. "My Lord?"

"You'll call me Elsworth as you always have. It doesn't mean a thing."

The meal continued pleasantly, and after-ward they played cards. It was Emily who said, "It's getting late. I'll have a room full of noisy, rowdy students tomorrow, all determined to remain unchanged."

They rose to go, and Elsworth said quickly, "Do you live near here?"

"Oh, it's not too far."

"Well, allow me to escort you home."

"That would be nice."

The two took their leave. It was cold, and when they reached her door, she turned and put out her hand. "It's been so nice to meet you."

"Yes, it has. It has been a good meeting. I

get lonesome here. I'm, more or less, use-less," he said.

"I felt the same way when I came. My purpose was gone."

"Do you suppose we could get together for a meal at the café and talk about England and things like that?"

She smiled, and Elsworth had warm feelings about this woman. All men, even the roughest kind, perhaps, had a picture in their hearts, fashioned by their desires, of the ideal woman. He was aware that few men ever found their ideal in reality, but it was one of the shocks of his life that this woman fit his lifelong dream of what a woman should be. He had never married, and although he had known women, none of them had formed any kind of an attachment with him. He had felt himself out of the mainstream of courtship.

Now as Emily Russom smiled at him, and he was holding her hand, he sensed that her vitality affected him powerfully. It fanned his inner hungers, which had been latent for many years and which he had learned to ignore. He felt like a very young man meeting a sweetheart for the first time, and it was a strange thing for him.

"Would tomorrow be too soon? he asked.

I don't want to rush you, but I do get lonely."

"Tomorrow would be fine. Why don't you come to my schoolroom tomorrow? You could talk to my students about England. They've heard almost all I've had to say."

"Well, I'll be glad to do that, although I don't know that I could add much."

"It will be a break for them. Come about ten o'clock in the morning."

"I'll be there. Good night, Emily."

"Good night, Elsworth."

He turned away, and as he walked back to his room in the hotel, he felt alive in a way he hadn't before, and he knew he would sleep little that night, for the woman brought an excitement he thought had escaped him.

Two weeks later Elsworth counted the times he'd had supper with Emily — four times, twice in the hotel dining room and twice with the doctor and Marzina. He recounted each moment, and he felt like a fool. "I'm like a schoolboy," he muttered as he walked along the street. "It's like something out of those awful romances some people write." He shook his head wondering at his own foolishness and stopped at the livery stable.

"I need to rent a buggy," he said to Evan Smith.

"Where are you going, Mr. Charter-house?"

"I've got to go over to a little town called Hemmings. I hope I don't get lost."

"Oh, that's on the main road. What's going on in Hemmings?"

"I've got to pick up two saw blades for Tremayne. He needs them for his mill, and he's busy putting the thing together."

"I've got just what you need."

Twenty minutes later Elsworth was in the buggy, and he stopped at Emily's boarding-house. She was waiting for him, and he helped her inside. When he sat back down and took the lines, he said, "I'm glad you're going with me. It would be a lonely trip otherwise. I hope they have a place to eat there."

She had been pleased to be asked. Life was dreary in this place. Men had courted her, of course, but none of them were appealing. Most of them had been rough farmers or trappers, all men who still seemed very foreign to her. Elsworth Charterhouse was like a breath of fresh air for her. "How far is it?"

"About a three-hour ride. We can pick up something to eat, I'm sure, there and drive back."

"It's nice to be free of the schoolroom. I

want to thank you again for coming. The students loved you," she said.

"I think they were just anxious to get out of doing their arithmetic," he grinned.

Emily's laughter made a delightful sound. "Well, you may be right about that, but I enjoyed it."

Later that day, after completing their errand, they were riding back to Oregon City.

"Well, we've had a successful trip. Got the saw blades, had a good meal, and now we're headed home for another good meal."

"We're going to wear out our welcome at Wingate's."

"I think not. They seem to appreciate the company."

"It's sort of a strange relationship, isn't it?"

"Well, as you know, she lost her husband. They weren't very close, I'm afraid," he said.

"Why is that?"

Elsworth shrugged. "As I understand it, she was rather forced by her father into marriage with a man not at all suitable."

"How terrible. I can't imagine such a thing."

The two talked on, and the road made a turn. Suddenly Emily heard a whizzing sound, and Elsworth gave a cry and leaned over. She was horrified; the feathered end of an arrow protruded from his upper body. It had hit him high in the shoulder, and she whirled to see three Indians coming on horseback. One of them had a tomahawk, and the other two were waiving spears. Quickly Emily grasped the lines and shouted, "Hup! Get up, boys!" The horses leaped against the harness and took off at a dead run. She could hear the yelps of the Indians.

"Are you hurt bad, Elsworth?" she cried.

"I don't think so." He straightened up and looked at the protruding arrowhead. "It went all the way through, but it's so high I don't think it hit anything vital. Can you drive these horses?"

"Yes, of course."

Elsworth looked back and saw that the Indians' horses were poor things, indeed, as were the Indians themselves. He couldn't see much, but he pulled out the gun Tremayne had insisted he carry. He couldn't hit much with it, but when he leveled the revolver and fired, one of the Indians jerked to one side. Whether it had hit him or simply come close, he didn't know. He continued to fire, and one of the horses suddenly fell, evidently hard hit.

"Well, that stopped them."

"Are you bleeding much?" Emily asked.

"No, I don't think so. Not very comfortable!"

"We'll have to get you to Dr. Wingate."

"I hope the thing's not poisoned. That would be a sorry way to end my life out here."

They made the trip back to Oregon City. Tremayne had come into town to pick up the saw blades. He helped Elsworth down and into Wingate's office. He watched while York removed the arrow and suggested that Wingate cut the arrowhead off to pull the arrow out. York finished by dressing the wound and gave Elsworth laudanum for the pain.

"No damage done. It went through the thick muscles here over the neck."

"You were pretty lucky, Elsworth."

"I was lucky to have Emily there." He shook his head. "She drove like a trouper."

"It could have been worse," Tremayne said. "We'll have to do something. I'll find out if there are any war parties in this part of the world. You be OK?"

"I'll be fine."

Tremayne found a group of men waiting outside.

"What'll we do, Tremayne? You fought the Indians before," Gwilym said.

"I'll get some of the men who know the

country to help. We'll comb the area and find out if there are any war parties around. The rest of you stake out here as much as you can. If we need an armed band, we won't have time to round you up."

"How long will it take?" Evan asked.

"Not long. I know exactly where they ambushed Elsworth and Miss Russom. I can backtrack from there."

He left at once, and, indeed, he found the signs where Elsworth indicated they had been attacked. He scoured the country quickly, and he found a group of Klamaths. They were rather peaceful Indians with whom Tremayne was in good standing. He knew the chief, a very old man with wrinkled features, but his eyes were still sharp. Tremayne explained what had happened.

Running Bear said, "There's a Blackfeet war party to the south of us. I expect it was them."

Tremayne tried to find the tracks of the Blackfeet party, but there was too much ground to cover. He returned to town and gave his report. "The Klamaths are all right. They're peaceable. These Blackfeet — they're different. They're a tough people, so we'll have to keep watch. If they're in this territory, I'll find them."

"You better! We don't want them running around and picking us off," Jack Canreen said. "Can I help you?"

"Sure, Jack. You've done some tracking. We'll go together."

"Good enough."

The next day Tremayne rode out with Canreen and three other men. They left Charterhouse to be cared for by the doctor and Marzina. The wound did become infected.

"Doctor, is it dangerous?" Emily asked.

"We just don't know about these poisons if that's what it is. Some of them are pretty rank."

"I'll help care for him. I know you're tired, Marzina."

"That would be kind. I have my hands full with these two boys."

Each night Emily sat with Elsworth. He developed a fever, and she put cool cloths on his head and upper body. She also learned to change the dressing, and the wound seemed to be healing well by the fourth day when Tremayne and the scouting party returned.

Elsworth was awake. "Did you find them, Casey?"

"No, but they're here somewhere. They're pretty stealthy. We'll have to be on guard.

How are you doing?"

"I think I'll get shot with an arrow every once in a while. I've never been so pampered in all my life. They cook me anything I want. Emily reads to me from some soupy poet."

"He's not a soupy poet! It's Alfred Lord Tennyson, a great poet."

Elsworth winked; he was recovering. "We argue about that, but I'll win her over, yet, to the Latin classics. We got the saw blades."

"I wasn't worried about the saw blades." Tremayne put his hand on Elsworth's shoulder. "You take care, old hoss. I can't do without you." He turned. "Nice of you to take care of him, Emily." He left the room.

"What a stalwart, virile man," Emily said.

"*Virile* isn't the word for it. He's the real article. I wish I was like him."

Emily brushed his hair back from his forehead. "No, you don't need to be like him. You need to be like yourself." She smiled, "Be happy with what you are, Elsworth."

"I never have been."

"Then I will teach you."

CHAPTER
TWENTY-TWO

Evan Morgan moved the plane carefully over one of the planks that would form the floor of his cabin. He had honed the blade razor sharp so that with each stroke a tiny wisp, thin and smooth, curled upward and then fell off. For a moment, Evan stopped, brushed the shavings away, and then ran his hand over the smooth board. It pleased him to make this floor, and he was aware that all his neighbors had been satisfied with a bare earth floor. Evan had better plans — or so he thought. He had planned the cabin to dovetail into a larger house, and this small cabin would eventually be a larder and a washroom and would have a fireplace for the wintertime.

Outside a brisk wind brushed against the cabin, and Evan looked out the door. Christmas was only a week away, and the weather had turned bitterly cold earlier in the week, but now the temperature had warmed, and he wore a light coat. Thankfully it was not raining. It seemed to rain more in Oregon in a day than it had in Pennsylvania in a week. It didn't bother him, however, and he moved back with a sigh, swept up the shavings, and put them in the fireplace. They made good kindling. There was no fire now, but he would build one when he came back to spend the night.

He felt restless, and he left his cabin with his rifle and bullet pouch and walked toward the Morgan cabin. They had adjacent homesteads, and as he approached, he saw Charity was boiling clothes in an iron pot. He hailed her, and she looked up.

"Well, the old man of the mountains," she smiled. "We haven't seen you lately."

Evan shoved his hat back on his head. "Been busy putting the final touches on the cabin. You've got to come over and see the floor I put in, Charity. Not a splinter in it, smooth as glass."

"I envy you. I don't feel at home with a dirt floor."

"When we catch up a little bit, I'll come over and put one in for you and the others. You can walk around barefoot all you please."

As they talked, Charity stirred the clothes boiling in the black pot over the fire. "You've worked so hard, Evan. Why don't you take some time off?"

"And do what?"

"Go call on a young lady."

"Don't know any."

"Don't be foolish!" Charity exclaimed. "You know Alice Brand."

"She's seeing Louis Manning."

"Alice has always liked you. You can beat Manning out if you put your mind to it." She put her arm around him and squeezed him; they were an affectionate brother and sister, close enough to share most things. Charity knew her brother was lonely, and it would get worse. He was living on his own homestead now, as the law required, and being accustomed to his family and lots of activity around, he found the solitude hard. "I'd love to see you get married and have a dozen children. That's what you'd like."

"Well, maybe not a dozen." Evan displayed a crooked grin, and a small dimple on his left cheek popped out. "Maybe you're right." He shrugged. "I'll go calling on Alice."

"Put on your best clothes and shave. A good-looking, young fellow like you — how could she resist?"

"All right. I'll give it my best shot. But Louis is a stout young fellow and hasn't been known to lose any fistfights. He may beat me up."

"I'll tell you what. If he starts for you, run and hide behind Alice. We women love to protect our men."

"Like fun you do!" He suddenly kissed her on the cheek. "You smell good," he said.

"You go see Alice."

Alice Brand was a pretty girl. Her parents, Nelson and Kate, had had one other child, Tom, but after his death from cholera, Alice was their pride and joy. She was eighteen years old, the same age as Evan. When she opened the door, she looked surprised, "Why, Evan!"

"Hello, Alice. Can I come in for a moment?"

"Yes, come on in. My folks are gone. My pa went to see Dr. Wingate."

Evan removed his hat. He was struck immediately by Alice's attractive features — warm dark eyes and an expressive mouth. Her dark brown hair was arranged to expose her white neck. Her demeanor was self-possessed, and he knew she had a great deal of imagination. Wearing a blue dress, she displayed a mature figure.

"What's wrong?" he asked. "I hope your pa doesn't have anything serious."

"I don't think so. Some of these winter colds have plagued us," she said.

"Yes, my pa got a case of that."

Silence followed, and Evan felt awkward. He had never shown any particular interest in Alice, no more than he had in half a dozen other young women, nor had she seemed to be drawn to him recently. But when the silence grew uncomfortable, he said, "I hear there's going to be a dance in Oregon City next Saturday. I'd like to take you. It might be fun."

"Why, Evan, I've already agreed to go with Louis Manning."

"Oh, well, I didn't know that."

Alice smiled archly. "It's a secret, but Louis and I are talking about getting married."

"But you're only seventeen."

"No, I'm eighteen. You've lost count, and Louis is twenty-three."

"Why, I haven't heard a word about it."

"No, I guess you might say, Evan, we're engaged to be engaged. My folks want me to wait for another six months."

"Well, he's a lucky man, Louis is, and a fine fellow. I've always liked him. He'll make you a fine husband."

"What made you come over here and ask me to that dance? You never asked me to go anywhere?"

"Just lonely," he said. "I'm used to being around people, family of course, and when I'm out there on my claim all by myself, I get lonesome."

"Well, maybe I can help you pick out a girl. How about Eliza Schultz?"

"Why, she's so skinny she could take a bath in a gun barrel!"

"That's an awful thing to say! She's a nice girl. You'd like her."

"Well, if I can't go with you, I'll stay home. Congratulations to you and Louis."

"Don't breathe a word of this, Evan. It's a secret."

"I won't." He shrugged. "I'm always a day late and a dollar short, but I'm glad for you."

He left the Brand homestead, and the thought of returning to an empty cabin wasn't pleasing. There was plenty to do — trees to fell, trim, and haul away to make the fields for spring planting and final touches to make on the chimney. But the loneliness felt overwhelming, so instead, he got on his horse and rode to the Krisova homestead. He found Stefan and Zamora working on the corral. Evan stepped out of the saddle, and they both greeted him.

"Hello, Evan," Stefan said. "That's a sorry-looking horse you've got there. Why don't you trade him to me? I've got a nice sorrel that'll suit you."

Evan laughed. He liked Stefan very much. "I've got better sense than to bargain with a horse trader like you."

"Why, I'm as honest as a man can get."

"Except with horses. I think that's in your nature, isn't it?"

"He's honest about half the time. You come and ask me, Evan," Zamora said, "and I'll tell you what day is one of his honest ones. Then you can trade horses."

"Good, you do that."

He looked at Zamora, still beautiful as a grown woman. She still wore more colorful clothes than any of the other women. Her dress was bright green with yellow trim, and her black hair was bound with a green scarf. He knew she was his age.

She displayed self-assurance and self-reliance, and she knew more about life, Evan realized, than he did. He had lived a sheltered existence while the Krisovas had come from the old country and had traveled extensively in the East. Evan admired her vitality and wished he had more of that quality himself.

An impulse overcame him. "There's a dance in Oregon City next Saturday. I'd like to take you if it's all right with your brother."

She laughed and asked, "Brother, is it all right? Do I have your permission?"

Stefan shook his head. "Since when did you ever ask my permission for anything? But I'm going to be there. I'll be playing my fiddle. Come on over. We'll go together and maybe stay over — make a night out of it."

"All right," Evan said, suddenly feeling good. "Let's see what you've done to the inside of your cabin."

Zamora led him inside, and he appreciated their craftsmanship. He touched a table Stefan made and said, "Your brother is a good carpenter."

"So am I. I'm making the chairs. See?" She showed him her work, and he was impressed. She poured him a cup of scalding coffee from a pot over the fireplace and poured herself one, and then they sat on boxes and talked for a while.

He finally said, "I never did tell you how sorry I was about your loss, the death of your grandmother. I know it was hard on you."

"She was such a wonderful woman. So wise. She had done everything, Evan. I could always go to her, and she always knew what to say."

"You are a little bit like her, I think."

"Oh, I don't know about that. You know, the night before she died, she talked to me a long time about what I ought to do."

"What did she say?"

"We've always been wanderers in our family, but when she was a girl she told me about how she lived in a house on a farm with her parents and with her brother and sister, and she talked about how wonderful it was to have roots. That's what she told me — to have roots."

"Well, this is a good country for that," he said.

She laughed and grasped his hand. "Now I've got to find a rich man — a good-looking one who likes Gypsy girls."

Evan was intensely aware of her hand. Then, revealing his own streak of humor and wit, he turned her hand over and said, "Let me read your fortune."

"I'm the one who reads fortunes."

"No, listen to me." He looked at her hand and said, "Ah, I see you have a long lifeline, and you're going to have a long and happy life and many children."

"What about a husband?"

He looked down to her hand, kept his eyes away from hers, and said, "You're going to meet a tall young man with red hair. He'll make you a good husband. Don't you let him get away."

"You fool! You're the only redheaded man I know. Wouldn't we be a pair? You're a farmer, and I'm a traveling Gypsy."

"Remember what your grandmother said."

"Maybe it's so. You'll have to come court-ing me. Do you know any love songs?"

"No, not a one."

"I wouldn't marry a man who couldn't sing me a love song. You go learn some."

"How would I do that?"

"Ask Stefan. He knows hundreds of them. He'll teach you. You can come and serenade me outside the cabin some night. Who knows? Maybe I'll fall in love with you, and we'll run off and get married. I've got to go to work."

He got to his feet and realized he was still holding her hand, and she didn't pull it away. He squeezed it then, "Never known a woman like you."

"You've never known a Gypsy."

"No, I haven't, but if you're a sample, I've missed something. I'll be here early Satur-day to go to the dance with you and Stefan."

The trouble came so suddenly that York had no time to react. He and Marzina had left the two young boys with Malcolm Douglas's daughter, Elizabeth, a reliable young lady of fourteen who loved babies. They stepped out of the office and headed toward the general store to buy supplies. York was telling Marzina about ordering drug supplies when suddenly a hulking figure blocked their way.

"Well, if it ain't the doctor and his lady friend."

York knew there had been gossip about him and Marzina. They lived on different floors of the house — but still it was the same house. He had seen this man before, a rough-looking character with an imposing bulk and a loose mouth. He had been drinking, and his tone was crude and loud.

"Let us pass if you don't mind."

"Well, ain't you got pretty manners now, Doc! I bet you show this woman here some pretty manners, too, don't you?" He grabbed Marzina by the arm. She tried to move, but he had a grip like a vise.

"Turn me loose, please," she begged.

"Why, I don't know why you'd be satisfied with a scrawny-looking specimen like this here doctor. He can't satisfy a woman, but I can."

"Turn her loose," York said. He knew he had no chance in a fistfight with this man. He'd never been good at that and never wanted to be, but now there was no choice since the bully was pulling Marzina away. He swung and struck the man on the forearm, and immediately a fist struck him in the forehead. The world turned to flashing whirligigs. He felt himself hit and tried to get up, but the blow seemed to have disconnected his brain from his muscles.

"Now, sweetheart, me and you will go have a drink."

"Let me go!" Marzina cried.

"Not likely. We're gonna —"

Suddenly, almost miraculously it seemed to Marzina, she saw the big man crumple and fall forward. She lifted her eyes and saw Sheriff Joe Meek replacing his pistol in his holster. "Hate to use my hands on scum like that. I might break a finger. He ain't worth it. Kind of hard on weapons though."

"Oh, thank you, Sheriff."

"Why, I wouldn't let this scum do anything to hurt our doctor or you either, missy." He pulled the big man to his feet. "Come along, Jed, and we'll put you where the dogs don't bite you."

Marzina asked, "Are you all right, York?"

"Yes, I think so."

"You're bleeding over your eyebrow. I think you'll need stitches."

"Well, I better go do it then."

He got to his feet, and the two of them

made their way back to the office. He went straight to the room where he saw patients. He looked in the mirror. "It will take a couple of stitches."

"I can't do that," Marzina said.

"I can."

Marzina watched, fascinated, as he used a strange-looking needle and, standing before the mirror, sewed up the cut without any sign of pain.

"Doesn't that hurt, York?"

"No, I think he numbed it. I'll put antiseptic on it. I'll be all right."

Marzina was troubled. York snipped off the end of the gut he had used to close the wound and said, "Don't let it bother you."

"The man was partly right, York. We are living together."

"Well, not in the way that usually happens."

Marzina shook her head, "I'll have to leave. I can't stay here. It doesn't look right."

Suddenly York Wingate knew he must make a decision. Her presence, as it had for some time, stirred a desire in him he couldn't ignore any longer. He had never loved his first wife as he thought a man should love a woman, although he had treated her well. But this woman was a treasure. He dreamed of her and didn't want to lose her. He took her hands, which were long, slender, supple, and very strong.

"You know every time I leave this house, Marzina, I want to come back — because you're in it. I know it's too soon, but I want to be a father to Ben and Rose, and I want you to be a mother to David and a wife to me. I love you, Marzina. Do you think you could ever learn to care for me?"

She stood very still, and York saw a change go over her face. Warmth illuminated her eyes, and her features displayed eagerness. At that moment he overcame his loneliness. He drew her forward, and she didn't resist but came into his embrace. He kissed her, and the richness and fullness of that experience unsettled him. When he lifted his head, her smile was soft and shining, and he comprehended her loyalty and capacity for love.

"Would you marry me, Marzina?"

"Yes," she said quietly and laid her head on his shoulder. "I've never loved a man, but now I know I love you."

Tremayne was working on the pulleys that would run his big saws. He had worked in a sawmill for only a short time, but he was quick to learn new skills by trial and error. He heard a horse approaching and looked up to see Gwilym Morgan.

"Hello, Gwilym. What brings you out in this kind of weather?"

"God sent me."

The answer came sharply, and the smile on Tremayne's face disappeared.

"Well," he said slowly, "you come well recommended. Come inside. I've got a fire going." The small cabin was exactly like the others on the homesteads. Tremayne said, "Will you eat something?"

"No, I didn't come for that. I've been praying, and the Lord has told me to come and give you His message."

"Well, let's have it, Gwilym."

"Jesus is your only hope, my boy. You've led a hard life. You've tried the ways of the world, and they haven't pleased you, have they?"

"No, they haven't. It was exciting being in the mountains — dangerous — but it didn't satisfy me."

"Nothing is going to satisfy you except the Lord Jesus Christ."

Tremayne was silent as Gwilym quoted Scripture after Scripture. He saw the compassion in the older man's face and knew this was not merely preaching that Gwilym felt was his duty.

Finally Gwilym said, "I want you to stop

running from God, Casey. You've run long enough. I know you care for my girl, but she'll never have you unless you're a Christian man. That's not the reason for becoming a Christian, but it could be one of the good things that God has been waiting to give you."

"She's a fine woman, Gwilym. I don't deserve her."

"No, you don't. Just like I didn't deserve my wife, but God can make you deserving. Now let's pray. Will you kneel with me here?"

Awkwardly Casey Tremayne got on his knees beside the older man. He felt the strong arm of Gwilym go around his shoulders, and it warmed him. And then Gwilym Morgan prayed a prayer such as he had never heard. Intense, powerful, and compassionate, it was as if Gwilym Morgan had God by the hand and was begging Him for a great favor.

"This man, Lord, needs You. He needs Jesus. He needs a life that's different. I pray that You would bring him to a halt. That You will make the world tasteless so that he doesn't care a pin for it, and I pray that he will see the Lord Jesus and learn to love Him as we all should, and it's in Jesus's name I pray."

When Casey got to his feet, he said quietly, "Thank you, Gwilym. I'll not forget this."

"I'll be praying, and others are praying too. Good-bye now."

For the next two days Casey could do little work. He tried, but he would find himself thinking of Gwilym Morgan's prayer. He had a Bible, and he read it almost without ceasing. He read through the Gospel of John three times, and each time he was drawn closer to the Christ portrayed there.

In the middle of the night when he had stayed up late before the fire, reading about the miracles of Jesus, the things He did, Tremayne woke up suddenly, startled as he had been in the mountains when danger was near. But there was no danger here. He sat straight up in bed and at once knew what he had to do. He fell on his knees and prayed what he had wanted to pray for some time, "Oh, God, I'm nothing but a sinner. I've done everything wrong that a man could do, and I can't save myself. But Jesus loves sinners, that's what Your Book says. I don't see how He could love me, but I feel drawn to Him, and I ask You to come into my heart, cleanse me from my sins, and make me a new man."

He prayed for a long time, and finally, as

dawn was breaking, he felt a peace come into his spirit. He stood up, walked outside, and watched the dawn. He knew his prayer in that cabin now determined his entire life, and he looked up and said, "God, I'm Your man. Whatever You'll have me do, that's what I'll do!"

Charity stared at Tremayne who had come to the Morgan cabin and found her alone for a change. She knew her father had talked to him although Gwilym had said little about the conversation. It was something her father often did. But she saw something different in Tremayne.

"What is it, Casey?"

"I called on God last night, Charity. I'm going to follow Him from now on. I don't know how to be a Christian, but your father will help me, and I'll do the best I can to be a good servant to the Lord Jesus Christ."

Tears came to Charity's eyes, and her voice was choked. "I'm so glad, Casey. So very glad."

"You'll have to be ready for one thing. I love you, and after I've proven myself to you and to the community, I want you to be my wife."

Charity blinked the tears away and stared at him. Although he was strong and tall, there was nothing in him now except a new humility she had never seen before. But still she was cautious. "I'll be watching you, Casey. Everybody will."

"I'm not going to be perfect, I don't think."

"I'm not sure I love you as a woman loves a man she'll spend her life with, but I'll be praying that you will find yourself so dedicated to God that we'll see where you go."

He leaned forward, kissed her on the cheek, and then left without another word. Her breast was stirred with shock and emotion, and she whispered, "Oh, God, don't let me make a mistake!"

CHAPTER
TWENTY-THREE

The smell of meat cooking and the aroma
of fresh bread filled the small cabin of Gwilym Morgan. The room was crowded now,
for the Morgans had invited Elsworth Charterhouse and Emily Russom to a meal with
them, and Tremayne had been invited as
well. Gwilym looked around the table,
which was made simply of planks on sawhorses.

"We're glad to have these guests in our
house. Now we will ask God's blessing on
the food." He bowed his head and began to
pray, and when he said, "Amen," Meredith
piped up.

"That's a long prayer, Pa."

"You mind your manners, girl," Gwilym
said. "My prayers are never too long. Just
the right length." He laughed. "All right.
This is the meal the Lord has provided.
Let's show our appreciation by eating it."

Charity and Bronwen brought in the food

and set it before the group. A great platter of smoking venison had been tenderized by soaking in salt water all day. Charity had also purchased a supply of potatoes at the general store, and of bread, there was plenty. She took her seat between Bronwen and Meredith.

She kept her eyes on Tremayne who sat on the other side of Meredith and answered her questions between bites of food. She could sense the difference in the man, for before there had been tension and restlessness, whereas now there seemed to be peace in his expression. He had spent a great deal of time with her father, learning from him the fundamentals of the Christian faith.

"Well now, Brother Tremayne, how does it feel to be a little lamb in God's great flock?"

Tremayne had placed a bite of the venison in his mouth. He chewed it for a moment and then swallowed. "It feels mighty good, Pastor, although I don't know much about how to go about being a Christian man."

"Well, you're learning fast," Charterhouse spoke up. He was dressed in more formal attire than the other men. He glanced at Evan and said, "You were lucky, Evan, to have a Christian family to grow up in."

"That I was," Evan said. "It must be hard to be as old as you and having to learn

410

everything all over again." His eyes sparkled as he teased Tremayne.

"You know, I've been reading a sermon by a preacher called Spurgeon."

"Ah yes, Charles Spurgeon," Emily spoke up quickly. "I've attended his church in London. He's probably the best preacher in the world, I think. Certainly the most famous."

"What did the sermon say, Casey?" Charity asked.

"Well, it was about prayer, and I found it very interesting. I never read the story he used. It's in the book of Nehemiah."

"A wonderful man of prayer and faith, Nehemiah was," Gwilym said. "What did Reverend Spurgeon say?"

"Well, the chapter started out with Nehemiah praying for his people at home, and it says he prayed and fasted for a long time and confessed his sins. But then the king asked him one day, 'What's the matter with you?' And Nehemiah told him he wasn't sick, but he was sad because the home of his father was in ruins. And then the king — must have been a pretty good king — said, 'What would you like me to do for you?' And then right there in one line, it says, 'So I prayed to the God of heaven,' and then he asked the king to help him

411

restore his city of Jerusalem. But the point Spurgeon made was that this prayer was so short — 'So I prayed to the God of heaven' — and Reverend Spurgeon went on to say that we ought to pray like that."

"I don't understand you," Evan said. "What's different in that prayer?"

"Well, Spurgeon said we need to pray immediate prayers. When something comes up, you pray right then. A quick prayer. Maybe only a few words. So that's what I've been trying to do. It's hard for a reprobate like me to remember to pray, but when I go work on the sawmill, I used to go straight at it, but now I say, 'Lord, help me to get these pulleys in right.' Or, when I get up in the morning, I say a little sentence prayer: 'God, help me to be a good man for you this day.' "

Charity listened intently as Tremayne spoke of how he had adopted Spurgeon's method of praying on the spot. She was impressed.

"I think that's a wonderful habit for a person to form," she said finally.

"Well, I feel like I wasted a lot of time in my life so I need a quick trip to catch up. One thing that bothers me, though," Tremayne said, "I keep remembering bad things that I did before I became a Christian.

412

Some of them go all the way back when I was just a boy."

"Well, now. That's of the devil," Emily said firmly. "When you came into God's family, He forgave you all those sins. They're buried in the depths of the sea as far as the east is from the west."

Elsworth was listening carefully to her, and she smiled at him. "I guess you think I've become a preacher as well as a teacher."

"I think you're right."

"Well, I'll have to learn how to do things," Tremayne said. They went on speaking for some time, and finally Elsworth laughed as Emily spoke of the way to serve God. "She's a preacher as well as a schoolteacher. I need to be on my good behavior when I'm with her."

"Nonsense," Emily snorted. "You need to be good in the dark when nobody's looking except God. Never mind what I think."

Finally, in a slight break in the conversation, Meredith said, "The doctor and Miss Marzina are married now. How long will it be before they have babies?"

Laughter went around the table, and Charity said in a flustered voice, "You can ask outlandish questions! It'll take at least nine months."

"That's a long time. When I get married,

I'm going to have two boys. They're going to be named Jonah and Gabriel, and I'm going to have two girls named Jemima and Bathsheba."

Tremayne laughed. "Well, good to make plans, and I see you've made plenty, Meredith. What about your husband? Have you got him picked out yet?"

Meredith paused and tapped her chin thoughtfully with her forefinger. She said slowly, "Well, I like Earl Allen."

"How old is he?" Tremayne asked.

"He's thirteen, but he's not good to his mother so I'm not going to marry him. If he's not good to his own mother, he won't be good to his wife."

"I think that's good sound theology, Daughter," Gwilym smiled. "Let that be a lesson to you men. Be good to your mothers."

The meal ended finally, and they sat before the fire, enjoying the warmth and the fellowship. Charterhouse and Emily left, and then Tremayne rose and said, "I've got to go too." Charity rose with him and walked with him to the door. He pulled her outside suddenly, shut the door, and said, "The sawmill is almost finished."

"That's good, Casey. You've done so well. You've worked very hard."

"The cabin's finished, but it needs a woman in it, and I'm still waiting on you to make up your mind about me."

Charity couldn't answer for a time. She could never remember when she had been so confused. She had a strong feeling for this man, more than for any man she had ever met, but she simply couldn't make up her mind. That had not been an issue before he was saved, but now that he was a Christian, she still couldn't decide.

"I'll have to have more time, Casey."

"Sure. You want to see if I'm going to hold out or just be a flash in the pan as a Christian." He grinned. "I don't blame you, but I want you to know that I'm ready when you are." He leaned forward, took her in his arms, and kissed her soundly. He laughed at her expression then said, "That's the way to say good night." He mounted his horse and rode away into the darkness.

She turned and went back into the cabin. She was silent, for the most part, while she and the girls were cleaning the kitchen, and when she went to bed in the loft with Meredith and Bronwen, she lay awake for a long time. She knew she was stirred as a woman by this man, but marriage was more than that. *Oh, Lord,* she prayed, *help me to know Your will in this important matter.* She went to sleep then, but it was a fitful sleep.

The following Sunday morning was the day before Christmas. Gwilym preached on the Child in the manger and what He meant. He also preached on the need for obedience to follow this Savior who had died to save the world. His voice rose as he spoke, "We are to obey the Lord, and He has given us specific commandments. The first thing He commands us to do after we have turned from our sins and enter the kingdom of God is to follow the Lord in baptism. I'll not trust a man who's a Christian who disobeys this first command. We may differ with some of our brothers on the mode of baptism, but there is no question at all that this is what the Lord intends for each of His young believers to do."

After the sermon Gwilym said, "We'll now have the closing prayer," but he halted for Tremayne had stood up. "Yes, Brother Tremayne?"

"I want to be baptized, Pastor."

Gwilym stared at the man. "It's freezing out there."

Tremayne shrugged. His face was rather pale, and he said, "I've trapped beavers when the weather was this cold and came out soaking wet. I did that for money. Can I do any less for God who has saved me?"

"You mean," Gwilym said, "you want to be baptized — right now?"

"The river's there and you're here. I hate to ask you to get in that cold river, but I'm ready."

"Well, hallelujah!" Gwilym shouted, and his face shone with joy. "That's the spirit I like to see in a new believer. Come along, everyone."

The whole crowd went to the river and watched as Gwilym waded out waist deep. Tremayne followed him. Tremayne stood with his head bowed while Gwilym said, "Now out of obedience to the command of our Lord and Savior Jesus Christ, I baptize you, Brother Tremayne, in the name of the Father, the Son, and the Holy Ghost." He grabbed Tremayne by the back of the neck, lowered him into and under the water, and finally pulled him up.

"Glory to God!" Gwilym shouted. "You won't forget this, my son."

The two men came to shore where the women had blankets. Charity said, "Pa, you go in and get dry clothes on right now. You, too, Casey. You'll catch your death."

While they were inside changing, Elsworth said, "Well, Charity, there's a man who means business for God." He shivered, shook his head, and added, "It would be hard for me to put myself in that river."

"He's a strong man," Emily said. "He's going to do something good for God with that kind of spirit."

Christmas was past, and the New Year was coming. There had been little celebrating. Tremayne went back to his mill afterward, but there was little work to do until the spring, and he knew he had to find more parts for the mill. Without much to occupy his time, he felt lonely, but one thought calmed him: *I've spent months in the mountains all alone and never knew I was alone, and here I am, two or three days, and I'm lonesome for people. I guess that's what God does to a man.*

For the rest of the morning, he tried to put his thoughts out of his mind but then gave up. By midafternoon he was riding into Oregon City where he met Charterhouse who invited him to eat with him. Afterward they discussed how life was different now for both of them.

"I never told you this," Charterhouse said, "but I was a barrister back in England."

"That some kind of a lawyer, Elsworth?"

"Yes. I could qualify here to be a lawyer without much trouble. Emily wants me to do it." He laughed. "I could become a judge. I might have you in my court. Now that would be —"

"Look, Elsworth, that's Frank Novak. He's not a man to abuse a horse like that."

Indeed, Novak was riding at a reckless, breakneck speed and flogging his horse, which was nearly staggering. He fell off the horse and yelled, "Tremayne!"

"Something's wrong," Tremayne said. He approached the frightened man. "What is it, Frank?"

"It's the Indians. They hit my cabin. We fought 'em off, but I seen smoke. I think they burned out the Wilsons."

"Which way were they headed?"

"Headed toward Gwilym Morgan's homestead."

Men started to gather as Novak gasped out his news.

Studdart exclaimed, "Tremayne, you're the only one who's fought Indians. Tell us what to do."

"Studdart, you raise all the men you can. I'm going on ahead."

"You can't go by yourself."

"I'll be all right." He ran to his horse, mounted, and yelled, "Meet me at the Morgan place with all the men you can get and as quick as you can!"

As he rode out, Tremayne found himself praying as hard as he could. *Lord, I'm not able to do much, but I'll do whatever You would have me do. Keep the Morgans safe. Help us to fight off these Indians.* He leaned forward and drove his mount at the utmost speed.

Charity left the cabin, calling out, "Pa, I'm going over to see Stefan and Zamora."

"All right, Daughter. Watch out now."

She saddled her mare and started down the road. She hadn't gone more than a few hundred yards beyond sight of the cabin, when she heard gunfire. Quickly she wheeled her horse, and fear gripped her. She rode the mare back, and when she saw the cabin, her heart grew cold. Painted Indians were firing at the cabin. There was only one window, but the door was open, and Evan and her father were returning fire. One of the Indians already lay prone, but there were many of them.

Charity tried to wheel her horse, but she heard a shrill yelp and saw one of the Indians jump on his pony and come after her. She rode as swiftly as she could, but the Indian caught up with her, reached out, and knocked her from her horse. She hit the ground on her back, which left her breathless. Instantly the Indian was on top of her. He was smeared with yellow paint, and there was an unholy expression in his eyes. He was grinning at her, and she fought him, but he cuffed her in the face and said something in a guttural language. He dragged her to his horse, removed some rawhide, tied her hands, and then threw her on her horse. He tied her feet underneath the mount so she couldn't escape, and then he mounted his own horse swiftly and called out. Three more Indians soon appeared, riding bareback. Her Indian captor was a tall man with commanding features. He uttered something in their native language and then rode off, pulling Charity's mount by the reins.

She heard more rifle fire and prayed for herself and for her family.

Tremayne pulled up in front of the Morgan cabin. Evan and Gwilym were stepping outside.

"Are you all right?" he yelled.

"Yeah, we fought them off. We had extra rifles loaded. We killed one of them and wounded another, I think."

Evan said, "But they took Charity. She had gone on her horse to visit the Krisovas, and they caught her. I saw four of them leading her away."

"We've got to catch her," Gwilym called.

"I'll go get her. Give me a fresh horse."

"I'll go with you," Evan said.

"No, you stay here. Studdart is leading a band here. When he comes, I want half of you to go to the west; the others to the east. Ride hard. They'll have to go through the pass over there so they'll be somewhere in that area. We'll pinch them in."

Tremayne checked his pistol while Evan changed his saddle to a fresh horse. Casey mounted and, glancing at Gwilym, said, "I guess it's time for God to do some work."

"But God uses men," Gwilym said; his face was pale but determined. "God be with you, my son."

As Tremayne left the homestead, Evan said, "I feel we ought to be going with him."

"He's done this sort of thing before, Son. We'll do what he says."

The Indians had ridden hard for more than two hours. It was growing dusk. They had stopped long enough to kill a cow that belonged to one of the settlers; they built a fire and were now roasting the meat on sharp sticks. They ate it nearly raw, and the tall Indian who had captured Charity threw her a chunk of uncooked flesh. He uttered something that must have meant she was to eat. She shook her head. He slapped her and issued another guttural expression. He spoke as if he had a mouthful of hot mush. His hot eyes frightened her. She took the meat, tried to cook it, and took a few bites.

The Indians had managed to get liquor, probably from a cabin they'd raided. She had always heard that they couldn't manage alcohol well. They began singing and dancing, and she hoped they would all pass out and give her a chance to sneak away. But the tall Indian tied a strip of rawhide around her neck, and he held the other end. He gave it a jerk to let her know he was in control. He said something and then grabbed her dress. He ripped the front of it down. She tried to strike him, but he doubled his fist and hit her in the forehead. She fell to the ground, and then he fell on her, tearing at her clothing.

"God help me!" she cried. The Indian merely laughed. She got one glimpse of the other Indians who had gathered to watch. They were laughing, too, and Charity knew that life was a very precious thing, and she could very well be about to lose it.

Suddenly a shot rang out, and the tall Indian fell across her. She heard more gunfire. She pushed the Indian off and saw

Tremayne riding and firing as he rode. The Indians tried to run, but he was too close. He shot two of them, but the last one dashed into the thick woods. He leaped off his horse and came to her.

"Are you all right, Charity?"

Charity felt him pull her to her feet and felt his arms around her. She held him tightly, and tears ran down her face. "Yes, you were in time, Casey."

The two stood in that scene of death, and as they did, Charity was suddenly aware of a great and startling truth. She had thought as the Indians had led her away, *I've lost everything.* She had thought of the things she would never have.

She looked up and said, "Casey, I almost lost you."

"You'll never lose me."

He kissed her and she clung to him. "I want to be your wife, Casey."

"That's a miracle to me." He stroked her hair. "God is good. He's a great Deliverer. Come, I'll take you home."

CHAPTER
TWENTY-FOUR

The sun high in the sky shed a bright gleam on the frozen earth. It was the first day of January in the year 1856. Tremayne and Charity had been married that morning by her father, and there had been a celebration. But the two left, and now they were approaching the cabin Tremayne had built.

Charity felt strange as if she had passed a milestone and could never go back again. Ever since Tremayne had saved her from the Indians, she had been rejoicing in the deliverance God had provided. He had asked her how long she wanted to wait before getting married.

"Not long. I'm ready to be a wife."

He had grinned at her and said, "I'm ready to be a husband."

They had wasted no time, and now on this first day of the New Year, they arrived at the cabin. He helped her off her horse and tied their animals. He said, "Let's look over your new home."

She had seen it before, of course, but he showed her the sawmill, which was in working order now, and then the cabin. It was almost exactly like the one she had been living in with her family.

He walked with her to the river at the bottom of a steep hill. "The boats come once a week, at least, but that's about the only people who pass by here." He turned to her and said, "You think you can be happy here, Charity?"

"I know I can."

He had worried about this. "You've lived with your family and with others. It'll be different up here." He hesitated, and she saw he was troubled.

She put her hand on his chest and said, "I'll be happy. You'll be here at night, won't you?"

"Nights and days too," he grinned. "I found a verse in the Bible that says the first year a man is married, he ought to stay at home and please his wife."

She laughed. "I think you made that verse up."

They walked along the perimeter of the claim. "You think you can have your children here and not be lonely?" Casey asked.

"Well, what do you think a marriage is?

You and me. Yes, I'll be happy."

They looked at the river and then at the dark forest. He said, "I'm going to build you a big, fine, frame house with glass windows one of these days."

Charity looked at her husband and knew she had found the man she could love all the days of her life. She took his hand, and her smile was tremulous, but with joy and happiness she said, "We've got each other, Casey, and that's all we need."

He took her in his arms then and held her, and the two thought of all the tomorrows ahead of them, and they were happy.

The employees of Thorndike Press hope you have enjoyed this Large Print book. All our Thorndike, Wheeler, and Kennebec Large Print titles are designed for easy reading, and all our books are made to last. Other Thorndike Press Large Print books are available at your library, through selected bookstores, or directly from us.

For information about titles, please call:
  (800) 223-1244

or visit our Web site at:
  http://gale.cengage.com/thorndike

To share your comments, please write:
  Publisher
  Thorndike Press
  295 Kennedy Memorial Drive
  Waterville, ME 04901